Awaiting Fate

by

J. L. Sheppard

Fated Immortals Series

Awaiting Fate

Cover Art by *Angela Anderson*

The Wild Rose Press, Inc.
PO Box 708
Adams Basin, NY 14410-0708
Visit us at www.thewildrosepress.com

Publishing History
First Black Rose Edition, 2015
Print ISBN 978-1-62830-877-8
Digital ISBN 978-1-62830-878-5

Fated Immortals Series
Published in the United States of America

"What?" She managed the strength to mumble.

He drew closer, pressing his chest against hers. The heat of his body caressing hers, she grew warm with craving. Helplessly, her gaze drifted to his thick full lips. Her mind wandered. What she'd give for a kiss, a single mind-blowing kiss?

Cheeks flushing, her gaze darted toward his again. "Why are you…" Her body's desires overwhelming her, she gasped for breath.

"Why didn't you tell me you were *leaving*?"

He wasn't just angry. He was livid, and he was livid with her because she'd left.

She didn't know what to say, had no excuse, not one she could tell him anyway.

Shutting his eyes firmly, his anger intensified, coiling rapidly against her until she not only felt it but tasted it.

Still, she wasn't afraid. With each passing moment, all she felt was heat, his and hers, and how badly she wanted him.

"Answer me," he demanded harshly. "Tell me why you left without telling me!"

His tone startling her, she jolted against him, her body rubbing his. A desire so powerful rippled through her and spiraled inside her, pooling liquid between her legs. It clouded her every thought and every action, so as she stared straight into his eyes, she couldn't remember what he'd said.

Clenching his jaw, he ground his teeth in anger, so close to losing it. "Olivia, tell me!"

Praise for J. L. Sheppard

"[*BURDENED BY DESIRE*] has all the great characters to make it exciting. It's a fast paced book of intrigue and shifter politics, but with a mating mixed in...Looking forward to other books by this author."

~*Night Owl Reviews*

~*~

"J. L. Sheppard knows how to create smoldering steam, sensual characters and brilliantly tense moments...Each scene [in *BURDENED BY DESIRE*] is detailed and the flow is always running hot, either from the action, the arguing, the battles or those intimate moments when I swear I saw smoke rising from my Kindle."

~*Tome Tender*

~*~

"The author brings [*HEAVENLY DESIRE*] to life with well written scenes that capture the imagination while the suspense and drama draw the reader into the story and the characters are strong, bewitching and ensnare the readers from the very beginning."

~*Night Owl Reviews*

~*~

"...Love this series...[*HEAVENLY DESIRE*] is full of romance, surprises and secrets..."

~*Paranormal Romance Guild*

~*~

"You'll laugh, you'll swoon and you'll fall in love with J. L. Sheppard's [*HEAVENLY DESIRE*] world, her words and her characters, whose diversities are like a melting pot of the supernatural!"

~*Tome Tender Blog*

Dedication

For John Andrew Sheppard

Prologue

Five Months Ago

The sidewalks near New York University were crowded with students making the heat more intense on this hot, humid morning. Sweat beaded on Cain's brow then slid down the sides of his face, but he paid no attention to the sweltering heat.

His senses were on alert. As always, when on duty, he read the emotions streaming off everyone he encountered and everyone who neared Jocelyn or glanced her way. It was his duty to protect her, ensure she wasn't abducted, again.

His king, Lucas, and queen, Jenna, Jocelyn's sister, had instructed him to do so and as a good warrior, he wasn't leaving anything to chance. If anything happened on his guard, he'd never forgive himself.

When a man eyeing Jocelyn greedily approached her, Cain stepped out from behind a concrete barrier and stalked toward him, his expression fierce, glaring at the mortal, who took one look at him and cowered away. At six-foot-five, Cain could be intimidating when he desired, despite his carefree personality and irresistible charm.

Jocelyn turned and neared him. Just a couple feet away, looking peeved she said, "Cain?"

He briefly glanced in her direction, knowing she

wouldn't be too pleased. She wasn't fond of being "stalked" as she claimed and unfortunately for him, the mortal alerted her of his presence.

His gaze still squared on the mortal, he said, "Yeah."

"Oh God, Cain! Really?" She sounded as irked as she looked.

Finally, shifting his attention to her, he asked, "What?"

Jocelyn was a beautiful woman with an oval face, chocolate-colored eyes and pouty lips. Her long hair was a shade lighter than her sister's, a dark honey brown. Right then, her eyes were narrowed and her brows drawn, mocking anger.

"Did you have to frighten the guy? I have a class with him and I think he likes me."

"Yeah, he likes you all right," he said amused, his stance still stone cold.

She quirked a brow. "Huh?"

Shaking his head, he said, "Trust me. You want nothing to do with that guy. He was lusting after you."

Lifting her brows, she asked, "So?"

"So? He was lusting after you in a demeaning way. He's the type that wants to rip and dip," he pointed out. "You don't want a guy like that, Joce."

A soft smile spread across her lips then she teased, "How do you know what I want?"

"I know you have a man who's destined for you and that's the one you should look for."

"I'm immortal, remember? It could take centuries or longer for me to find that guy. Besides, I'm twenty-one. I'm not looking for Mr. Right. I need Mr. Right Now."

He chuckled, unable to help himself. He had never met a woman quite like Jocelyn. She was, for all intents and purposes, the female version of him. He'd never looked for his fated mate, the one person destined for him, and enjoyed time with the opposite sex. Although he doubted Jocelyn ever slept around like he did, she enjoyed men fawning over her, complimenting her and taking her out on dates. Despite her being abducted less than three months ago, she paraded around New York City without a care in the world. She left the past in the past, also very similar to him.

"Joce, you're too much to handle sometimes," he admitted.

She shrugged, not denying his comment. "Thanks for letting me spot you by the way," she said, then winked. "You know how much I love giving my brother-in-law hell about it."

That was the understatement of the century. Jocelyn wasn't fond of being guarded twenty-four-seven, the reason his queen, her sister, had instructed them to remain incognito, but being undercover wasn't as important as keeping her safe. Everyone agreed. When Jocelyn spotted her guards, she'd run home and fuss to Lucas. It never got old watching a twenty-one-year-old Elemental, who hadn't come into her powers, ream a seven-hundred-year-old immortal who also happened to be king of the most reviled immortal breed.

"I didn't let you," he pointed out. "The mortal—"

"Yeah, yeah, whatever," she smiled, cheekily. "I gotta get to class."

He watched her walk away and into her classroom, chuckling to himself. When she was out of sight, he leaned against the building's wall, scouring his surroundings, relentlessly ensuring nothing escaped his attention.

Then it happened.

A sweet pine scent wafted into his senses. The scent coursed through every cell of his body, soothing him as deeply as it enticed him. His heart beating rapidly in his chest, he frantically scanned every person in his vicinity, desperate to discover the origin of the scent that captivated him.

His eyes caught a glimpse of a brunette with shoulder-length dark hair flowing freely in the wind. The air in his lungs escaped him. Everything in sight faded away until she was all he saw.

Never had he feasted on a more beautiful sight. Her features were striking yet delicate, the soft angles of her face angelic. Her eyes were a piercing blue matching the halter dress she wore that fit snugly to her hips, accentuating her plump breasts, small waist and round hips. Her legs were long, sleek and powerful, like a predator's.

"Beautiful…" he whispered under his breath.

His pulse jackhammering at the base of his neck in sync with his heart made it hard to hear anything but the harsh, erratic pounding and his shallow breaths. It didn't matter much. He was entranced, enthralled by her beauty, her allure—*her*. As if he'd been created to behold her, he couldn't find the strength or will to look away.

A low growl escaped him as desire for her coursed through him so deeply, so forcefully, he thought he'd die if he didn't ravish her at that moment. He released a breath as he rubbed his sweaty palms against his jeans.

Could it be? Had he founded her—his fated mate?

His body responded, his heart clenching painfully in his chest.

He knew then it was true.

"*Mine*," he said in awe as a smile spread across his lips. "She's *mine*."

He'd found her, and he couldn't move because he could barely breathe. Unable to take his eyes off her, he devoured her repeatedly, inch by breathtaking inch as possessiveness flowed off him in waves. He knew his own eyes were no longer blue but engulfed in crimson.

His longing intensifying with each passing moment, the need to follow her gnawed at him, finally forcing him to act. He reached for his phone and dialed.

"Yeah." Cain heard Benjamin, one of the demon Guardians, say as his eyes continued to trail his fated mate who seemed to strut across the street, taunting him with her curves.

"Need you here. Emergency."

A second later, Benjamin was at his side. Cain didn't let him speak. He blurted, "Joce in class. I gotta go."

Not a moment later, he ran into the road. A horn blared. A car collided with him flinging him ten feet. He landed hard on the pavement. Disregarding the pain throbbing down his legs where the car had struck him and his back where he'd landed, he instantly leapt to his feet, angry his eyes lost focus of the woman fate granted him.

The driver of the car who'd hit him pulled open his door and neared. "I'm fine," he barked not sparing a glance in his direction. His eyes greedy for his fated who'd captured his heart moments before.

He spotted her and dashed onto the sidewalk. Only

twenty feet behind his mate, her scent infiltrated his senses once again. The unique scent of her so captivating, so enthralling, he thought it'd take him to his knees.

Need her, want her, his demon chanted.

She paused in front of a restaurant. Not a second later, a male strode out then wrapped his tattooed arm around her. In that instant, jealously coursed through Cain, searing the memory of the negative emotion into his soul, one he'd been privileged to have never felt until now. In its wake, unmanageable rage churned, boiling his blood.

I'll kill him, he thought clenching his jaw painfully. He fisted his palms, every muscle in his body fighting for control. His face growing flushed from the effort. Involuntarily, a deep growl escaped him, drawing the gaze of several passersby.

More than anything, he wanted to kill the male who dared touch his mate. More than that, he wanted to wrap his arms around his fated and take her away, far away where he could admire the angles of her face for days on end and run his fingers through her dark, silky hair.

"Hey, Liv," the male said. "Get any shopping done?

Subconsciously, he recognized the voice but too enraptured with her he didn't bother to attempt to place it.

"Yeah," she spoke, so softly.

The sweetest voice he'd ever heard soothing the anger coursing through him. In that moment, he knew he could never kill the male if his mate cared for him.

"Landon, can we go to the movies? I haven't been

in ages," she asked, so sweetly.

Landon? He blinked, forcing his thoughts to focus. His mind swirled. The tattoo along the length of the male's arm, the voice, the name, it was all familiar, so familiar he was intrigued, so he summoned the will to peel his gaze away from his mate and shifted it to the male.

His jaw dropped. The male wasn't a stranger. He was the arrogant alpha werewolf who'd recently joined the Guardian League, the league of various immortal breeds Lucas, his king, created to combat Malum Inmortalis, rogue immortals. It was the alpha, Landon, who'd helped them rescue Jocelyn when she'd been abducted three months ago.

Fuck. It was just his rotten luck.

Landon shrugged. "Sure, we should go today though. Tomorrow, I want you to come with me to the Guardian meeting."

"Really?" she asked. Her eyes had gone round and wide, her excitement clear. "So I'm going to meet immortals from other breeds?"

"Yeah," Landon replied, chuckling.

Her face brightened as a smile tugged at her lips, enough to render him immobile and breathless. His heart, he was sure, stopped beating.

"I can't wait! Thank you so much for letting me. You're the best brother ever!" she exclaimed.

Brother? What do you know? He wouldn't have to kill the werewolf after all, breaking his vow to his king and the Guardians.

Cain started toward her then hesitated, pondering his next course of action. Run after her? Tell her she's his?

No, his conscience advised. He couldn't.

She was a werewolf, and werewolves were reclusive by nature, had always been. In fact, he'd never heard of a werewolf mating an immortal from another breed. To top it off, she was the alpha's sister, a princess within her pack while he was a demon warrior. Not only were they worlds apart in class and breed, Cain knew the hot-tempered Landon, her brother and alpha, wouldn't be pleased a demon had found a mate in his sister.

She was now his most important duty, protecting her, his top priority. If he wanted to win her, he had to play his cards right.

She'd never met immortals from other breeds. That alone was enough to advise caution. He couldn't confess she was his mate—not yet. There was no way to know how she'd react. Perhaps with time if he befriended her, she would accept him.

But what if she didn't? What if she ran?

His chest ached with the thought. He couldn't fathom it, and he wouldn't think of it now.

Of one thing he was certain: his mate needed time.

Landon and Liv took a step away from him.

His heart tightened in his chest and involuntarily his muscles twitched, his heart and body battling his mind.

I'll see her tomorrow, he chanted silently attempting to soothe his desire, his need, his worries along with his heart and body.

He watched her until she was out of sight, sadness too powerful to describe overwhelming him.

Letting her go was the hardest thing he'd ever had to do.

Chapter 1

Present day

The sun had begun to set, glimmering off the large skyscrapers in New York City. As the sun's rays turned a lovely shade of orange and pink in the sky, Cain breathed deeply enjoying the sight and sounds of cars flying past.

This had been his home for more than a century now. Although quite different from his home in the demonic plane, Treconomia, where five moons shined in the night sky instead of one, he'd grown to love New York and the human plane where it was housed.

His job as second in command to Demon King Lucas Thaler had granted him access to this plane, its people and its life. He, along with the Guardians of various immortal breeds, protected humans and immortals from Malum Inmortalis, rogue immortals, whose purpose was to rule immortals and mortals alike. Lucas started the Guardian League to combat Malums centuries ago and asked him to join. Cain agreed because he owed Lucas his life, and because Lucas was his brother, if not by blood then by conviction.

He'd never regretted his decision. He loved his king like a brother, believed in their purpose—a safe place for immortals and mortals without wars, battles and death. He took pride in his duty to his king, their people and the Guardian league, and above all, it soothed him to know he was, in some small way, avenging the family he'd lost more than four hundred years ago.

But his life had changed months ago when he'd laid eyes on his fated mate, the woman destined for him, *Olivia*.

Over the course of five months, he'd befriended her, grown to know and admire her. Despite his need to mark her and claim her as his, that grew more pressing as the days passed, he'd waited—for her, because she needed time. He'd waited and waited, but he was done waiting.

Today, he would tell her she was his.

With just the thought, excitement surged through him. He materialized outside the alpha werewolf's estate, a large colonial, three-story mansion in northern New York, where Olivia lived with her brother, the alpha of their pack, Landon and his fated female, Jocelyn, Cain's good friend. Jocelyn was an Elemental, a new breed of immortals who possessed the ability to control the classic elements: earth, wind, water and fire. Elementals, like other immortals, possessed super-human strength, agility and heightened senses, but they weren't able to control the elements until they met their mates. Before Jocelyn mated Landon and gained her power over the elements, Cain had been her personal bodyguard. Naturally, a friendship evolved. Landon and Jocelyn had mated a few months ago and were now expecting twins.

The doors to the estate parted before he had the chance to knock. Ethan, head of security at the estate, greeted him.

"Cain, welcome."

"I came to see Olivia," he said, unable to hide his smile.

"Cain," Jocelyn called.

He glanced up and spotted her on the second floor landing, beside the large winding staircase. Her golden brown hair parted in the middle and styled in soft curls. He smiled her way, but she didn't return the smile. Her brows were drawn, her eyes beseeching. It wasn't the fun-loving, hardheaded Jocelyn who usually greeted him. Immediately, he reached out with his senses and read her emotions, a gift demons possessed; concern and worry coursed through her.

"Come up," she said simply.

Worry beginning to override his excitement, he materialized next to her then asked, "Joce, what's wrong? Are the babies okay?"

She patted her belly and nodded, avoiding his stare. "Yes, they're fine. Let's go talk."

Her solemn demeanor unnerving him, he prodded, "Is Landon okay?"

Nodding again, she avoided his gaze and led him into an office decorated with wood panels and dark blue tones. She took a seat. Too worried to sit, he remained on his booted feet. When her eyes finally met his, the sorrow in them had dread crawling up his spine.

"She's gone," Jocelyn whispered.

His heart clenched painfully in his chest. He knew, his body had told him so and still he needed to hear it, so he croaked, "Who?"

"Liv."

And just like that, his plans were shot to hell. The light in his life went out. As the color drained from his face, he parted his mouth wanting to speak, but no words resonated.

His Olivia was gone.

Gone.

He looked away from Jocelyn, feeling numb inside and out. He knew it to be true. Jocelyn had said it, his body and heart responded to it, and still his mind couldn't fully grasp the concept: his mate, his werewolf, his Olivia had left, leaving him behind.

Shaking his head in denial, he whispered under his breath, "No." He said it aloud because it *couldn't* be.

Olivia cared for him.

He knew.

He felt it.

She wouldn't leave without telling him. They were friends, good friends.

Jocelyn stood and neared then whispered, "Cain…"

His head shot up to meet her gaze realizing her face was solemn, and her eyes were misted with unshed tears. That look alone proved it. Taking everything in stride, Jocelyn wasn't much for tears or sorrow.

It's true. He was sure he still stood, unmoving, but the room spun and swirled around him. No, not the room, it was his whole world spinning out of control. Without Olivia, his life was nothing.

"She left late last night. Left a note for Landon," she continued.

He barely heard her words. *She's gone. She left, left you. She doesn't want you,* his conscience sniped. "But…" He grumbled as dread churned through him muddling his shock.

Jocelyn shook her head. "I'm sorry, Cain. I really am. She didn't leave anything else."

Pain too deep, too profound, pain he'd never thought possible, filled him, agony searing him alive from the inside out.

He shut his eyes, angling his head toward the heavens and clenched his teeth, praying for the strength he needed to keep the ache at bay.

He had to go to her. Letting the pain consume him wouldn't do any good because when he saw her again, he'd tell her the truth and he needed his wits to do that.

Gaze shooting to Jocelyn, he wondered aloud, "Your overprotective mate let his sister go, *alone*?"

"It's not like she asked for permission. She left late last night, left her cell phone and you know Landon. He's upset, trying to run off his frustration."

Fuck. She left late, left her phone. Was she in trouble? Was she safe? Worry for her now gnawing him, he snapped, "Where did she go?"

Shocked at his abrasiveness with a woman he considered his dear friend, he flinched. Still, he held her gaze waiting for the response he so desperately needed.

"She didn't say."

Panic seized him, leaving him without words, without a conscience, without life.

It just kept getting worse. Not only had she left without telling him, he didn't even know where to start looking. "How could she…Why would she…" His thoughts tumbled frantically through his fragmented mind.

The months since he'd found her he lived in torment. He'd found his fated, the one woman destined for him, but she'd still been out of his reach, and yet she'd been near. Now, he couldn't see her or feel the warmth of her presence or watch her face light up when she smiled.

He had to find her, couldn't live without her, didn't want to bear a life she wasn't in.

"I don't know why she left. All the note said was she needed a vacation."

Because stringing words together was now beyond him, he parroted, "A vacation?"

"I'm sorry, Cain. I know she's yours, and I have a feeling she cares about you, but—"

Jocelyn didn't need to tell him that. As a demon, he was an empath. He'd felt her feelings for him intensify over the last several months, but still he'd been extra cautious. Perhaps, he'd been too cautious because he hadn't thought she knew him well enough, and especially because a part of him had been terrified of how she'd react knowing the truth. He was a demon, after all, and she grew up isolated from the other immortals, thinking she'd find her male, the man destined for her, in a werewolf. Only recently had the pack begun to acknowledge mates from other immortal breeds. Besides that, he was a demon, an orphan, a warrior, so different from her, a princess within her pack. He hadn't wanted to ruin their budding friendship or cause her to run if he admitted the truth, so he'd waited but she *had* to know how much he cared for her. He'd done everything in his power to show her.

Had she figured out she was his and run from him? *God, no!*

"But what?" he asked impatiently, fisting his palms painfully.

"Have you told her?" Jocelyn asked.

He shook his head, his cheeks flushing in shame. "No," he admitted, reluctantly. "I was waiting for the right time. I wanted everything to go smoothly, so I waited…"

"You've waited five months," she pointed out as if he hadn't realized it, as if he hadn't been counting the days himself.

He glared in her direction, then instantly regretted it. He had no right to take out his frustrations on her. It wasn't Jocelyn's fault. No one was to blame but him.

"Yes. I waited because you and Landon got together. Olivia's new to this whole world. Landon kept her away from other immortals, from everything. She's…"

Closing his eyes tightly, he took a deep breath hoping it would soothe him. It didn't. His chest throbbed and ached. He couldn't ignore it, so he met Jocelyn's stare again and said, "I thought she needed time to adjust. I thought if I told her right away, she would freak and bolt. I wanted to give her time to get to know me. I just thought it—"

"Okay. I get it. You were doing it for her," she interrupted.

Eyes hardening, he said, "*You* know I've waited for her far more than just *five* months. I've waited centuries for her then she was right there and I held back because I thought she needed time…Do you have any idea how hard holding back my need has been? I…" His words trailed off, and he ran his hand over his face.

"You have to tell Lucas to give you some time off—"

"I know. I can't…" He shook his head. "…go on like this. I've been a wreck for months. Lucas…he knows, but…*Fuck*! I was coming over to ask her out on a proper date. I figured I had given her enough time to get used to everything and get to know me. I was going to tell her, and now…*Fuck!*"

Jocelyn strode toward him and placed her hand on his shoulder. "It's going to be okay," she assured.

He wasn't so sure. His heart had just been wrenched out of his chest, and he ached all over. The agony was all he felt despite his attempts to keep it at bay. Without his Olivia, he wouldn't last long.

Immortal men waited their entire lives to find their mates, the one woman destined for them. When they did, their souls instantly recognized them as theirs. He'd denied his desire and his need for her for five months. His heart and soul yearned for Olivia, knowing she was just within his reach, yet doing nothing because he felt his mate needed time.

He shouldn't have waited.

He should have told her.

Perhaps, she would have accepted him, and he would have spent the last five months enjoying her, romancing her with words, flowers and actions. He could've enjoyed quiet dinners while he held her and loved her.

Could've, should've, would've.

Too late now, and rehashing his mistakes wouldn't solve a damned thing.

I screwed this up.

Worst part was he should've known. The past several weeks, he'd sensed a deep sadness in her. It pierced through him worse than if it were his own, dislodging something deep and primal in him—the need to safeguard, protect as it was with fated immortals. He wanted to ask but hadn't. Instead, he'd done all he could to distract her, attempting to make her laugh and smile. She had laughed, but deep down that sadness never faded.

And now…She was gone.

Why hadn't he done more? He should've. She was his, and it was as much his job to keep her happy as it was to keep her safe. So not only was he a damned fool but he was to blame. Over the past months as he'd gotten to know her, he'd felt he didn't deserve a female such as her. Now, he knew he had a right to feel that way. She deserved so much more than him.

His bitter thoughts, his faults, sparked his anger. Attempting to temper his rage, he exhaled heavily. He couldn't let his emotions overwhelm him or else risk turning demon, and he couldn't do that. He wasn't in his home, so he didn't have the luxury of turning.

Trying his hardest to ignore his rising fury, he asked, "How do you know?"

"I know because these things always work themselves out," she said, softly.

It had worked out for the Elementals and their mates, but he wasn't so sure it would work out for him because his mate was gone. Why she left and where she'd gone, he had no idea, but he had to start looking.

Unable and unwilling to control his emotions any longer, he said, "I gotta go, Joce."

"I'll let you know if I find out anything, okay?"

He nodded then dematerialized.

****

Olivia was exhausted. She'd flown half the night and half the morning to reach her destination—Greece. Thanks to her parents, Landon and she co-owned property in Santorini, part of the Greek Isles.

As a kid and later as adults, she and her brother

often vacationed on the island but during the last decade or so, they hadn't travelled much.

If she was being honest with herself, in a hundred and two years, she hadn't needed a vacation as badly as she needed one now. It hurt her to leave the home she was fond of behind indefinitely, but she needed to get far away from Cain, whom she'd fallen madly in love with.

The demon she'd met months ago had somehow managed to wedge himself in the deepest part of her heart. So deep, when she closed her eyes it was his face she saw: his golden hair, his bright blue eyes, high cheek bones and full kissable lips. He was burrowed so deep, it was him she dreamt of, him she wanted to be hers—her fated male.

But he wasn't.

Immortal men had an instinct—the ability to sense and recognize their fated females the moment they laid eyes on them. When they recognized their fated, they were incapable of suppressing their need for them. The desire to mark and claim them as theirs was powerful and unrelenting, the need to protect and guard them fierce and unyielding. They couldn't leave them, couldn't stand to be away from them—ever.

Unfortunately for immortal women, fate and destiny only granted men the knowledge of who their fated females were. She wouldn't instantly recognize the male destined for her, only he would.

Finding one's mate was viewed by all immortals as a gift, the one person who complemented you, someone you could love forever and share your long existence with. No immortal would wait to claim what was destined to be his, except for her stubborn brother,

Landon, who'd tried to deny his female and had for three months, nearly losing his mind with desire for her. It had cost him, dearly, but she supposed he'd gotten what he deserved for fighting with fire and fate. In the end, destiny had won as it usually did.

She met Cain five months ago, and Cain was the same jovial, lighthearted man he'd always been. Further proving she wasn't his. No way could he deny his need to mark and claim her for that long. No way any immortal male could.

Despite her brother, Landon, mating outside their breed, she doubted she would as well. Less than a handful of werewolves had found their mates in other breeds.

Regardless of all the overwhelming evidence lingering in her mind, Cain wasn't destined for her. She often found herself thinking of him, and feared she was becoming infatuated. His muscular frame, his good looks, his mannerisms and his fun-loving, kind-hearted personality, everything about him drew her to him, and it wasn't fair to her or him.

Although she'd never dated and had no experience with men because of her domineering, overprotective brother, and alpha of their pack, she knew her feelings for Cain intensified with every passing day. She couldn't completely trust her instincts because of her inexperience, but in her heart, she believed she loved him and feared if she wasn't already in love with him, she was close to it. That alone had her running away from home.

Only Landon knew where she was now. She hadn't written it in the note she left for him, but expressed she was taking a vacation, like the ones they used to take.

Regardless, she knew her brother would attempt to track her and call her, so instead of flying *Eternal Air*, a private airline immortals often used, she'd flown commercial and consciously left her cell phone behind.

As she deboarded the small plane on the island and retrieved her luggage, she was glad for one thing—the trip was almost over. Soon, she'd be able to lie in her bed on the gorgeous island and sleep.

Perhaps she was foolish to think distance would diminish her feelings for Cain, especially considering ever since she'd left, he was all she thought about. But there was hope that, with time, she'd get over what she hoped was just a school girl crush, her first in a century.

Chapter 2

His mind in shambles, his heart in shreds, Cain materialized just outside his king's office. Taking a deep breath, he strode through the doorway. His gaze gravitated toward the chaise at the far end where Lucas sat, his arms tight around his mate, Jenna, who sat on his lap, seductively running her fingers down his chest. Staring into each other's eyes, they looked so much in love, captivated with one another.

A glimpse of what he so desperately wanted and had let get away, so Cain knew he should look away. He knew he should attempt to erase the sight from his mind.

But he couldn't.

A part of him knew he deserved what he got, deserved to feel jealousy churning his gut, and ripping open his chest. That same part of him felt he deserved to suffer for his cowardice, for his many mistakes. The other part of him wanted to memorize the sight so he could fantasize that one day Olivia would love him half as much as his queen loved his king.

The sadness that had clung since hearing the truth compounded, choking him. He fisted his hands in an effort to keep it at bay, though he knew it would be useless. Nothing would erase the grief, nothing until he found her.

He'd give the world to have Olivia in the same

room. He'd sell his soul to the devil to have Olivia on his lap. No, that wasn't true. He'd gladly sell his soul to simply know where she was.

If he'd been braver…If he hadn't been a foolish coward, he could be enjoying her or maybe, he thought ruefully, it would've caused the same outcome, only sooner. If, as he feared, Olivia had figured out she was his and run from him, it wouldn't have mattered. She would've just run sooner.

"Cain," Lucas said in greeting without tearing his gaze from his mate.

Jenna quickly turned to face him, her long brown hair swayed as a warm smile spread across her heart-shaped face.

"I need time off," he blurted without greeting.

Jenna stood and quickly closed the distance between them. "Cain? Are you okay?"

She didn't give him time to respond, instead, she took him by surprise when she asked, "Did something happen to Olivia?"

He knew a demon's ability as an empath meant Lucas, Benjamin, and Jacob were all aware of his feelings for Olivia, but he never guessed Jenna or Jocelyn would've known. Had one of the demons told them?

"Cain, is she okay?" she asked again, concern marring her expression.

"How did you—"

"It's obvious. I've watched you with her. More importantly, is she okay?"

His eyes held hers for several moments before he looked away and admitted, "She just…she left."

Lucas materialized beside his mate as Jenna placed

her hand on Cain's shoulder in a comforting gesture. "Oh, Cain, I'm so sorry."

Pity, everyone pities you more so than before, his conscience sneered.

"Take all the time you need," Lucas said.

"I'm fine. I just need to find her," he said through clenched teeth.

"You're far from fine, Cain," Lucas advised. "It's normal...anything relating to our mates is...difficult. I know," he said giving him a level stare.

"You have to stay calm through this. Just keep in mind that wherever she is, she's safe. Landon would ensure it," Jenna said.

The anger he'd kept at bay boiled over. "*Calm*? How am I supposed to stay *calm*?" he shouted, unleashing his frustration. "She left *me* behind! I thought we were friends! I thought—"

Lucas's eyes ignited, burning a deep crimson shade. He took a menacing step in Cain's direction.

Cain felt the anger his king projected spilling from him, hitting him full force. He knew he deserved it, just as he knew Lucas couldn't fight the instinct to defend his mate, to punish him for disrespecting her.

Jenna placed her hand on her mate's stomach stopping him from lunging forward and asked, "Friends? Didn't she know?"

Cain turned away from her. Unable to admit it aloud again, he shook his head.

"So she *didn't* leave you," she pointed out.

His anger further seeped through his resolve. Turning to face her, he snapped, "Yes." He fisted his palms then took a deep breath, attempting to control the rage coiled inside him. "She left in the middle of the night. I…" He ran his hands through his hair in frustration.

Lucas growled, taking another step in his direction. Jenna glared at her mate, then shifted her attention to him, her eyes softening. "No, she didn't leave you. Find her and tell her. I know she has feelings for you. I'm sure of it."

He wanted to admit his fear, that she'd run because she couldn't stand to be the mate of a demon—of an orphaned demon at that, but he held his tongue.

She closed the distance between them and wrapped her arms around his waist, hugging him tightly. He returned the hug knowing he didn't deserve her comfort, not after he'd taken out his anger on her.

As she pulled away and met his gaze, she said, "Cain, if you need anything. We're here for you. Anything you need, okay?"

He nodded. "Thanks, Jenna."

As he walked out, he heard Lucas grumble. Jenna's voice resonated moments later. "Oh, for God's sake, Lucas!"

****

Drowning in a sea of regret, the days that followed were long and draining. Cain fought harder and harder to get hold of his emotions. After the initial shock and anger came defeat and now anything and everything set him off.

He had no leads as to where Olivia could have gone. He'd tried to find Landon and ask him, but the werewolf took off the moment he found out Olivia had left and only returned for brief periods. During those times, Jocelyn asked Landon, but he hadn't admitted where she went, which made Cain think he didn't know, so he'd taken the matter into his own hands. He searched property records under Landon's name and Olivia's across the country. He also hacked into her bank accounts to see if she'd used her card for any purchases. But he had no luck with either. Jenna and Lucas visited him daily, encouraged him to continue searching for her.

Over and over, he replayed his conversations with Olivia in his mind, but they'd never discussed anything regarding vacation spots or where they'd run if they wanted to get away.

His conversations with her over the past five months were usually about the Guardians. She asked him loads of questions about other immortal breeds, and he found it fascinating how her eyes widened, and she smiled when he told her something she hadn't known.

That's when he realized he'd spent his time admiring her instead of truly getting to know her, the root of her. While he memorized the angles of her face, every expression she made, her mannerisms and every curve of her body, he never thought to ask her anything about her past, primarily because he knew Landon had kept her stowed away.

Her brother treated her like a child even though she was one hundred and two. By all accounts, she was still twenty. In comparison, Jocelyn, who was merely twenty-one and had just recently been thrust into the immortal world, knew much more about it than Olivia because of Landon. Cain hated that Landon had sheltered her so much because, despite the fact his intentions were for her wellbeing, Cain felt Olivia's hurt at being kept out of werewolf affairs, Guardian business and the reality they all lived with—that a war between good and evil was undoubtedly nearing.

Although, recently, Landon allowed her a glimpse into the real world, Cain feared it too late. He often sensed her disbelief over reality, which was quickly followed by remorse. He wanted to ask so many times why, but held his tongue in fear she'd flinch at his intrusion.

The question that continued to plague him was why she'd left. He didn't want to believe it was because of him, but his heart continued to tell him otherwise.

Sighing heavily, he closed his eyes tightly, hoping the action alone would magically block out the sense of defeat threatening to take hold. Not for the first time he thought: if he would've known the last time he saw her would be the last until he found her again, he would have looked at her longer, closer and most importantly, he would've held her. He would've run his fingers through her hair as he inhaled her scent and kissed her for the very first time then maybe she wouldn't have run away. Then again, if he knew it would be the last, he would have never let her go, not without him.

He shook his head to dispel the thought because the past was lost, and there was no use rehashing it. It would only serve to make him believe the present could be changed when it couldn't. The only thing that could be altered was the future: what he did when he found her.

Closing his eyes, he relived their last moments together, just the day before she left. They'd sat outside in her garden and talked. Before he'd left for the night, looking thoughtful, she did something she had never done before. She walked up to him, wrapped her arms around his waist, and hugged him tight. He enclosed her in his embrace, bending over and angling his head so he could bury his face in her hair. Inhaling the scent of her, he'd smiled against her, thinking that one action in that single moment was a sign, a sign she was ready to know the truth about them. Because of it, he had decided to confess she was his. Now, looking back he knew better. It had been a sign, but not the one he thought. It had been her goodbye.

Hating the realization, it made him feel like a bigger idiot. Anger coursed through him so powerfully, he had to find a way to release it without unleashing his demon. In his state, the demon would take over, and his ability to think rationally would vanish. He'd never find her then.

He did the only thing he could think of. He stood, and punched his fists through the wall repeatedly. When he was done, the entire wall laid at his feet, utterly destroyed.

Staring at the mess he'd made, paying no mind to his bleeding knuckles, he pushed his thoughts elsewhere. He forced himself to fantasize, the only thing that seemed to calm him, if only temporarily. Going back to the same fantasy, the moment he found her. He imagined she would be overjoyed, run toward him, and hug him. He would tell her how much he missed her, and he loved her, and finally he would muster the courage to tell her she was his, then he'd kiss her for the very first time.

That was just a fantasy though. There was no way to know how she'd react. Odds were, she'd run again because she'd run once.

Of one thing he was sure: he would find her. He'd

find her because he had to. And when he did, he'd never let her go.

Chapter 3

Olivia slept for three days. After arriving at the vacation home in the southern part of the island, she had crept into her room, and lay down. Soon after, she'd drifted to sleep.

The moment her eyes slid open only one thought prevailed—Cain. She'd dreamt of him, and recalled the dream as if it were real.

In that dream, his blond hair, usually styled in a crew cut, had been longer and disheveled. His gaze pierced through her, but his blue eyes had lost the glimmer she admired so much, and his torn expression had pleaded. She couldn't recollect why. He'd uttered no words, said nothing just stared at her, as if waiting for her to do something. She didn't know what. Thinking of it made her chest ache just as the sight of him in the dream had.

She rolled over in bed and hopelessly covered her head with a thick blanket as if it would shield her from her thoughts, wondering how much longer the pain would last.

Now, she was wide awake, exhausted from too much sleep and no food but had no desire to get out of bed or eat.

A knock on her bedroom door startled her. She leapt off the bed and opened the door.

"Miss Olivia," Maria, the maid, said in greeting.

She was an older woman, a mortal, with long midnight-black hair.

"Oh, h-hi," she replied. "Sorry, I wasn't expecting anyone."

"Your brother told me you'd be coming. I assume I arrived shortly after you, but you were asleep and I didn't want to bother you, but he's called about ten times during the past three days and I wanted to give you the message before I head out for the day," she said sweetly. "He's been very worried about you."

She felt her cheeks flush, ashamed she hadn't thought about her brother at all. She left in the middle of the night, only leaving a note then spent three days without word. The least she could've done was call him. It seemed there was only room for Cain in her overactive mind and heart.

"Yes, of course. I'll call him right away. Thank you, Maria."

"I'll be back tomorrow," Maria said.

"Oh, no," she blurted too quickly then attempted to rephrase. "There's no need, really. I mean, it's just me. I won't be doing much at all. Take the weekend off."

"Thank you, Miss Olivia," Maria replied then turned and strode away.

Olivia walked out of her room into the living room, and reached for the phone, pausing briefly as she gathered the courage to call her brother.

She wanted to call him, but knew he would be upset and would demand answers, answers she couldn't give. She couldn't admit the real reason she'd left, and hated to lie to the brother she admired, the only family she had.

Releasing a breath, she dialed.

He answered on the first ring, his voice harsh. "Olivia Clare Waden."

Swallowing the lump in her throat, she managed, "Hi."

On cue, he demanded, "Why?"

Closing her eyes, she pictured him running his hands through his hair as he often did when he was upset. "I...I'm calling to tell you I'm fine."

"Why, Liv?" he repeated, his voice growing louder.

"I told you I needed a vacation."

"Why would you leave in the middle of the night without discussing this with *me*? Do you know how worried I've been? Do you realize how worried Joce has been? Everyone—"

Guilt overwhelming her, she said, "I'm sorry for worrying you and Joce, but you know if I had discussed this with you, you would've never let me come."

"That's not true," he denied.

"Yes, it is. It's true, and you know it, and Joce knows it, and I'm an adult," she reminded him. She often had to remind him because he always forgot.

"It's been three days! You're lucky I'm not there right now! If Maria hadn't told me you were alive and sleeping, I would've—"

"I'm fine," she interrupted.

He sighed heavily, which he often did when he was frustrated with her.

"She's right, Landon." She heard Jocelyn's voice drift through the phone. "Let me talk to her."

Landon grumbled. A moment later, she heard Jocelyn's voice, "Liv, are you okay?"

Olivia hated most she'd worried Jocelyn, pregnant

with her niece and nephew, and in no condition to worry about her. "Yes," she said, swallowing the guilt eating at her. "I'm sorry I worried you. I just needed some time away."

"I understand. Your brother understands, too. Don't you, Landon?"

She heard Landon groan "yes" in the background.

"So…you're okay?" Jocelyn asked again.

"Yeah. I'm fine," she assured.

"You're in Greece?"

She hesitated briefly then admitted, "Yeah, Santorini."

Immediately, she wondered if Cain had asked for her. She had the urge to ask, but bit her tongue instead. She knew he probably had. As her friend, he'd wonder where she'd gone to. It meant nothing, except the fact he was a good friend. He visited her often. They talked and laughed and hung out, so she knew he cared for her. Still, it wasn't the way she cared for him. The reason she'd had no other choice but to leave, knowing she'd never get past her crush unless she put distance between them.

"How exciting. I've never been. How's the weather?" Jocelyn said, distracting her.

"It was nice when I arrived. I haven't been outside today. I've been catching up on sleep."

"Make sure you enjoy it for me, too. Keep in touch, okay? Let us know if you need anything."

"Will do. Thanks, Joce."

"No problem, but don't stay away too long, okay? You'll give your brother a stroke," Jocelyn said then laughed.

"Okay."

She placed the phone back on the receiver and exhaled, relieved Landon hadn't demanded she return. Perhaps, he was finally learning to let her go or maybe not. Maybe Jocelyn was the reason he seemed calmer than she'd expected.

****

"Cain." Jocelyn's voice resonated behind him, startling him.

He hadn't been able to eat or sleep in days. It was beginning to show. No one had ever snuck up on him before. It didn't bode well for his state of mind.

He swiveled his desk chair, and spotted her. Her eyes widened as sorrow emanated from her. Jaw dropping, she quickly placed her hand over her mouth.

"Yeah, yeah. I look like shit, and I feel like it, too," he said, running his palm over the beard he'd allowed to grow.

"I never said that," she said, her voice solemn.

"You're a bad liar, which is why you didn't say anything, but your expression said it all."

Crossing her arms over her chest, she said, "As your friend, I'm going force you to shower, shave and eat."

"I don't need to shower, shave or eat, and I won't until I find *my* Olivia," he retorted.

"You haven't found anything?"

It was a stupid question. If he'd known, he would be with her. Fighting the urge to scream at Jocelyn through clenched teeth he said, "*No.*"

He'd searched bank statements, credit card receipts for both Olivia and Landon. He searched property records, sealed files in every state, across the country, Europe and even Russia, Japan, and China.

Hope choking him, he swallowed the lump in his throat. "Have you heard…anything?"

She looked away from him and shook her head.

So much for hope, his was just shot to hell.

"Shower and shave while I make you something to eat then we'll discuss some options, okay?"

"No," he said, then dragged his hands through his hair in frustration.

"Cain, you're not a child, and I have very little patience for grown men who act like children," she said firmly.

Quirking a brow, he asked, "Oh, yeah, how do you deal with your mate then?" A snide retort, one that made him ache with guilt despite the fact it was kind of true. Landon was a handful, often acted like a stubborn child, especially when it related to her. Jocelyn was his friend, only trying to look out for him and undeserving of his spiteful remark, no matter his state.

"Very funny," she said, taking it in stride. "Now shower."

Reluctantly, Cain stood and headed toward his room removing his shirt then jeans. He had no desire to shower, shave or eat, but he hated upsetting Jocelyn, hated that he had, and didn't want to make it worse. He knew seeing him in this condition affected her, and he regretted being the cause of it. Lord knew she deserved an apology for his remark as well.

After he showered, shaved and dressed, Cain strode into the kitchen and spotted two foot-long subs with ham, turkey, bacon, lettuce, and onions. His stomach recoiled at the smell.

Standing against the counter, Joce ordered, "Eat. I made them myself."

Reluctantly, he sat then took a sub and shoved it in his mouth, eating only to pacify her. After the first bite, he continued. Despite knowing he needed food or he wouldn't last much longer, he didn't have the strength to trouble himself with chewing, but he did.

"You still need to sleep, but at least you don't smell like a foot anymore," she commented, looking amused.

"I didn't smell," he retorted with difficulty, his mouth full.

"Maybe not like a foot, but you didn't smell clean."

"Whatever," he shrugged. Not like it mattered much anyway.

Jocelyn's eyes studied him. She waited patiently, seemingly disinclined to leave until she was sure he'd eaten.

He cursed silently. In a matter of days, he'd become someone he didn't recognize, a man who needed his friends to force him to eat and shower, a man pitied by everyone he admired. The cruelties of life never ended.

After the last bite, Jocelyn released a breath then blurted, "She's in Greece."

He heard her clearly, but the words seemed to slip through his mind and swirl, uncomprehending.

She's in Greece, the words resounded and replayed inside him like a broken record. If by "she" Jocelyn meant his mate, he'd wasted precious time.

Finally, the meaning hit him with full force.

His answer was Greece.

His mate was in Greece.

Anger ignited and pulsed inside him, flushing his face a bright shade. "What?" he screamed, and stood suddenly. The stool he'd been sitting on crashed against the marble floor. "You knew and you didn't...I can't believe...I'm so fucking angry with you!" Never had he cursed a woman, but his temper at her deception hindered his manners.

Her expression hardened. "Calm down, Cain or I won't give you the address." After he took several deep breaths, she continued, "Now. Do you want to win her, or don't you?"

In fear he'd lose his temper again, he didn't speak. Clenching his jaw, he nodded once.

"If I would've told you right away, you would've materialized in front of her looking and smelling like shit. I'm trying to help you—"

Eyes flaring, he pointed out, "But you *lied*—"

"A-ah," she interrupted. "Cain, I love you like a brother, and she is my sister by marriage. I want this to work out for you and her."

All he heard was blah, blah, blah. His nerves, anger and desperate need to find her wouldn't allow him more.

"You can't mess this up. You need time—"

He smashed his fists hard on the granite countertop. It broke to pieces, shattering. Over the sound, he yelled, "Oh, for God sakes! Tell me where the fuck is she!"

Her eyes blazed silver, using her power over the wind to fling him backwards. He struck the wall, his back slammed against it then he landed hard on his butt. He deserved it, he knew, so instead of screaming and shouting, demanding she give him what he needed like he wanted to do, he took a deep breath then stood and met her stare.

"I really didn't want to do that. Really." She paused again.

Cain exhaled. Patience. He needed so much of it now. *Why is she torturing me?*

"She has feelings for you. The 'you' she's gotten to know over the past five months, not the man staring at me now. So before you go over there as angry as you are now, remember that. Be the man she would never run from."

He wanted to laugh in her face. Tell her, her advice was useless. The scales were tipped against him. Olivia had *already* run. She didn't want him. Instead, with the remainder of his control, through clenched teeth he reminded her, "She already ran from me once."

"She wasn't running from you. You weren't romancing her. You weren't treating her any differently than you treat me or Ash or Jenna. You were being her friend."

He nodded, knowing he'd heard all this before from her sisters, Jenna and Ashley. The Elementals were alike in more ways than one.

"She's in Santorini, one of the Greek isles. She and Landon own a home on the southern part of the island."

Before she finished the last word, he was gone.

Chapter 4

Four months ago

"Hey, Liv." Cain's voice resonated behind her.

She turned quickly, spotting him leaning against the door frame to the library in her home and smiled. He wore a pair of loose-fitted jeans and a t-shirt that highlighted his muscular frame.

Staring straight into her eyes, he smiled that amazing smile of his.

Her chest tightened. She realized then, although she had seen him the night before, she'd missed him.

Cain was a demon warrior, part of the Guardians. She met him only a month before, after her brother had joined the Guardians and allowed her to meet them, she'd become acquainted with a variety of immortals from different breeds, Cain being one of them. He was handsome. Well, he was beyond handsome, in her opinion. Tall, broad-shouldered, muscled, strong jaw, full lips, blond hair styled in a crew cut and eyes so blue they almost looked fake, everything a woman, any woman found appealing. Despite the fact he was a warrior, he was easygoing and carefree. Another great thing about Cain—unlike most males in her pack, he didn't shy away from her because she was the alpha's sister. He was good friends with Jocelyn, destined to mate her brother, which meant he was often around.

Him being around had given them a chance to get to know one another and they'd become friends.

"What are you up to today?"

Shrugging, she said, "Not much as you can see." She turned away from him, placed the book she'd just read on the shelf then faced him once again.

"Are Joce and Landon here?"

Shaking her head, she said, "Nope. They went out…not sure where. I kinda tune them out sometimes."

He laughed, the twinkle in his eyes glimmering. "Do you want to watch me turn?"

Her eyes widened. Was he serious? Excitement rushed her. She couldn't keep it from her voice. "Really?"

Smiling wider, he nodded.

One of their earliest conversations, he promised to teach her about the immortal world she lived in but knew little of. So far, he'd kept his promise. She was now well-versed in demons, vampires, elves, fairies and the little immortals knew about angels. Of all immortal breeds, she was the most intrigued with demons. She thought that might have something to do with Cain. Now, he was keeping another promise he'd made— letting her see a demon turn.

She smiled wide then teased, "Not afraid I'll be hurt or scared away anymore are you?"

His smile faded suddenly then he cleared his throat. "I am, but I made you a promise."

Shaking her head, she said, "I was joking, and I'm a werewolf, remember?"

As she closed the distance between them, he nodded in agreement and said, "Lucas, Jenna, Benjamin, and Jacob will be there, so you have nothing to worry about."

She rolled her eyes playfully and assured, "I'm not worried, Cain."

He smiled softly then opened his arms. "Come here."

She did, nestling her body between the warmth of his arms. Feeling his chiseled chest rub slightly against hers, sent shivers through her. Her face flushed. She couldn't help it. She'd never been so close to a man that wasn't her brother. Not a moment later, he wrapped his arms around her back, the warmth of his body soothing her.

"Are you cold?"

Though her face was plastered against his chest, she shook her head then met his stare and said, "No."

"Close your eyes."

Pressing her cheek back against his chest, she inhaled and couldn't help but marvel in his scent. She did as he asked.

"Okay, open."

When she did, they were no longer in her home, the estate where she and Landon lived. He'd materialized them in the demon compound's gymnasium where Cain and the demons trained. The demon compound was a fifteen-story building in Manhattan, where Cain lived with his king, queen and two other demon warriors. Also where Jocelyn lived before she'd mated Landon.

"Hi, Liv," Jenna said in greeting.

Praying the flush in her cheeks had dissipated, she pulled away from Cain then greeted Jenna and the rest of the demons.

"Liv," Cain said, drawing her attention toward him

again. "I'm going to stand at the end of the gym." His voice grew serious.

She turned to glance where he pointed. "Wait, all the way over there? That's really far. I won't be able to see anything." She would, her eye sight like that of any other immortal's was beyond excellent. Still, she wanted a closer look.

His expression turned grim, confounding her. "You'll be able to see just fine. Trust me," he said in a way that silenced further rebuttals.

Her brows drawing together, she blurted, "Are you worried?"

He sighed. The breath he released came out in waves like he was nervous. With no qualms, he admitted, "Yeah, I'm worried, Liv."

It hit her then. He was worried because he cared. It was sweet, so sweet and endearing her heart clenched, even though she couldn't understand why he was so concerned. She might be a sheltered werewolf princess, but she trained for battle regularly.

His gaze holding hers captive, he said, "Please, don't come close. Stay here with Jenna, Lucas, Jacob and Benjamin, okay?"

Smiling, she nodded.

He materialized at the other end of the gymnasium. In a split second, he shifted.

She stood immobile, awe-struck watching his already towering frame stretch, growing a foot bigger as his muscles expanded, ripping his shirt. His horns, black in color, emerged from his scalp. His eyes glowed, engulfed in red, no blue remained, and his skin had grown a darker shade.

He looked feral, vicious, a monster. He'd been

right to worry because she knew had it been anyone else she would've been terrified.

It wasn't anyone else though. He was Cain, so she wasn't. She couldn't be. She'd come to know him, trust him, the man who'd saved her once before, the very first night they met.

After the first Guardian meeting she'd attended, where she'd learned her brother was destined for Jocelyn, she and Landon had gone to a bar, knowing Jocelyn would be there. For her brother, she'd mustered the courage and asked Cain to dance, only to give her brother and Jocelyn privacy.

They'd been on the dance floor when a bomb was dropped and detonated. Cain had noticed moments before the explosion and pushed her out of harm's way, saving her. He hadn't been so lucky. Terribly burned, it'd taken two days for his body to heal.

So, even though Cain looked deadly in demon form, even though she'd been taught to fear demons, the most reviled of the immortal breeds, she wasn't afraid. Instead she was enthralled, without thought she ran toward him, wanting to get a closer look. When she reached to touch him, he dematerialized. She turned and spotted him, his expression worried.

"Liv, don't please," he said. "You could get hurt."

Smiling she said, "You're not going to hurt me, Cain." Of this, she was sure.

Then she lunged toward him again. Finally reaching him, she placed her hand over his heart and felt it beat.

Seconds later, his body shifted. His demon was gone.

The man standing before her was the Cain she'd

grown to trust, the man who'd saved her, the one who opened up a new world for her, the one she admitted to herself she cared for deeply.

Smirking, she teased, "See, told you, you wouldn't hurt me."

He exhaled, seemingly relieved, then he leaned into her, coming inches from her and in a serious tone, he said, "You're right. I'll never hurt you, ever."

The way he'd said it, delivered in such a heartfelt tone, and the fact she'd heard the truth in his words made her chest ache. She couldn't grasp why.

Chapter 5

The cool air hit him immediately as Cain materialized in southern Santorini.

He'd come for one reason, Olivia, bringing nothing but the clothes on his back and his wallet. Everything else he needed was already here.

Quickly, he perused his surroundings. One road with two lanes led away. Bushes and shrubbery grew sporadically around him, for miles it seemed. He couldn't see the beach from where he stood, but he smelled the sea's salty water and heard the waves pound the shore. This far south, he only found two houses off the beach. One was more secluded, fenced in, partly concealed with trees and more grand than the other. Knowing the alpha and his expensive tastes, Cain chose to inspect the lavish home first.

One whiff and a hint of Olivia's clean pine scent penetrated his senses. He shivered, enjoying it for what it meant. She was near. He sighed in relief, then followed her scent. It led him toward the back of the two-story home past an infinity pool and hot tub and toward a private beach.

His mate was nowhere in sight. But her scent was stronger there, which meant Olivia must have gone for a walk, so he sat on the sand and waited.

He wondered briefly where she had gone and how much longer until he saw her again. He supposed it didn't matter. She was on the island and sooner or later would return. But because it had been days since he'd seen her and missed her terribly, he needed to see her more than he needed the air to breathe and the earth to roam.

The aching in his chest, that had begun the moment Jocelyn admitted Olivia had taken off, hadn't subsided as the days passed. On the contrary, the throbbing intensified ten-fold. When he discovered her location, the pain had deepened, burning a hole in his heart. Honestly, he wasn't sure if he'd ever be the same. The memory of her loss was carved into his heart and would live in his soul until his days on earth were over.

Figures Landon would have taken precautions to ensure they couldn't be found in spite of all the documents and sites he'd hacked into. He didn't know an immortal who didn't conceal their true selves, and everything belonging to them. It was a prerequisite to being an immortal, learning to hide and living invisible.

He had Jocelyn to thank for leading him to Olivia. Because he'd been angry with Jocelyn for withholding and frantic to get to his mate, he'd forgotten to thank her but supposed she understood. In hindsight, she'd done the right thing. The last thing he needed was to show up in the disastrous condition he'd been in.

For Olivia, he wanted to be better and worth more than the orphaned demon he was. He wanted to care for her, protect her, hold her and love her as he should have been during the last five months. And above all, he wanted to be the one she ran to, not the one she ran away from.

As the sun descended into the horizon, his thoughts wandered again, reliving the moment they'd first laid eyes on each other, the same night she'd cared for him after he'd been injured. Although it seemed so long ago, it hadn't even been half a year. All the memories had led him to that very moment.

Knowing he'd waited too long, he scolded himself. He'd done so countless times the past three days.

When the last of the sun was swallowed by the ocean, a breeze carrying Olivia's scent wafted into his senses, his mangled heart thumped wildly.

Immediately, he stood, his eyes greedily scanned the beach until he spotted her. His gaze bored into her, searing the image of her into him. She was as beautiful as the image of her in his mind but somehow, that image paled in comparison. In person, she was so much more: simply breathtaking.

She wore a blue empire waist dress that flowed around her. Her dark hair, two inches longer since they met, spilled around her oval face. When those blue eyes he dreamt of, met his, they widened. Her rosy lips parted, and her breath hitched.

At last, as it had for days, the air he breathed no longer singed his lungs. His chest swelled in relief, no longer aching in anguish.

Because he wanted to memorize every part of her anew and because he wanted to remember that moment of triumph—the moment he'd found her, he stalked toward her slowly, silently vowing: *Never will I part from Olivia again.*

Chapter 6

It was improbable he would look for her and implausible he would find her, but he had.

Cain, the demon she'd fought to forget since the moment she laid eyes on him.

Although she would recognize him anywhere, it wasn't the man she'd come to love and admire. The man staring back at her was a shadow of the man she'd become too familiar with, the same who'd haunted her dreams the night before. His hair was disheveled, and the sparkle in his eyes gone.

And yet it was Cain.

It was his blue-eyed gaze that bore into her, burning her with awareness, and his fierce expression laced in torment, pain and grim determination that unnerved her now as he patiently strode to her.

I'm mistaken. He had to be a figment of her overactive imagination, a trick of the mind showing her what she most desired instead of reality. But as he neared, mere feet from her, the wind shifted and his scent permeated her senses. Her skin tingled as it always did when he neared. She knew then he was real, not a creation of her deepest desire.

His gaze trailed up and down her body. When it met hers again, his eyes glowed deep crimson.

Her heart pounding, her pulse quickening, she held her breath. Her mind spinning, jumbled with questions.

What had happened to him? Why had he come? Was he not needed by his king? She knew he'd never hurt her, but why then was his burning gaze centered on her? As far as she knew, a demon's eyes only glowed when angry and close to giving into his demon.

Instead of asking all those questions, she asked, "How…" Her voice cracked. "How did you find me?"

His eyes burned a brighter, deeper red, unnerving her further. Instinctively, she took a step away.

His face transformed in a split second, his features hardening. Placing his palm over his heart as if her words and actions caused him ache, he asked with a rough voice, "Are you afraid of me? You think I came here to hurt you? You think me capable of hurting *you*?"

Hands shaking nervously, she pressed her palms against her thighs then admitted, "I'm not afraid of you, but you…you're angry…and I don't know…"

He tore his gaze away from her and recoiled, looking pained.

"I just don't know what you're doing here," she finished quickly.

He ran his fingers through his hair then cleared his throat and met her stare. "Why do you think I'm angry?"

She paused, considering how she should answer. They were friends, comfortable with each other, and she'd always been honest with him, but he seemed so different from the man she'd fallen for. He looked different, but it wasn't just that. It was his expression, the air around him. Jovial, jesting Cain was gone. In his place was this man, defeated and solemn, a shell of the man she'd known.

Choosing her words wisely, she admitted, "I don't know...I—"

"I'm not angry," he said and took a step toward her. "I came here for you."

"But your eyes—"

"What about them?" he interrupted, impatiently.

"They're glowing. You told me..." She faltered. The longer she gazed at him the more she felt the inexplicable urge to comfort him.

He shook his head once, then said, "It's not because I'm angry."

Why else then? she wondered, then asked, "Why are you here?"

"Because you left," he said simply and didn't elaborate as if the matter wasn't for further discussion.

Still, her heart lurched. She shook her head attempting to rid herself of the hope his words spurred, knowing in her heart, he couldn't care for her like she cared for him.

"And?" she prodded.

"Why did you leave, Liv?" he asked, ignoring her question. His eyes were bleak yet seeking, searching for something though she didn't know what.

She hated the question because she couldn't admit the truth—he was the reason she'd left. She didn't possess the courage to say it, and she was too inexperienced with men, immortal or otherwise to serve her heart on a platter.

"Because I needed a...break," she blurted a version of the truth. The same version she'd told her brother.

"From what?" he prodded but didn't wait for a response. "From *me*, Liv? Did you need a break from me?" His voice had gone solemn.

Her heart nearly shattered, still confounded by the man who stood in front of her.

Yes, the answer to his question rested on the tip of her tongue, but she couldn't voice it. "I…I needed a break from everything. There's been a lot going on and I just wanted to…" She paused.

He sighed seemingly in exasperation, but the resolve in his expression never left. He came for a reason, for a purpose, and she needed to know why.

"Did my brother send you?"

He chuckled humorlessly. "No, he didn't send me, and he doesn't know I'm here." He said the latter firmly.

"How did you find me?"

Instead of answering, he asked, "Why didn't you tell me you were leaving?"

"Why does it matter?"

He clenched his jaw. "Because I *care*," he said firmly in a tone he'd never used with her in the past, rough and unrelenting.

Of course, he cared. It was in his nature. He was kindhearted, always more concerned for others than himself, one of the many reasons she'd fallen for him.

"You shouldn't care," she blurted before she thought it through.

"I *care*, and I *can't* stop," he said decisively, then his eyes trailed up and down her body, causing a shiver to run through her. "Are you hungry?"

"Um…yes." *Liar*, her conscience sneered. She hadn't been hungry for days.

His shoulders relaxing, he said, "I'm starved. Do you know of any good places to eat?" Then he smiled for the first time, but the smile never reached his eyes.

Still, it gave her a glimpse of the man she loved.

She nodded.

"Come. It's on me."

Finally, the red in his eyes dissipated. She caught sight of that blue color, but the glimmer hadn't returned.

Chapter 7

The reunion he'd envisioned thousands of times since she left didn't go as planned. After the endless days without her, he needed to hold her, but her reaction stopped him from dragging her into his arms. The shock then sadness streaming off of her stalled him. Now his body ached for what should have been— her body against his, her warmth even if it had only lasted a measly moment.

He spent days wondering how she'd react.

Now, he knew.

When she found him on the beach, the strength of her shock blasted through him. He hadn't sensed fear, but her actions spoke for her, said she had been afraid of his glowing red gaze. Unfortunately, there was nothing he could've done to control it. His mate left him, and he spent three days wondering and worrying. The instant he spotted her, his eyes glowed. A demon's eyes glowed for a number of reasons: any strong emotion did the trick. His had glowed with every ounce of love he felt for her.

But she didn't know that. What she knew about demons, he'd told her because he'd taught her about other breeds. At the time, he thought it wise to leave that tidbit of information out.

Too quickly her shock morphed to sadness, that same deep-seated sadness he sensed weeks before she left. Perhaps, his fear wasn't just a fear. Perhaps, she knew she was his and didn't want him. Perhaps, she'd envisioned loving a werewolf and couldn't stand the thought that her demon mate had come in search of her regardless of the feelings he knew she possessed for him.

What he wouldn't give for a glimpse into her mind. He could ask, but he knew it'd get him nowhere. She wasn't answering any of his questions. Go figure, he wasn't answering any of hers.

Olivia gave him the address of a seafood restaurant on the island. He insisted he drive instead of his usual mode of transportation, materializing, figuring it would give her time to get used to his untimely arrival.

Besides her directions, the drive to the restaurant was quiet. When they reached a small establishment near Black Beach, he opened her door and led her inside. The hostess seated them on the outside patio near the ocean. He pulled out a chair, and she sat.

She waited until he took a seat across from her before she spoke. "Cain, what are you doing here? Doesn't Lucas need you?"

Wishing she'd stop questioning his reasons, his gaze on the menu in front of him, he muttered, "I'm on vacation."

"Really?" She sounded doubtful.

"Yeah, a much needed one. Haven't been on a vacation in..." He looked up to her and admitted, "Well, I've never been on vacation."

"Why here?"

Eyes narrowing, he replied firmly, "Because you're here."

Looking uncomfortable, she glanced away.

His gaze hardened further, then he asked, "Do you want me to leave?" He didn't know why he bothered to ask because there was no way in hell he'd leave. Still, he supposed a part of him wanted to know.

Her gaze landed on his again.

When she didn't answer, he asked, "Did you have plans with someone else? Am I crashing a hot date?" Some of the anger the thought sparked leaked into his voice, despite his attempts to sound nonchalant. *Is it with a werewolf? Cause I'll kill the bastard.*

On cue, her eyes went wide, and her face flushed, tinting her cheeks a lovely rosy shade.

God, how he'd missed that, even the simplest of things, watching her face flush.

She swallowed visibly then, finally, she shook her head.

He released a breath then smiled and said, "Good."

Looking down at her menu, she asked, "How long are you on vacation?"

He shrugged then admitted, "As long as it takes."

Her head snapped back up, those crystal clear blue eyes under her furrowed brows met his. "As long as what takes?"

As long as it takes for you to love me, he thought.

Pausing, he analyzed her expression and demeanor realizing she continued to cower away from him and flinch every so often.

What had happened? What had changed? Days ago, they'd been friends, good friends, who joked, laughed and teased often. There had been no uncomfortable silences, and no imaginary walls causing the cold distance that existed between them now. There had been trust, respect, attraction and love, on his part at least.

"Why do you look scared of me?"

She looked away from him then said, "I...I—"

"You've never been scared of me before," he pointed out, interrupting her.

Meeting his stare again, she said, "If you were reading me, you'd know I'm not scared of you. I'm uncomfortable...I've never seen you like..." Her gaze scanned him from top to bottom, then she finished, "...*this*."

Like I went through hell and back in three days? Because you never left me before.

Even as he thought it, guilt and remorse washed over him because in that moment, he realized he was screwing up his second chance.

Reaching for her hand, he clasped it in his. The small touch was meant to comfort her, but the instant he felt her soft smooth skin, it soothed him. "I'm sorry. I've been through a lot the past several days. Hence, this much needed vacation."

Her eyes softened and saddened simultaneously, she asked, "Do you want to talk about it?"

The tension in his shoulders dissolved. Because her eyes gave her away, because he knew she cared, he found himself genuinely smiling for the first time in days. "It's my burden, Liv."

The waitress placed their drinks on the table and took their orders. Though he hated to do it, he knew he had to. He released her hand then took a sip of whiskey and felt the alcohol burn down his throat, partially soothing his nerves.

Hoping to rid them both of their moods, hoping they'd overcome the barrier, he asked, "What have you done since you've been here?"

She sipped her martini then said, "Nothing, really, just catching up on sleep."

"We should go dancing tomorrow night."

Her eyes widened, a soft smile spread across her lips. "Really?" She couldn't keep the excitement from her voice.

He chuckled, loving her reaction to the simple invitation. "Yeah, you love dancing."

"How did you—"

"I remember from that night we danced."

"Oh," she replied.

The sadness returned. He heard it in her voice, read it on her expression and the emotion struck him anew. He barely controlled the need to cringe, hating the emotion altogether.

Even though over the last five months he watched her, constantly learning everything he could about her, there was so much he didn't know. Like the sadness that came so unexpectedly, so quickly. It wasn't the first time. Weeks ago, her moods began to shift, sadness coming suddenly. What went on in that head of hers? Why did she keep it from him? Repeatedly sensing it in her caused havoc in his soul, shredded pieces of it little by little. Because he'd sensed it so often, he was sure he had no soul left, sure he was damned.

He did what he always did when it came. He tried to fix it, ease it or erase it altogether. "We don't have to go if you're not up for it."

"No, I just…" She paused, took a deep breath then admitted, "I hate remembering that night."

He remembered that night well because he'd seared it into his mind, because he loved that night. The night of the Guardian meeting, the night she'd seen him for the very first time.

After the meeting, after seeing her and being unable to hold her, talk to her, he'd been disillusioned and contemplative. Because he was guarding Jocelyn, he ended up in a bar in Manhattan, talking to Jocelyn about nothing important, but the entire time he'd been trying to come up with a plan, a way to get close to Olivia. He hadn't needed one. Half an hour after they arrived, Landon and Olivia had, sealing his fate.

That night, he'd gotten to talk to her and dance with her, though her brother protested. That night, he'd even proved he could care for her. During their second dance, a group of Malums had attacked, dropping a make-shift bomb on the dance floor. He'd pushed her out of harm's way, risked his life and almost died doing it, but he'd saved her. He remembered that night fondly because even thinking he would die, right before everything faded away he knew she would live. Knowing she would, knowing his last act on earth was saving his mate as the darkness engulfed him, he smiled. He was glad when he woke the next morning, but had he died, he would've been content.

Because of all of those reasons, hearing her say she hated that night made panic claw him. "Why?" *Because you met me?*

She took another a sip of her martini as if summoning the courage to respond. With each second, his heart drummed louder until finally she said, "Because you almost died."

Releasing a breath, he smiled. "Yeah, but it was still a great night. I met you. I danced with you." *One of the most memorable nights of my life,* he left unsaid.

"But you almost died trying to save someone you barely knew," she pointed out, sounding so sad.

"It was worth it, and I would do it again in a second," he said quickly.

The sadness in her returned, then looking resigned, she said, "I guess you're used to risking your life for other people because it's part of your job."

Silently cursing, he clenched his jaw, then took a deep breath wondering why she couldn't understand what he meant. She was very smart, he knew. She spent all her spare time in her library, yet she never seemed to grasp his compliments.

"It's part of my job, but that's not why I'd do it again."

The waitress neared with their food and set their entrées in front of them. The whole time, he watched Olivia, waiting for her next words.

When the waitress left, she took her first bite then asked, "Have you talked to Landon or Joce?"

She changed the subject, completely disregarding his words. So typical, it was predictable. She did it all the time, but now, more than ever, it made him think she knew the truth—that she was his and chose to ignore it. The reason she left. Why she ignored every one of his compliments and pretended he hadn't said them. The worst part was he couldn't do much about it. For the time being though, he had to get them back to where they'd been.

"Joce, yeah," he answered, belatedly.

"Was she really upset I took off?"

"I think she understands." *I don't*, he thought then asked, "You've called since you got here?"

"Today. Landon was upset, but..." Her words

trailed off then she took a bite of food.

"It's only natural. He's your brother. He cares."

"No, it's my fault. Because of the way I left. I just…I knew if I discussed it with him he'd never let me come alone, so I left in the middle of the night, only left a note."

He nodded, unwilling to speak, so she would continue.

"It's more than that, too," she said, sipping her martini.

She shrugged, and he could tell she wouldn't say anymore unless he asked. He placed his hand over hers again. "You can tell me, Liv," he urged. "Anything and everything, you know you can trust me. You know I won't tell anyone."

She sighed heavily then admitted, "When I was two, our dad was killed during the vampire werewolf war. Less than a year after, our mom died. Doctors said it was from a broken heart, from losing her male. I didn't take any of it well."

His eyes widened. Though he'd known her father had been killed during the war, he hadn't known her mother followed such a short time later.

"Landon is four hundred years older, but I was just a baby. I was terrified I'd lose him too, so I wouldn't let him out of my sight. I would latch onto him and go everywhere he went. If he tried to leave without me, I'd cry bloody murder. If I woke up and he wasn't around, I'd suffer awful panic attacks, wail and scream until I threw up. It lasted until my pre-teen years. Even after that, I needed to know where he was at all times. He is my brother but acted like a father. He never complained and treated me like a princess no matter what he had to do, his responsibilities with the pack. He didn't care. I was his number one because I needed him."

She paused and gazed away from him and toward the ocean. Two emotions streamed from her at once: overwhelming guilt and fierce admiration—for her brother, for everything he'd done for her.

"He's overprotective because of me. He sheltered me and kept the realities of our world from me because he thought I couldn't handle it, but the fact is there was a time when I couldn't even handle being away from the only relative I had left. On some level, I encouraged his behavior. I can't ever repay him for what he's done for me, and I can't express how much it means to me, but I am over a century old now. I'm not afraid of the things I used to be afraid of, but I am afraid of living in a self-created fantasy."

And there it was again, remorse gushing from her, and he finally understood why. She regretted not being strong enough, causing her brother to shield her from the realities of life.

"No one knows the sacrifices he's made more than me. It's why I don't fight him." She laughed humorlessly. "Well, I suppose I should rephrase that. When I found out all he kept from me about the Guardians and the war, I did fight him. I was angry, really angry in a way I'd never been before. I grew a temper and took it out on him. Honestly, looking back now, it wasn't just him leaving me out of things. It was the fact he was so lucky to have found his fated and he denied her. You remember. That was around the time we met. After that, he started to include me in our breed's affairs and even let me join the council."

Pausing for a moment, then she said, "Still, I feel

like it's not enough. I know there are still things he keeps from me, and I want to be more involved. I want to date and—"

Date? His heart slammed against ribs, so hard he thought it had cracked open his chest.

His mate *couldn't* date. He wouldn't tolerate it. His palms beginning to sweat, he fisted the napkin on his lap. Breathing deeply, he asked, "Don't you want to wait to find your male?" He hoped his voice didn't sound as panicked as he felt.

Lifting a brow, she asked, "Have you waited?"

He held her gaze for several moments then finally, unwilling to lie, he shook his head.

Despite the fact he hadn't bedded another woman since he'd found her, he hadn't waited before that. He'd taken pleasure in women hundreds of times, never searched for his mate, never thought twice about the fact she could've been waiting for him. When Olivia was alive and within a fifty mile radius of him, he'd slept with numerous women and the knowledge tormented him. He shouldn't feel like he'd cheated or slighted her in any way, but the guilt was undeniable. She'd been right under his nose, and he hadn't bothered to look.

"I'm sorry," he said.

"For what?"

For not looking for you, he thought, instead he uttered another truth. "For your loss, for losing your mom and dad at a young age, I know how you feel."

Lifting her brows, she asked softly, "Do you?"

He nodded then reluctantly admitted, "I was orphaned at a young age." He paused wondering if it was worth confiding in her knowing she'd pity him, knowing it'd only serve to further prove how different they were. "In the demon plane, there was a war much like the one brewing now. Lucas's father taught and urged my kind to control their demons. He believed we could control ourselves and not live in fear of our demons taking over, and he was right. However, some disagreed. They preferred being reviled by other breeds. They preferred being feared. We called them Hellions. They killed Lucas's family. We recently discovered his twin, David, is responsible for the rise of the Hellions as well as the rise of the Malums in this plane."

His gaze drifted away from hers, unwilling to see the pity in them when he knew he would sense it spilling from her as well.

"At the time, Lucas created an army to combat the Hellions. During a raid of one of the homes of Hellions, they found me in a house nearby. My mother, father and brother were killed. I was four. I have no idea why they left me alive. Lucas took me in, treated me like his own."

When he was done, he held his breath as he reached out to sense her feelings.

It wasn't pity.

It was sorrow—for him.

His gaze darted to hers.

Tears rimmed her eyes. "I'm so sorry, Cain," she said as a tear slid down her cheek.

He smiled then reached out to grasp her hand in his, again comforted by her touch. "Don't cry, Liv. It was a long time ago."

She wiped away a tear. "That's why, isn't it?"

Her question caught him off guard, the meaning just out of his reach. "Why what?"

"Why you chose to become a Guardian? Why you risk your life every night?"

Revealing his tragedy, she'd inadvertently understood why he'd chosen his path. "One of the reasons," he said then admitted, "Yeah, the main reason...I couldn't save my family, but I can save other families, other kids from becoming orphaned. I've been lucky though. Lucas has been my family."

She nodded, and he waved the waitress for the check.

"How do you feel about doing some shopping?"

"Shopping?" she repeated, a look of confusion marring her face.

As the waitress neared, check in hand, Cain pulled out his wallet and handed over his credit card. "Yeah, I need some clothes. I didn't bring anything with me. You can help me pick out some stuff."

"Sure. We should go to Fira, the capital. They have tons of stores there."

"Great. Then tomorrow night, I'll take you dancing," he promised, grinning widely. For the first time that night, it was a real grin. He knew because the barrier between them melted away.

"Wouldn't you rather go dancing alone, so you can meet someone or—"

Jesus! Was she serious? "No," he said, firmly. "I came here to be with you."

She blushed, then looked away from him. Hesitating only briefly, she smiled and nodded.

He was familiar with the rosy tint on her cheeks and loved it. It occurred often, anytime he complimented her, flirted with her, or told her a simple truth that expressed how he felt as he'd just done.

Then she did what she did best, she completely disregarded the compliment. "So my brother sent you?"

Grabbing her hand again, he squeezed it lightly. "No, I came here to spend time with *you*. Your brother didn't send me."

Confusion muddling her expression, she asked, "Are you assigned to guard me?"

Shaking his head, he patiently said, "No. I'm on vacation, remember? I'm not assigned to guard you, and your brother didn't send me. I came here to be with *you*."

Her piercing blue gaze fell away from his, in thought, then met his again. "I just don't—"

Leaning in, placing both elbows on the table, his hand still firmly holding hers, he asked, "You don't understand why a man wants to spend time with a beautiful woman?"

Eyes widening, her cheeks turned a rosier shade.

He bit his tongue so he wouldn't chuckle. He didn't find her discomfort amusing, but it was about time she got used to it. She was his. He would have her. When she accepted him, he planned on spending the rest of his life complimenting her.

The waitress returned with his card and receipt. Releasing her hand, he took both, added the tip, signed the receipt then shoved his copy and card in his pocket.

"But—"

"But you don't want me here?" he wondered aloud.

"No, I just—"

He didn't let her speak. "No, you don't want me here?"

Looking flustered, she tried again, "That's not what I meant. I just—"

"Good. Let's go," he said then stood quickly silencing any other rebuttals.

Grabbing her hand again, he pulled her toward him and led her to their car.

Chapter 8

Three and a half months ago

The end of his shift. Finally.

It'd been so long. Ten hours he'd been hunting. Ten hours since he'd seen her.

He hated what he'd come to, but he had no other choice, so he closed his eyes and materialized in Olivia's bedroom, his gaze gravitating to the bed where her sleeping figure lay.

His heartbeat pounding at the base of his neck, he sighed in relief, finally having glimpsed her.

His work had once been his salvation. He'd taken solace in knowing he fought for justice in honor of the family he had lost.

That all changed with his first glimpse of her.

His nights became an agony of craving, a countdown. Each night he counted the hours until he saw her again.

His life became a waiting game: waiting to steal a glance, sometimes even a touch.

It was the way it had to be because she needed time. Time once seemed to fly, now crawled at a snail's pace, taunting him. He lived in a hell where his mate was just within reach yet untouchable, so he wasn't proud of what he'd become—a voyeur, but he had no other choice. He needed her presence to soothe him.

After his long shifts, when everyone was at rest, he appeared in her room and watched without her consent.

He'd been there every night for weeks; regardless, he knew nothing of her room; couldn't describe the color of the walls or furniture. He had no idea if she had an en suite bathroom or the size of her closet, but he had memorized the angelic features of her face, the glow of her skin in the moonlight and the small mole on the corner of her lip. He knew she kicked off her sheets often. It made her shiver moments later, but she still did it, and he knew she tossed and turned and mumbled incoherently in her sleep.

His voyeurism was salvation, satisfying his minimal needs. It wasn't enough, not for him. Honestly, he didn't know how much longer he could withstand it, being so close and yet so far away. Torture of the worst kind, a torture he suffered gladly night after night because his mate needed time.

As his gaze moved to her, he wondered once again how it was possible for anyone be so beautiful, so perfect, how it was possible any female had been created just for him.

What he would give for just one touch, just to feel her silky skin against his?

Anything and everything.

But things remained stagnant, as they had for weeks. She didn't know she belonged to him, granted to him by fate. She didn't know she was his. It was his privilege to know, his duty to tell her, but he couldn't, not just yet. She needed time.

Only minutes had lapsed in her presence, yet he was overwhelmed with his desire to touch her, to feel her skin against the palm of his hand. A desire so deep and primal, his arm extended regardless of his will. His fingers so close, he could feel the warmth permeating her body. He caught himself before he was discovered, and slowly and regretfully withdrew his hand.

She's not ready, he reminded himself. *She needs time.*

The battle inside him waged and he continued fighting his desire for her. Still, he tilted his head back as if in surrender and thanked God, heaven and fate for his precious gift—his Olivia.

Chapter 9

Because it was a small island with only few roads, the drive to Fira seemed longer than it should. She was still in shock over his arrival and still couldn't understand why he'd come.

I came here to be with you, his words continued to replay in her mind. While they partially explained why he had come, they also surged emotions in her she wanted to forget.

Her feelings for him were her reason for leaving home, but he'd found her. There was no escaping him now without telling him the real reason she left. It would hurt him to hear the truth, and she couldn't stand to see the look on his face, the torment and pain she witnessed before.

Something had happened to him while she'd been away, something he wasn't revealing. He'd come to her needing a friend, and she didn't have the heart to turn away the man she loved when he needed her the most.

They were friends and had been for months. She wasn't a fool to think he didn't enjoy her company, but their relationship was what it had always been, a friendship, and it wouldn't lead where her heart wanted it to go.

Hearing his words though, every time he uttered, "I came here to find you," or "I came here for you," her heart fluttered with hope. That hope crashed and burned when her conscience reminded her, the inevitable truth: he cared for her as a friend.

She knew because she was his friend as he was hers. Had he been attracted to her, he would've made a move months ago. It was for the better. Had he kissed her, she would have fallen much sooner only to be broken when he reminded her she wasn't his.

When they arrived in Fira, he once again opened the car door for her. They walked briskly and entered several shops. Cain purchased at least two weeks' worth of clothes including swim trunks, shirts, jeans, shorts and shoes. She assumed he'd spent at least three thousand dollars. The man had expensive taste and it showed.

"Do you want to grab a drink somewhere?"

"Sure."

He shifted the bags in his hands and grabbed her hand, pulling her away from the locals and tourists. She shivered from the warmth of the simple touch. Her hand in his felt right. As soon as the thought reared its head, she shoved it away reminding herself again they were only friends.

With that beautiful grin on his face, he joked, "Did I sting you?"

Not sting, she thought, shaking her head and smiling.

Not a moment later, he pulled her into him, pressing her body against his and wrapping his arms around her.

The length of her body against his, his warmth consuming her, she fought how good it felt and stilled, unsure.

He pulled away from her slightly, his eyes seeking

and finding hers, confusion in his expression. "I think we should drop this stuff off first," he explained.

That made sense to her, so she asked, "Where?"

He grinned widely. "Your house... You don't mind if I crash at your place, right?"

With her? *Shit.* That was a bad, bad idea. Being so close to him, seeing him constantly, she wouldn't be able to get away. Still, she couldn't say no, so she lied. "Of course not."

"Good." He smiled then pulled her head toward his chest. "Close your eyes."

She did. A moment later, her lids drifted open. Her gaze scanning her surroundings, noticing they stood outside her home. She pulled away from him quickly because she didn't want to think about how good it felt in his embrace, but she instantly regretted it, missing his warmth.

Leading him inside, she showed him to a spare room where he placed his bags. He then materialized inches from her face and wrapped his arms around her again. This time, he leaned down, and buried his face in the crook of her neck, each of his breaths burning her skin. She shuddered as goose flesh erupted.

He pulled away from her slightly, his lower body still pressed against hers. "Are you cold? We can go back."

"Back?" she asked, disoriented. Scanning the area, she realized they were once again in Fira near the shops, bars and restaurants. "Oh," she mumbled. "N-no, I'm fine."

Still too close to her, he placed his hand on her forehead. His brows drew together. "You're hot, actually."

Flushing, she admitted, "Yes." *And it's your fault!*

"Are you getting sick? Can werewolves get sick?" he asked quickly.

She hated that he sounded so concerned. It would be so much easier if he could care less. Flustered, she answered truthfully. "No, we can't get sick. I'm warm because..." *No!* She couldn't admit that.

There were three reasons a werewolf's temperature spiked, a need to shift, anger or craving. She was scorching with need.

After a long pause, she said, "It's a weird wolf thing."

"Do you need to shift? We can go back—"

"I'm fine." She interrupted him harshly, then instantly regretted her tone.

He nodded, but she didn't miss his clenched jaw. "Where to?"

She took a step away from him, avoiding his gaze. "There's a bar overlooking the ocean. It's down this way," she said then turned and led the way.

He caught up to her, walking close to her side. Just then she felt it—tension, lots of it, making the air nearly unbreathable. Confounded by it, she spared a glance in his direction. Her jaw dropped when she realized his eyes had begun to glow in public. *Not good.*

"Cain, your eyes," she whispered.

"Fuck," he hissed, sounding as angry as he looked.

He grabbed her hand and led her away from the crowds and into a narrow alleyway. Not a moment later, his body enclosed hers. Without touching her, he closed in until her back was pressed against the wall. His arms went to each side of her head, trapping her in a touchless embrace as his eyes swarmed a deeper crimson.

Shit! She was in trouble, and she knew it. Cain wasn't one to lose his cool and anger, yet he was angry, angry enough he would lose it any moment. The fierce expression marring his face, the ticking muscle in his jaw, his glowing eyes, all bore testament to his anger, anger that knotted every muscle in his powerful body. The air around them was so thick with tension it was suffocating, and she knew she felt it only because he couldn't control it.

Softening her voice, she asked nervously, "What's wrong?"

The tension surrounding them heightened, so she couldn't breathe. His eyes hardening to slits bore into her then a rush of anger hit her square in the chest, leaving her breathless.

His anger.

He projected it as only demons could. What she didn't know was whether he'd done it intentionally. She hoped he had because if he hadn't it meant he'd already lost it and that meant he *would* turn.

"Why didn't you tell me *you* were leaving?" he barked. His breath hit her with each word, laced with rage.

"What?" She managed the strength to mumble.

He drew closer, pressing his chest against hers. The heat of his body caressing hers, she grew warm with craving. Helplessly, her gaze drifted to his thick full lips. Her mind wandered. What she'd give for a kiss, a single mind-blowing kiss?

Cheeks flushing, her gaze darted toward his again. "Why are you..." Her body's desires overwhelming her, she gasped for breath.

"Why didn't you tell me you were *leaving*?"

He wasn't just angry. He was livid, and he was livid with her because she'd left.

She didn't know what to say, had no excuse, not one she could tell him anyway, so she said nothing.

Shutting his eyes firmly, his anger intensified, coiling rapidly against her until she not only felt it but tasted it.

Still, she wasn't afraid. With each passing moment, all she felt was heat, his and hers, and how badly she wanted him.

"Answer me," he demanded harshly. "Tell me why you left without telling me!"

His tone startling her, she jolted against him, her body rubbing his. A desire so powerful rippled through her and spiraled inside her, pooling liquid between her legs. It clouded her every thought and every action, so as she stared straight into his eyes, she couldn't remember what he'd said.

Clenching his jaw, he ground his teeth in anger, so close to losing it. "Olivia, tell me!"

She should be afraid, trapped in an angry demon's embrace, but she wasn't, as unbelievable as it was. All she felt was him so close to her, and that was all she'd wanted for months. It was crazy, even to her it sounded crazy, but then again, she knew deep down Cain would never hurt her.

She pressed her hands against his chest, praying she possessed the strength to push him away. Without his heat, his touch, him inciting her, she would regain the ability to hear, to think.

He didn't budge, not an inch. Instead, he growled, low and guttural. The sound resonated in her chest. She shut her eyes, clenching them, naïvely attempting to force herself to ignore the longing inside her.

"Olivia." He pronounced each syllable of her name. "Why did you leave without telling me?"

She finally heard his words, and still she hesitated because she couldn't tell him the truth. Knowing she had to say something before he scented her desire, she blurted, "I didn't think it mattered."

His eyes narrowed further. His arms, blocking her escape, trembled with anger. "Why would you think it didn't matter? I've seen you every day for months. I thought we were friends—"

"I'm sorry. I just...I didn't think you'd be..."

Her words fell away when he placed his big hands on her cheeks, rested his forehead against hers, staring deep into her eyes. His lips millimeters from hers, he gasped for breath.

Slowly, the anger around them dissipated. When it did, he placed a soft kiss on her cheek. His full lips trembled against her, amplifying her desire so much she couldn't hold her weight. Her knees buckled beneath her.

He wrapped his arms around her, catching her, further pressing the length of her body against his. He held her for moments too long. She fought not to give in, her body tense against his until, finally, she gave up. She couldn't fight the need inside her anymore, the need to be held by him, something she'd wanted for so long. She rested her cheek on his chest, closed her eyes and enjoyed the feeling of his arms around her, enjoyed that with every breath, his scent seared its way into her.

"Olivia, forgive me," he rasped, his voice tormented.

For what? For making me melt? For making me want you? For making me love you?

"I'm sorry. I just…I was angry you left. I thought you were running…" His voice sounding choked, he finally said, "…from me."

Her heart clenched. She swallowed the lump in her throat, knowing now she'd never summon the courage to tell him the truth. She had been running from him, from the emotions he kindled in her.

She wanted to ask why he cared but couldn't summon the courage for that either, not while he held her so tenderly, cradling her against his chest.

One of his arms trailed up her side then cupped her cheek and pulled her face even closer to his. "I'm sorry, Liv. I have no reason to treat you this way…I feel like…you're pushing me away. I'm trying to…"

His voice laced with anguish tore at her. Inside, her heart broke to pieces, crying for him.

Who was this quick-tempered man? He wasn't the man she'd grown to love. She should be glad he was giving her reason to push him away, but she couldn't stand the thought, not after he'd come such a long way for her, not after whatever had changed him. She yearned to make it better, to help him find himself again because, regardless of his newfound temper, she loved him.

I'm pushing you away because I love you, she thought. Staring into his eyes, so blue and so sorrowful, she finally found the courage to mutter, "Cain, you don't have to apologize."

His expression was bleak when he said, "I owe you much more than an apology, Liv."

His body shuddered against hers, making her crave

him more. "Yes…a drink. You promised me a drink," she said and smiled despite her desire.

He nodded and then slowly released her. As her feet hit the ground, she wobbled. He quickly placed both hands on her hips to steady her.

In minutes, they reached the bar. Cain ordered a round of drinks, apple martini for her and a whiskey straight for himself. She took two large gulps of her martini, then together they headed toward the balcony overlooking the ocean.

He stood beside her, the heat of his eyes on her when he said, "Liv, I'm so sorry I lost it."

She turned to meet his gaze and said, "There's nothing to be sorry about." She meant it. Deep down, she knew she deserved it, for running from him, for not telling him the truth. Most importantly, there was no need for an apology because she'd enjoyed it, enjoyed it so much she craved him even then. Hoping to keep that thought at bay, she said, "Landon used to bring me to this island as a kid, at least once a year."

Cain exhaled, seemingly relieved for the change in subject. "What did you do here?"

She turned to look at the ocean. Its breeze wrapped around her, taking with it the warmth of him that'd still clung to her. Now it seemed like the moment never happened, like it had been an illusion—one of her best created fantasies.

"We spent most of our time on the beach. The water's cold, but still enjoyable. We also climbed the Mesa Vouno mountain several times and visited the ancient Thira settlement."

"Did you ever vacation anywhere else?"

"Yes, we went to California, Miami and Barcelona

as well but only a handful of times, not nearly as often as we came here. Since we have a home here, it's easier. Plus it's an island. My parents bought the property because it's isolated. We have a private beach, so we can shift when we want."

"I haven't seen much of the island, but I think it's beautiful."

She smiled and looked his way then said, "It is. Oia, the northern part of the island, is made up of cliffs." Looking back toward the ocean, she continued, "There's a small church on a separate cliff where people go cliff diving. It's lovely in an unconventional way. I always pictured myself getting married there."

"You will," he said, definitively.

She turned to look at him. His eyes seemed somber; the glimmer usually present had once again dissipated. Again, she wondered what could've altered Cain, a carefree man, so drastically in such a short period of time. She couldn't help the words spilling from her lips.

"What happened to you? What happened when I was away that changed you?"

His face hardened then he shook his head.

"You can tell me, Cain. We're friends."

As if she said something to anger him, his eyes briefly sparked red.

He shut his eyes for a moment. When he opened them, they were once again blue. "I know I can, and I will, soon, just not tonight."

She nodded, acknowledging he may have changed, but she hadn't. Her love for him hadn't faded. She needed and wanted him more than ever, which only made her wonder if she'd ever get over him. Her instincts told her she wouldn't, and that was what she feared. Today, they were still friends. Nothing changed between them, but the minute he found his mate, it would.

He finished his drink and ordered another round. She took another sip of her martini, noticing for the first time it was strong. The alcohol burned her throat as she swallowed. The music blared inside the bar distracting her from her thoughts.

"Would you like to dance?" a voice behind her asked.

She turned and spotted a man, around six-feet-tall with dark hair and green eyes, hazy from drinking. The scent of alcohol filled her nostrils.

Tension coiled around her, and she turned to look beside her where Cain stood. His muscles were bulging, his face stark with anger, appearing inhuman like the powerful demon he was.

Could he be jealous? As quickly as the thought appeared, she batted it down. He was just being a friend trying to protect her from a mortal, drunk beyond reason. She placed her palm on Cain's chest, a futile attempt to stall him.

Turning again to face the mortal, she said, "No, thank you."

Immediately, she turned back to Cain. Jaw clenched so hard it was a wonder he didn't crack his teeth, his gaze still locked on the mortal walking away from her.

She patted his stomach until his eyes met hers. "Do you think I'm stupid?"

His face blanched then he asked, "What?"

She heard his heart hammer, quickening more so

than when he'd been ready to fight. *Weird,* she thought. "You think I'd consider dancing with an intoxicated man? I mean I could. It's not really like he could hurt me, but…"

He sighed. "Liv, I…That…" He turned away from her, facing the ocean.

"What?"

When he turned to her once again, he leaned down bringing his face an inch from hers. His eyes blazing red, he spoke. "Do you even realize…" Releasing a breath, he snapped, "I could kill him!"

Grabbing the hem of his shirt, she angled herself so her back faced the ocean and he stood in front of her, his eyes away from the mortals in the bar then she asked, "Why?"

Clenching his jaw, he snapped, "I'm an empath, remember? I know what he was feeling…he was…*fuck*!" His jaw ticked once then twice, his face beginning to darken, darken in the way it did when he turned demon.

Shit. It meant he was getting angrier, angrier then he'd been before, angry enough to fuel his demon, making him start to turn.

She wasn't afraid for herself because demon or not, Cain would never hurt her, but she was terrified of what it would mean for him, blowing his cover in front of mortals.

"Cain, please…just…calm down." She paused, watching him attempt to control his temper and helpless with no idea what to do.

He was failing and fast. His face was now fully flamed, a tone darker, as it was when he turned, and his eyes brightened to a deeper crimson.

She panicked and did the only thing she could think of. Placing her hands on each side of his face, she forced him to meet her eyes. "Nothing happened, I'm fine," she reminded him.

His hands went to her hips, his fingers clutching her, digging into her skin. "Stop...I don't want to hurt—"

Shaking her head, she said, "You *can't* hurt me, Cain, even if you wanted to. It's not in you to hurt a woman." She swallowed suddenly aware she was millimeters from his lips.

He closed his eyes firmly then opened them. The next minute, he wrapped his arms around her waist, pressing her pelvis toward his.

His lengthening shaft throbbed against her stomach. She gasped, her heart palpitating wildly ready to break free of her chest.

He wants me, she thought, her mind swirling. *It doesn't mean anything*, she chanted in her head. A man could be attracted to a woman. It didn't mean he wanted a relationship with her. It didn't mean she was his.

Oh crap, I'm in so much trouble. He'll never fit me. Her last thought startled her. Was she considering bedding him? Would she have sex, her first time, with a demon she loved but could never keep?

No, she couldn't; it would break her.

He leaned in, burying his face in the crook of her neck, then he ran his tongue along the sensitive flesh below her earlobe.

Her eyes closed, her breathing hitched as a soft moan escaped her lips. Heat engulfed every inch of her stirring desire. She couldn't fight it. Her fingers clutching his face, her body molded to his, melting against him.

He then feathered a light kiss under her ear, and held her for several moments until her breaths slowed.

"Meae deliciae, meus sodalis," he whispered against that same spot, his breath heating the skin on her neck.

Ignorant of the meaning, and too enthralled in the moment to ask or to push him away, she didn't, instead she fought a tremor and failed.

He pulled away slightly, only enough to meet her eyes. "Darling, we should go."

Darling? She nodded.

Still, he didn't release her. He held her for several more moments staring into her eyes as if no other woman existed.

Her heart clenching in her chest, her mind whispered, *I love you.* She so desperately wanted to force the words out, tell him the truth.

Just when she parted her lips to speak, he released her hips, wrapping one arm around her shoulders, and led her out of the bar into the night.

Chapter 10

The scent of the ocean and the familiar scent of the peach candles she burned inside her home told her they'd arrived. Quickly and regretfully, she pulled away from Cain's embrace and hurried inside. Rushing into her room, she closed the door behind her then slumped against it in relief, catching her breath, futilely attempting to dispel the emotions running through her.

After several moments she turned, intent on taking a cold shower and nearly collided with the man she hoped to escape.

"Oh!" She gasped, clutching her chest, her scare forgotten the moment her gaze climbed to his.

She wasn't an empath, but the forlorn drawn expression marring his face made his emotions clear. Her stomach knotted as the need to comfort him gnawed her raw.

"I didn't mean to scare you. I just…I'm sorry for—"

"Stop apologizing to me. You haven't done anything wrong."

His face hardening, he said, "I held you in an alley and demanded answers from you. I almost lost it again at the bar then I licked…"

She felt herself flush.

His face aghast, he asked, "You're ashamed?"

"No," she said instantly wondering why in the

world he'd think that. "I'm not ashamed. I'm…" Her words fell away, feeling heat climb down her neck and chest. "…embarrassed we're discussing it."

Running his hand through his blond hair, he said, "I'm sorry I'm ruining this. It's my fault. I can't seem to do anything right—"

"Stop!" she yelled, exasperated with his apologies. "I'm a werewolf. I can handle myself! I didn't stop you because it felt good. You make me…"

She trailed off again, then cringed when she realized what she'd admitted. Turning away from him, she was sure her face was as red as a tomato.

What did it matter? Why should she care if he saw her blush? He was an empath and could feel how badly she wanted him. And still, she felt embarrassed. No, it was more like humiliated because he knew how she felt and he didn't feel the same, but also because of her own inexperience.

"Liv," he said, closing the distance between them. Only a foot away, he asked, "Can I hold you?"

Yes, please, hold me forever, she thought then nodded. She was digging her own grave but at the moment she couldn't care less. She wanted, no, she *needed* him to hold her, to comfort her. As reckless and foolish as it was, she wanted to pretend, just for a little while, what she felt wasn't one-sided.

He slowly closed the remaining distance between them, grabbed her hand and turned her then wrapped one arm around her back and cupped the back of her head with the other, pressing her cheek firmly against his chest.

It felt so good, the heat of his body against hers; she closed her eyes tightly and sighed.

He exhaled. "My behavior today has been...I have no excuse. I promise tomorrow will be better."

Today was great. Them together, alone with no other immortals, she'd almost felt like they were a real couple. At times, her heart had chanted they were.

She lifted her head to stare in his eyes. "I had fun today."

Chuckling humorlessly, he whispered, "You're just saying that to make me feel better because you're special like that."

He was doing it again, making her love him even more. She swallowed. "No, I'm not. I hadn't left this house in days before you came. Thank you for dinner and drinks."

It was the truth. Regardless of her dilemma, Cain made everything worthwhile. She loved him; there was no changing it and little use in denying it. She hadn't tried to fall in love with him, but it happened. She couldn't control her feelings for him any more than she could control his. No way around it, so in that moment, she decided to accept what he offered, friendship, without wallowing in misery. She'd have plenty of time to think of how unfair life was when he left. For now, she wanted to take advantage.

"Let's watch a movie," she said.

He kissed the top of her forehead, the heat of his lips making her shiver. "You are an amazing woman. No man I know is worth you," he whispered, then drew his finger down her cheek. Pulling her against his chest until her cheek lay flat against him, he rested his chin on the top of her head and said, "Meae deliciae, meus sodalis."

The words wove themselves around her in a soft

caress like a revelation. Still, she had no knowledge of their meaning. She knew it was Latin, the native tongue of demons, and she didn't care to ask because their meaning didn't matter. At the moment, she was content with believing he'd said something that had the power to change both their lives forever.

****

Well past one a.m., the movie they'd watched ended. With Olivia draped across his chest fast asleep, Cain couldn't summon the strength to move.

Shortly after they'd turned on the movie, he heard the familiar sound of her slow and even breaths. She'd fallen asleep. Not a moment later, he pulled her against him, held her as she slept. Now, he sat as still as he could, admiring her in sleep as he'd done many times before, unbeknownst to her.

He'd done it so often he'd lost count. The first time he'd done it, he hadn't planned it. His fierce craving to see her had demanded it. The desire pierced through him, forcing him to undermine his will. Although he knew she needed time and had vowed he wouldn't destroy his chance with her, he couldn't stay away.

The few hours a day he spent with her weren't enough to soothe his need. After the first night he watched her sleep, he couldn't find the strength to stop. It was destiny's fault, but he couldn't blame fate because he'd been given the best gift of all—someone to share his long existence with. The only solution had been to watch her sleep. It gave them both what they needed: her time, and him, peace.

Tonight as he watched her sleep, his fragmented mind was in shambles. He couldn't believe what he'd done to her, his gift, his mate. He led her in an alley, pressed her against the wall and held her there as he demanded answers. All the while his anger whirled around them, unable to shield her from it. His control lost, gone along with his mind. The first time he'd lost control in more than four hundred years.

Jocelyn was right to have made him wait. It seemed he hadn't waited long enough. The moment he sensed she pushed him away, rage began to bubble. At times as easily as it began, it ebbed. All he had to do was use his gift to read her. In the alley, he thought he'd find fear, instead he found desire. That was all it had taken to soothe him.

His Olivia desired him and had been hot to the touch because she craved him. Although she hadn't said as much, he'd felt it. Now, he'd always know. He'd never forget.

If only he'd read her before she pushed him away, he wouldn't have lost control.

Then when she was opening up to him again, that damn mortal had asked her to dance. The man, too stupid to realize Cain would kill him for even glancing at his mate, was beyond intoxicated, desire had gushed off of him and that desire had been for *his* mate. Even now, it made his blood boil just thinking of it.

You think I'm stupid, she had asked him and his heart nearly stopped. For that brief moment, he thought she'd admit she knew she was his, but she hadn't. Because she didn't know or just refused to admit it, he still didn't know.

To top off the night, he'd licked her! He had actually licked his mate's neck before pressing his lips against hers. He knew she enjoyed it, but that didn't make it right. Licking his virgin mate in a bar to control his demon? The most selfish, inconsiderate thing he'd done in his entire existence.

I'm losing my fucking mind.

It was getting late, and regardless of how he wanted to continue to hold her in his arms, he'd already committed one too many selfish acts. Olivia needed a bed where she could sleep comfortably.

One arm under her legs and the other behind her back, he rose, carrying her, then materialized in her room and laid her in bed. As he pulled away, her nails lengthened, tearing his shirt. He tried to pry her nails away, but she wouldn't let go.

She wants me to stay. A smile spread across his lips. Although he wanted nothing more than to sleep with his mate wrapped around him, he couldn't and wouldn't. She was his, but she was a virgin. Waking with him in her bed would probably scare the crap out of her.

With her hand still firmly grasping his shirt, he pulled it off and let her hold it. Still, he couldn't summon the courage to leave her. He'd been less than a gentleman that day and wouldn't blame her for leaving him again but couldn't fathom waking to find her gone. That fear was overwhelming, earth shattering and undeniable. He'd be destroyed more so than he was already, so instead of heading to the spare bedroom, he lay on the small loveseat in her room. It wasn't big enough for his six-foot-five frame, but it would do.

He laid his head on the armrest facing her, so he wouldn't lose sight, his legs dangling over the other end. Exhausted because he hadn't slept in days, with his eyes still locked on her, the stress and worry overwhelmed him, and finally, he fell asleep easily comforted with the thought she wouldn't be able to run because the minute she tried he'd notice even in his sleep.

****

Olivia stirred in her sleep enjoying the comfort of the soft mattress but not nearly as much as the smell of Cain that still lingered. Eyes still closed, the memory of the night before flooded her.

Cain, he'd come. She was no longer alone hiding from him and how she felt.

Her lids, heavy-lidded with sleep, drifted open, realizing she lay in her bed instead of on the couch where she'd fallen asleep. He must've moved her while she slept. It was so him, considerate and thoughtful.

She sighed. His scent washed over her once again. Finally, she noticed the shirt clenched in her hand, his shirt, the one he wore last night.

Sitting up in bed quickly, she scanned the room. At the far end, her eyes landed on a figure of a shirtless Cain sleeping on the small loveseat. What a picture. His size and stature too big for it, his head rested on one armrest and his legs dangled at least a foot over the other. A giggle bubbling inside her, she clamped her mouth shut afraid the smallest noise would arouse him.

So many questions…Why did she have his shirt? Why was it ripped? Why had he fallen asleep in her room uncomfortably on a couch when he could've used the spare room?

Questions tumbling in her mind and plaguing her, she hopped off the bed and neared. His chiseled features were relaxed in sleep, yet still he was undeniably handsome, too handsome and striking in an obvious way, the type of man every woman wanted, and the type no woman could deny, and she was just "lovely." That's what everyone always said: "Olivia's lovely. Olivia looks lovely tonight. Olivia's dress is lovely."

What she'd give to be more? To be beautiful or sexy or exotic? What she would do to run her fingers through his golden hair then down his muscled chest? What she'd give to place her lips over his?

Anything. Everything.

Conscious of her thoughts, Olivia shook her head and berated herself for gawking at a sleeping man, the man she loved but wasn't hers. *I'm hopeless*, she thought. *Time for Plan B.*

Chapter 11

Cain's eyelids slid open the following morning, locked on where Olivia had been. Her bed was now empty.

Dread and fear prickling through him, he lunged from the sofa, and sprinted toward the bathroom.

It, too, was empty.

His breaths coming rapidly, he materialized in each of the bedrooms first. Finding them empty, he searched the first floor living room, bathroom, study and kitchen. It took mere seconds but already full-blown panic seized him.

She left you again, his conscience sneered.

He materialized outside; instantly scenting her, his nerves began to soothe. Still, he sprinted toward the sandy beach. There, he found her lying on the sand, sunbathing—topless.

Mouth gaping open, his eyes devoured her inch by breathtaking inch. Unable to help himself, he stopped dead and stared at her perfectly rounded, plump breasts. His gaze then trailed down her flat stomach to her legs, admiring her smooth, unblemished skin. Only a skimpy hot-pink bikini bottom covered her and barely.

Mine, he thought, adjusting the bulge in his pants.

He glanced around the beach wondering who else had been privileged enough to enjoy watching what was only his to see.

There was no one in sight.

Good, I won't have to kill anyone.

He growled. As if stung, she sat up quickly, covering her breasts with a folded towel beside her. Her eyes were wide as they met his, her face flushing bright red.

She was a werewolf, part of a pack. Werewolves shifted and hunted in groups, and before they shifted they removed their clothes. Because of it, they were comfortable with nudity. He knew all of this, so the fact she covered herself to hide from him was all it took to snap his control, that now too familiar volatile anger rushing him.

Looking away from him, she said, "Good morning."

Fisting his palms tightly, his eyes hardened then he managed, "Morning." He hadn't meant to bark the word, but realized he had when her gaze shot to his as she clutched the towel against her chest tighter.

Hating her reaction, hating more she'd shielded the body meant for him from him and knowing he was on the verge of turning, he paused, took a deep breath and attempted to rein in his temper. "I thought shifters were comfortable with nudity."

Her eyes widened. "It's different. Landon would protect me. He wouldn't allow anyone—"

"You need protection from *me*?" he asked harshly. Fuck, so much for controlling his temper.

Looking every which way, she said, "No, it's just…it's not like that. I meant when we shift with the pack, I usually shift elsewhere. Landon doesn't let anyone stare at me."

No one had ever seen her naked? How was that

even possible? Wait, who cared? The point was no one had ever seen her naked. He already knew she was a virgin, and he doubted she'd ever even been kissed. It meant she was his, *all his*. He smiled then decided he might start liking Landon after all.

Still, he found the need to point out, "You're shifters."

"Yes, but you've met my brother. You know he's—"

"Cain." Lucas's voice beckoned from behind him.

Immediately, he materialized in front of Olivia, covering her from view. He then grabbed the towel unfolded it and wrapped it around her, concealing every inch of her from her shoulders to mid-thigh.

Then he turned and barked, "What the *fuck*? Olivia's—" He sighed.

Olivia grasped his arm and said, "Cain, stop it." He looked at her, now standing at his side, realizing then she looked worried.

Eyes snapping back to Lucas, he schooled his tone then said, "You could've called."

"Called you on your cell?" Lucas asked, then flung his phone at him. Cain caught it a second before Lucas said, "Your queen was worried about you."

"Sorry, Cain," Jenna said, standing just behind Lucas.

Too distracted with concealing Olivia, he hadn't even spotted his queen.

He was being a dick. He knew it. The thing was he knew nothing would fix it until Olivia was his. Still, he felt bad about it, remorse overwhelmed him.

He closed the distance between himself and Jenna and kneeled before her. "No, I'm sorry."

"Oh God, Cain. You know I hate it when you do that! Get up."

He did, and she hugged him then smiled. "We just wanted to make sure you were okay," Jenna whispered then she turned to Liv and said, "Hi, Liv. Sorry to crash your vacation. We'll be leaving."

"Oh no, why don't you stay for breakfast?" Olivia asked, much to Cain's surprise.

"We can't stay. We're headed to Treconomia for the monthly council meeting, but when you come back into town, we'll have dinner," Jenna promised.

Lucas patted Cain on the back then Jenna wrapped her arms around him. Not a moment later, they were gone.

Olivia closed the distance between them then asked, "What was that about?"

Knowing he couldn't tell her the truth and hating to lie, he gave her half an answer while avoiding her eyes. "They're worried about me."

"I am, too," she admitted.

His gaze shot to her. He didn't need to use his gift because in her eyes and in her too somber expression, he read the sincerity of her words.

"I don't know what happened to you, Cain. You're so...different. I know you're not ready to tell me but just know that whenever you are, I'll be here for you."

He knew she meant it because she was perfect, a perfect woman with the perfect smile, perfect body and sweet beyond reason.

He smiled genuinely. "How about I make you breakfast?"

"I'd love that."

****

Sitting on a stool at the kitchen counter, Olivia watched a shirtless Cain make strawberry pancakes, her favorite. As he moved, the muscles in his back stretched and tightened, her greedy gaze devouring him, enthralled. She had the urge to trail her fingers along the outline of his chest down his rock hard abs and then kiss every inch of him.

Stop dreaming, she thought then exhaled, knowing if she had the chance she wouldn't even know where to start. She'd never been on a date. She'd never even been asked out…She'd never explored a man's body, never even been kissed.

"Are you getting excited?" he asked.

Her face flushed. Scolding herself for her lascivious thoughts, she mumbled, "W-what?"

"The pancakes. They're your favorite, aren't they?"

She exhaled, relieved he'd been referring to food. Of course, even if he had sensed her hormones, he was too much of a gentleman to bring them up.

"Um…yes, of course."

He plated the pancakes, poured two cups of coffee and two glasses of orange juice, then sat on a stool beside her.

"Has Ashley taught you anything new in the kitchen?" she asked. Ashley was Jenna and Jocelyn's sister. Only recently, she'd been reunited with her sisters. Like them, she was an Elemental.

"Yeah, some stuff, but you know her and Clyde are official now, so they've been spending lots of time alone."

"Figures," she said. "I remember when Jocelyn and Landon first got together. They wouldn't leave their room…" She laughed. "They still don't."

"I remember, too. I took advantage of that though," he said and smiled then shoved a large piece of pancake in his mouth.

Her brows drew together in confusion.

He swallowed then explained. "I knew Landon would be preoccupied, so I'd swing by to spend time with you."

What? That was news to her. "I thought you had official business to discuss with Landon and Joce?"

"I did." He shrugged. "Sometimes, but I could have just called them."

She took a sip of coffee, forcing herself not to read into what he'd said, forcing herself to remember he spent time with her in a platonic way.

He took another large bite then asked, "What time did you get up this morning?"

"Around six, I went for a run then sunbathed, but you already know that part," she said, her cheeks heating with the memory.

"Why didn't you wake me?"

"I thought you should sleep." She paused, summoning the courage to ask her next question. "Why were you so upset with Lucas?"

"I wasn't upset with him. I was just…" He sighed heavily. His eyes snapped to hers and hardened then he said, "You were *naked*."

She flushed with just the reminder, then pointed out, "Technically, I wasn't naked." She hadn't been, but she had been topless when Cain found her.

After last night, she didn't think she could be more humiliated. She was wrong. Him catching her topless was worse. Then again, she supposed she deserved it.

She should've been paying attention, listening for him. Instead she'd been daydreaming, so deep into one of her fantasies even with her keen senses she hadn't heard him near.

He clenched his jaw.

Looking away from him, she said, "Sometimes, you're worse than my brother. You do realize Lucas is mated. If he accidentally saw anything, it wouldn't matter. He's not interested. He only has eyes for Jenna."

This was true. In fact, she would've preferred Lucas catching sight of her topless rather than Cain. Because Lucas was mated, he wouldn't prefer anyone over his mate. His opinion wouldn't matter. Cain, on the other hand, as an unmated male, mattered. As the man she'd fallen for, he mattered much more, and she knew his opinion wouldn't be good.

She had no illusions about her looks. She was average: average height, average-sized breasts and average-length dark hair. The one thing she had going for her—her eyes. They were crystal clear blue. She wasn't being insecure, it was just a fact of life. She'd never been called anything but "lovely" and that didn't count because every time she heard someone say it, it wasn't said directly to her but to her brother. "Olivia looks lovely," they'd say, barely sparing a glance at her. Besides that, she'd never been asked out on a date, she'd never been kissed, so needless to say, she was a virgin. The first fifty years of her life, she thought it had to do with her brother's alpha status, overprotective and domineering, but as time passed, she realized it had to be more than that. It had to be *her*.

"It matters to me," he countered, his tone firm.

It was endearing he cared and, in part, the reason it had been so easy to fall in love with him. The problem was it made her think he cared for her as more than a friend. And although she had decided to stop wallowing in self-pity that she'd fallen for a man who wasn't hers, she didn't want him encouraging her feelings for him.

Her gaze snapped to his and narrowed, she said, "Yeah, I can tell, but here's the thing, I don't need another Landon in my life. I already have one overprotective brother. I know it doesn't look like it, but I can handle myself. You don't need to attack random drunk mortals because they asked me to dance."

He flinched, immediately causing her to regret her snide retort. She didn't want to hurt him. She hadn't meant to either. Whatever he'd been through the last several days had been traumatic enough. His king and queen were concerned, and she'd made it worse.

"Why?" he asked.

"Because you…You're making me…" She sighed, then shook her head, shrugged, and mumbled, "Nothing."

"I can't help myself. It's instinct."

It was—for him, protecting was an instinct because he was good, kind, sweet and to top it off—irresistible. And *she* hurt *him*, the man she claimed to love.

She placed her hand over his. "I'm sorry," she confessed.

"It's fine. Hell, it's nice to know you can lose it, too."

A glimpse of the Cain she knew, lighthearted and jesting. She was so relieved to hear it, see it, she threw her head back and laughed.

When she gazed at him again, the intensity in his eyes had tripled. It seemed his gaze hadn't left her. For the first time in her life, she felt like the prey instead of the predator. It unnerved her, and yet it felt great because for some inexplicable reason, it made her feel desired, too.

She couldn't peel her gaze away, so she stared at him, staring at her, then she was suddenly overcome with emotion, a love so profound and intense it brought tears to her eyes, overwhelming, excruciatingly beautiful, deep and meaningful love.

She recognized it instantly because it was how she felt for him. Still, she couldn't explain why she felt it radiate into her as if it wasn't her own.

"Liv." His voice came out hoarse.

Trembling from emotion streaming through her, making it hard to breathe, her gaze met his, then a tear floated down her cheek. "Kiss me," she begged. "Just once, please." After she said it, she couldn't believe the words had escaped her lips.

A moment later, he stood. Towering over her, he wrapped his arm around her waist and lifted her, placing her butt on the countertop. Standing between her legs, eye to eye, he pressed the palm of one hand against her back, pushing her body against his. She fit, melding perfectly against him. He then cupped her cheek, his thumb caressing her as he stared deep into her eyes. Finally, he leaned in and placed his lips firmly over hers.

She opened her mouth and his tongue met hers. Their tongues entwined, making her temperature spike and her core grow moist.

The kiss was passionate, sensual and unnerving,

making her toes curl with desire. He tasted sweeter than she'd ever imagined.

She had no idea what she was doing or if she was doing it right, but she couldn't find the strength to pull away because it was Cain, the man she loved, and he kissed her like he wanted her to be his.

Her first kiss was worth the wait. It hadn't been a random immortal, it was Cain. The man who'd saved her, protected her and befriended her, that she'd remember forever as her first.

There were no regrets.

Chapter 12

Two Months Ago

The day had drifted by slowly. It didn't happen often, only the days she didn't see Cain. Going on four days now, she'd begun to worry.

Over the course of the last three months, since she'd met him, she hadn't gone more than a day. They'd become friends who saw each other, not just often, but daily. They talked, laughed, sometimes even shared meals and trained together.

So it was only natural that she be worried, natural that she was a mess. She couldn't help it. Day in and day out horrible scenarios filled her mind—all ended with him hurt or worse. She knew it unlikely, considering bad news traveled fast, and she was sure Jocelyn would have told her.

With certainty she was sure of two probable scenarios: he was busy on an assignment and couldn't spare time or he didn't want to see her. Both scared her a bit: the first because he always found time for her before, and the second because she wanted to see him. She couldn't blame him though, she knew her feelings for him were growing and felt, perhaps, he felt her feelings for him grow. Perhaps, he didn't want to encourage them and hoped distance would cure that.

In an effort to distract herself, she headed to her

garden to water the flowers. As hard as she tried, she didn't succeed. Her attempts to keep thoughts of Cain at bay were fruitless. The image of Cain injured, as he had been the night he'd saved her, kept sneaking up on her.

Walking through the rows of flowers, watering each she chanted: *He's fine.*

After half an hour, she was exhausted, from the sun's heat and from her frazzled mind. Taking a seat on a bench, she sighed and closed her eyes. Seconds later, his familiar scent permeated her senses. *Great, I'm losing it*, she thought.

"Liv." His voice startled her.

Parting her lids and meeting his too blue eyes, she sprang off the bench. "Oh God," she whispered, her eyes scanning him from head to toe. He wasn't injured; he was safe, standing inches from her, comforting her wrecked, worried mind. She released a breath.

Looking startled himself, he held up his hands. "God, Liv, I'm so sorry, I didn't mean to scare you."

As he stared at her with unhindered concern clear in his eyes, she realized: *I've fallen in love with a demon.* How else to explain why her mind was constantly filled with thoughts of him? How else to explain why she'd been out of her mind with worry?

Shit.

How could this have happened to her? She was inexperienced, had never been kissed or been held or made love, yet here she was in love with a demon.

"Liv, I'm sorry. Are you okay?"

She meant to answer quickly, but the realization she'd fallen for a demon, made her ache and mute, so she nodded.

The sun's rays darkened, she wobbled on her feet.

Cain materialized beside her and wrapped a strong arm around her, steadying her.

"Jesus! Are you okay?" He sounded panicked.

She shook her head hoping the tightening in her chest would dissipate magically, hoping it was a just a school girl crush and it would fade.

She couldn't possibly be in love with the first man she'd felt attracted to—one she could never have. And she was sure she could never have him. He had a mate somewhere waiting for him. It wasn't her, and she knew with certainty because immortal men instantly recognized their mates. In that moment, they were overcome with the instinct, the need to mark and claim them as theirs. She'd known Cain for three months. During those months, he'd never treated her as anything more than a friend, and that meant no matter how much she wished it, she would never be his.

Her vision swirled. Panicked, she glanced around, realizing belatedly she wasn't standing. Once again, she sat on the bench with Cain beside her. "Did you—"

"Yes, I did," he admitted then paused, his eyes scanning her face. "Damn, you're pale." He pressed the palm of his hand against her forehead then cursed, "Shit, you're hot."

She nodded. "I'm overheated."

He wrapped one arm around her waist then gripped the back of her neck with the other, pulling her face against his chest. "Close your eyes, Liv."

She did, and as she did she inhaled, his scent spread through her like wildfire, soothing every inch of her.

"Open your eyes."

Glancing around, she realized she was at the

demon compound on Cain's floor. She had been there once before, the night he'd saved her.

He disappeared then reappeared moments later with a wet towel. Pressing it against her forehead, he released a breath and said, "You're scaring me."

"I'm fine," she insisted.

"You're in shock. I feel it," he said.

Shock? Well, that explained it. She couldn't blame herself either, having just realized she was in love for the first time in her life. "That's very sweet of you, Cain. I'm fine."

As he continued to dab the cold wet towel on her forehead, she watched him. His face riddled with concern, his brows drawn together, worry lines marring his forehead. He anxiously and repeatedly scanned her from top to bottom.

It was only natural that it dawned on her at that moment why it had been so easy to fall for Cain. He was sweet, kind, thoughtful and caring. It didn't hurt that he was handsome, gentlemanly, joked often and never angered. Since the moment she met him, he'd taken her under his wing, patiently taught her about the immortal world she knew so little of but craved to know everything about. On the very first night they'd met, he risked his life to save hers. A week later, when Cameron, werewolf council member, lost his temper, and shifted, Cain had been at her side, blocking her from harm with his towering frame. When Jocelyn trained for battle, he stood beside her like a shield in case anything should go awry. He was her very own bodyguard, ensuring no harm came her way, ever. All of it had drawn her to him like a moth to a flame.

She should have seen it coming. Every time he

taught her, protected her, shielded her and encouraged her, she'd felt her feelings for him grow. Every night before she went to bed, she prayed for his safe return knowing as she drifted to sleep he fought Malums. Every morning, she dreaded finding out he'd been injured or worse.

She should have known.

Stupidly, she hadn't.

She was too naïve, immature and inexperienced to recognize it until it was too late.

"Liv."

"I'm okay, Cain. I promise." *Just helplessly in love with you*, she thought, but left it unsaid.

He disappeared again and reappeared with a glass of water in hand. "Here, drink," he instructed, taking a seat beside her.

She took a sip of water, felt herself relaxing.

"Sorry I haven't been by to hang out," he said. "I was in Treconomia, the demon plane. We're trying to get new recruits."

"For the Guardians?"

He nodded. "How are Joce and Landon? Are they getting along better?"

She rolled her eyes. "You know how they are. They fight like cats and dogs and the next minute, they're going at it like rabbits."

He chuckled. "Yeah, I've seen this mate thing transpire a couple of times already."

She had often wondered if the fighting was part of the mating or if it was exclusive to Jocelyn and Landon. If it was part of the mating, she wasn't sure she wanted anything to do with it, but perhaps that was just the inexperienced part of her talking. She couldn't help the question spilling from her lips.

"Do Jenna and Lucas fight as much?"

"I'm sure they have arguments just not in front of anyone…Jenna's headstrong like Jocelyn but more laid back, too. She was more accepting of the mating thing. I guess she figured there was no use in fighting something you can't control."

"And Jocelyn wasn't accepting," she concluded.

"Yeah, for about a week." He chuckled. "You feeling better?"

"Yes, sorry about that damsel in distress thing."

"You're apologizing for that? I love being your hero," he said, then that amazing smile spread across his lips.

Her pulse quickened. She felt her cheeks flush. Being so inexperienced sucked, especially at times like this because she couldn't tell if he'd just flirted with her.

"You mean you like being the hero. I mean, of course, you do, you're a Guardian," she said quickly.

His smile faded. Briefly, she wondered why, then just as easily disregarded it completely.

Chapter 13

It had been Cain's intention to tell her she was his the moment he unleashed his feelings for her, giving her a glimpse of how he felt, but she'd asked for a kiss and it was a kiss he'd craved for months.

There had been no stopping him.

His mate, Olivia, was finally in his arms, firmly pressed against him. Her temperature spiking, he was overwhelmed with the longing he'd battled for months. All he'd dreamt of was a single kiss, and finally the time had come. It had been worth the wait. His mate had beautiful full lips. Pressed against his, nothing existed but her.

As he kissed her softly and slowly, his demon demanded he mark her, chanting in his head he'd waited too long. Simultaneously, he battled another desire—the need to intensify their kiss and make up for lost time.

He couldn't give in to either.

This was his first kiss with his virgin mate. He had to take his time.

But she was making it harder and harder. Every soft moan, every flick of her tongue drove him mad with craving. As she wrapped her arms around his torso to deepen the kiss and raked her fingers down his back, he growled deep in his throat. She shuddered, her body grazing against his, making him groan.

He ran his hands down her neck, and she arched her back in invitation. He couldn't help himself then. His hand trailed farther until it grasped her breast over the shirt she wore, squeezing lightly. His mouth trailing down her cheek toward her neck, he kissed and licked her softly, searing the taste of her into him, knowing he'd never tasted anyone so sweet.

When the scent of her need wafted into his senses a moment later, he groaned. The instinct to take her nearly took him to his knees. *I can't take her,* he chanted as a reminder, because at any moment he swore he'd lose control.

No matter his restraint, how hard he battled his demon's desires to claim her, his body moved of its own accord. Tugging her closer, he reclaimed her lips again, then hungry for the taste of her skin, he dragged his mouth down her neck. Gums aching, a moment later, his fangs sprang to life for the first time, proving again she was his.

Mark her. Mark her now, his demon purred.

His lips parted; his fangs throbbed. Seconds from giving in to his deepest desire, he materialized feet away from her.

His eyes locked on his mate's. Her lips were swollen from kissing his, her face flushed. *God, she's beautiful,* he thought.

Her shoulders slumped as an expression of disappointment flashed across her face.

She wanted him. He needed her, but pleading and torn, he wavered. Still consumed with his desire, words escaped him.

Her gaze fell away from his then she whispered, "It wasn't good."

His eyes widened. Instantly, he closed the distance he'd forced and clasped her hands, locking them in his. "Why would you say that?"

"You pulled away."

"Because I need to tell you something."

Moments passed. Olivia stared at him expectantly.

The time to tell her had come, but he found his courage fleeting. He feared she'd run—again.

Without releasing her hands, he took a deep breath and shifted his weight then finally, he admitted, "You're mine."

She didn't react. She didn't say a word. Honest, he wasn't sure if she heard him, so he repeated, "You're mine...Or well, I guess I should phrase it differently. You are my fated mate...or female if you prefer."

Then she did react. A soft gasp escaped her kissed lips.

He held still, waiting for her to say something...anything. During those endless moments, he felt emotion streaming off of her—disbelief.

When several more moments passed and she didn't speak, he did. "I've known for a while. I didn't tell you because I knew you...I thought you needed time to adjust to life among other immortals and your new responsibilities among the pack and..."

Pulling her hands away from his, she croaked, "W-what?"

Because he still felt her disbelief, he repeated, "You're my mate, Liv. I know I should have told you before—"

"I'm *what*? I'm *not*. I *can't* be," she said rapidly then pushed him away, making room for her to hop off the counter, turn and walk away from him.

He moved as she did, grabbed her hand, spun her until she faced him again, then he placed his hands on the sides of her face, forcing her eyes to meet his. "Yes," he contradicted. "You *are* my mate."

"But...*No*," she said firmly, shaking her head. She grabbed his hands at her face, pulled them away then turned from him again, walking away.

Running, she's running again. I can't let her get away, not again.

Panic clawing him, he materialized in front of her, blocking her escape. His eyes hardened to slits before, in a grim voice, he said, "Olivia, if you run from me *again*, I promise you I will *chase* you until I *find* you, and you know I keep my promises."

He meant every word. She wouldn't escape him, ever. Claimed or not, she was his, and he vowed he'd never part from her again, no matter what it cost him.

Chapter 14

Her wildly thumping heart stilled the moment he uttered the words that continued to replay in her mind: *You're mine.*

Everything she wanted, everything she needed.

He was all she'd thought of for months, but it couldn't be true. Her mind couldn't grasp it. They'd been friends and only friends for months, and during those months, not once had he done or said anything to make her think she was his.

"I *can't* be your mate. I'm your friend. You've never...you've never been interested in me that way," she said in denial, her voice cracking.

He parted his lips, baring his fangs. Unconsciously stepping away, she gasped. Before she could take another step, his fingers bit into her wrist.

"You *are* mine. My fangs still ache with the need to mark you. I stopped kissing you because I was a second away from sinking them into your neck, and I just showed you how I feel about you."

There it was, an answer to why she'd felt an emotion so powerful radiating through her moments before she'd begged him for a single kiss.

Her heart clenching in her chest, she brought her hand to cover it. "That was you?"

He nodded.

"But...but you...you told me...demons knew right

away when they find their mates. You told me—"

"I *did* know right away!" He paused to run his hand through his hair then he said, "Do you remember the first Guardian meeting you attended?"

Swallowing the emotion clogging her throat, she nodded.

"I saw you for the first time the day before. You were walking across the street from NYU. I was there guarding Jocelyn. I followed you then spotted Landon and overheard your conversation. I knew you'd never met immortals from other breeds, and I knew werewolves are reclusive by nature, so I waited, knowing I'd see you the very next day. It was the best option for me—for *us*."

She remembered the moment well because she'd been overjoyed with the chance to finally get a glimpse of the immortal world. Still, that had been months ago, so she pointed out, "But it's been months since then!"

Eyes hardening, he shot back, "Don't you think I realize that? Do you think I haven't been counting the days myself? Do you realize how hard this has been for *me*?" He sighed heavily. "The moment I met you, you claimed me, and all I wanted and needed was you, but I *couldn't* because I would've risked losing you altogether."

No. I can't be his, she thought, shaking her head in denial. She couldn't be *his* because immortal males couldn't bear being away from their fated mates, the need to mark them was unyielding, overwhelming and overpowered every thought, every action. He'd been able to stay away for *five* months, and for *five* months he hadn't marked her, claimed her.

"Five months? You waited five months? It's *not*

possible. You wouldn't have been able to control your need. Landon almost went crazy denying Jocelyn, and that was only three months."

His eyes sparked, tinting their blue shade blood red then he snapped, "I never *denied* you. I *waited* for you. There's a big difference, and I made every excuse to see you, to spend as much time with you as possible. You *are* mine."

"No, no," she said adamantly, shaking her head. She simply couldn't believe she'd suffered for months for a male she belonged to.

"Yes. When I found you yesterday, you saw my desire. That's why my eyes burned. I had spent days craving you without a glimpse, not knowing where to search. You *are* mine." He tapped his chest forcefully. "*My* mate."

Losing her patience, she shouted, "Stop saying that! I'm *not* your mate. You have—"

His eyes widened, clenching his jaw before he asked, "Olivia, why is this so hard for you to believe?"

Why? Had he really asked her why? Because it didn't make any sense. "Because you...you're an empath. You knew how I felt about you, yet you never told me."

"I knew you were attracted to me, yes, but I wanted it to be more than physical attraction. I knew your feelings were growing, yes, but I didn't know if you could accept a male who wasn't of your kind. I wanted you to get to know me and trust me, maybe love me then when I told you, you wouldn't be able to deny *us* a chance. You wouldn't run, but you *did* anyway."

"I ran because I was trying to forget you," she blurted, then slapped her hand over her mouth as if the action would erase the words.

He recoiled, releasing his hold on her wrist. His expression hardened further, his eyes glowing a brighter red. "To further prove my point, you have no idea what I suffered for three days not knowing where you were or if you were safe, fearing what you just admitted, that you ran from me. *Me!*"

His eyes stark with pain shredded her composure. Tears welled in her eyes, threatening to spill. He'd willingly provided an answer to her lingering question, the reason he was a fraction of the man he used to be. And the answer was her. It was *her* fault. The realization drew grief so thick it choked her.

She gasped for breath as images of him assailed her: when he'd saved her from the explosion at the bar, when he turned in front of her, when she'd almost fainted after realizing she was in love with him. In every image, his jovial expression had transformed, replaced with fear—for her. While she'd lived in misery believing she loved a man she'd never keep, he'd lived in fear of losing a mate he never had.

Finally, she understood. His fear had stalled him, in turn hurting her. But she'd hurt him, too, by running away. Three days, she had been gone before he found her. He'd suffered. She wondered why he'd changed, and now she had the answer, an explanation for his moods, his demeanor and his quick-temper.

Without blinking, tears spilled down her cheeks.

He flinched, drawing his gaze away from hers briefly as if her tears pained him. "You *are* my mate, so there's nothing I can do but follow you wherever you go. I can't stay away from you, ever, and I won't."

In that moment, all the things he'd said she

convinced herself meant nothing rushed her:

"You are beautiful. I thought so the first time I laid eyes on you."

"You're right. I'll never hurt you, ever."

"I love being your hero."

"I know this one werewolf who's not just pretty, she's beautiful."

"I'm not assigned to guard you, and your brother didn't send me. I came here to be with you."

Why hadn't she realized it before? How could she have been so dense? She was inexperienced, and he'd never made a move, but he spent hours with her every day. He complimented her every chance he got. He patiently taught her everything she knew about the immortal world. But he'd shielded her from his feelings for fear she'd run, and she had. Would he ever forgive her? Could he?

She'd hurt the man she loved the most, and knowing it caused a deep pain in her chest, so searing she was sure the ache would kill her.

"You are *mine*. I want you. I need you, and I *love* you. I've never loved another. I'll never forget you, and believe it or not, you will *never* forget me," he said firmly, his eyes still ablaze, holding hers captive.

He was angry, angrier than last night, angrier than she'd ever seen him: his eyes afire, his jaw clenched, a muscle ticking, speaking to her in a way he never had. Still, she wasn't frightened. In her heart, she knew, as she knew the day he'd turned demon for her to see, he'd never hurt her.

A sob escaped her then she wiped the tears streaming down her face and admitted, "I ran because I love you. Because I hoped I could forget you—"

"Because I'm not a werewolf!" he screamed, cutting her words off before she could explain then he unleashed his emotions.

Pain, anguish, torment, anger and rage...The intensity of his emotions struck the middle of her chest. The ache inside her fused with it, making the pain too much to bear. She swore any minute her chest would burst. Overwhelmed, her legs wobbled as useless tears continued to flow down her cheeks, recklessly bearing her river of misery for him to see.

"No," she managed to say between sobs. "Because I thought...I thought...I could never have you...I thought you...were destined for someone else."

In a split second, the anger, pain and anguish surrounding them vanished. His face paled, the red in his eyes dissolved. He stood still, staring at her in disbelief until finally his arms encased her. Holding her head tenderly against him, he rubbed her back ever so softly. He rested his chin on top of her head, and waited patiently as she sobbed against his bare chest, unleashing the agony she'd suffered and the agony she'd caused him, the man she loved.

"I'm sorry, Liv. I'm so sorry. Please forgive me, deliciae," he whispered every so often.

Please, please let him forgive me. I can't live without him. I don't want to live without him, she prayed.

"I'm sorry, Cain," she said between sobs. "I'm sooo...sorry."

Cupping her cheeks, he angled her face to his and whispered, "Shh...shh...darling. Everything's fine." He then pressed his lips against her forehead softly and pulled her against him again.

The warmth of his body soothed her as deeply as the words he'd uttered.

She knew he'd forgiven her.

She knew he'd never hold it against her.

She knew he loved her.

He said so, and she believed him. Just like that, the ache in her chest dissipated and her sobs quieted.

Then he whispered those familiar words, "Meae deliciae, meus sodalis."

She pulled away from him slightly to stare into his blue eyes. "You realize I don't know what that means, right?"

His eyes on hers, he rubbed the tears from her cheeks ever so softly then nodded.

"Well, are you going to tell me?"

He chuckled, and despite the tears streaking her face, she couldn't help but follow. His laughter was contagious. He possessed the ability to make anyone forget their troubles and laugh.

"It means, 'my darling, my mate,'" he replied, then kissed her lips softly.

The tender kiss, coupled with his heat, rekindled desire in her.

My darling, my mate, she thought.

Perfect.

Chapter 15

Smiling, excitement coursing through him, the anger and rage Cain felt moments before were now nothing but a bleak, forgettable memory.

It couldn't have been more perfect if he'd dreamt it. That was a lie. If he had it his way, Olivia wouldn't have shed tears, but the end was all that mattered. After five months, Olivia knew she was his, and she remained in his arms. To top it off, she loved him. He couldn't be more thrilled.

Reaching for him, she hooked her arms around his neck and placed her lips over his firmly. He was as enamored, captivated, by them as he'd been before he ever kissed her. The willpower he learned over the last five months granted him the strength to pull away slowly.

"Don't you need me?" she asked, her cheeks flushing, a stark reminder she was a virgin.

Despite his need for her, the need to mark her and claim her, the need he'd battled with for months, he couldn't and wouldn't take her now.

He stared into her puffy eyes, his body strung tight unable to believe the words he was about to utter. "Yes, darling, I need you, but I can wait."

"Why?" she asked, then immediately looked away from him, flushing a brighter shade.

He lifted her chin with his finger then said

somberly, "Because I want it to happen when my mate hasn't shed tears I caused. I want our first time to be special."

In all honesty, it was more than that. He had held back his need for months. Because of it, he feared he'd lose control, take her roughly and make it painful instead of pleasurable. Making matters worse was the fact she was a virgin. He needed to take his time with her, introduce her to sex slowly.

"You didn't...I did—"

"No, darling, I did. If I had been braver, if I hadn't been such a coward...I should've told you long before today and spared us both pain. I will repay you for every hurt I caused you. I promise."

"I forgive you," she said softly. "But I hurt you, too. I'm sorry. Will you f-forgive me?" she stuttered, nervously.

"There's nothing to apologize for, nothing to forgive. If I had told you sooner, you wouldn't have run." He rubbed his palm against her back. His mate, responsive to his touch, arched. He smiled, pulling her into him until her cheek rested against his chest. "I think I promised you a day at the beach," he whispered in her ear.

He didn't wait for a response. Materializing at the shore carrying her, he ran into the ocean then dropped her in the freezing water.

She shrieked and laughed. "That was not nice," she said, standing in front of him, then splashed the cold water on his face.

She removed her wet shirt, inch by inch uncovering her glorious flesh. His eyes ravished her body.

Her gaze raked his body, stopping when it met his

eyes. "Umm...I think you didn't think this through," she said, pointing to his wet jeans.

He'd been too consumed admiring her to notice. Smirking, he said, "You're right. I didn't."

Closing the feet between them, he wrapped an arm around her, pulled her against him and materialized in the spare room. She wobbled slightly.

He placed his hands on her shoulders to steady her then mumbled, "Sorry."

Heading to the bags of clothes he'd left on the floor, he rummaged through them.

When he heard her ask, "Think I'll ever get used to that?"

He turned and said in assurance, "Yeah, you will."

Finding one of the beach shorts he'd purchased the night before, he ran into the bathroom to change. He then materialized an inch from her, planted a wet kiss on her lips, snaked his arms around her waist and materialized on the shore. She tensed only briefly before her body molded against his.

Pulling away, he asked, "Was that time any better?"

Quirking a brow, she said, "That's cheating."

"Yeah? How so?"

"You kissed me, so I couldn't feel the world shifting around me."

Leaning into her, a hair's breadth away, he shot back, "Darling, that was the point. For the sake of ensuring you don't get dizzy every time, I'll kiss you."

She smirked, then pushed him away, and treaded seductively toward the water wearing that hot pink bikini well. She had no idea how well. His feet willingly led him to her.

For over an hour, they played, splashing water on each other like kids. When they were both exhausted from their games, they strolled toward the sand hand in hand. There, they lay side by side.

She lifted her weight on her elbow, and faced him as she twirled her fingers in the sand. "Do you remember the time you were gone for days in the demon plane?"

He shifted his weight and faced her then ran his hand down her shoulder, enjoying her skin's softness. He couldn't seem to keep his hands off her, but then he supposed it didn't matter anymore. She'd accepted him, so he could caress her all he wanted, all he needed.

"Yeah."

She looked away from him then continued, "You found me in the garden."

He scoffed. "As I recall, I scared the crap out of you in the garden."

Gaze darting toward his again, her expression softened. "I had been worried about you. I was used to seeing you every day. As the days passed, I kept thinking the worst. I kept getting this image in my head of you burned like the day you saved me. When I saw you again, it hit me. I realized I was in love with you."

His heart tightened in his chest. He remembered the moment well. He'd scolded himself for hours afterward. Now, he was doing the same because that had been two months ago. She'd loved him for two months, and he needlessly stalled.

"Liv, I'm sorry. I tried not to read you, but sometimes I caved and felt your attraction, I just...I thought you needed more time."

She leaned in and kissed him. A quick thoughtful

kiss that shouldn't have had him imagining her naked beneath him, but it did.

"I didn't tell you so you'd apologize. I told you so you'd know," she said, smiling.

"You're sharing?"

She nodded and smiled.

"Then I'll reciprocate," he said, his fingers trailing down to her waist. "When I found you, I fought my baser instincts. That first day, when I let you walk out of sight, it was the hardest thing I've done in four hundred and fifteen years. Then I saw you the very next day, I was thrilled. That night I was injured, so you were around for several days. I grew so used to having you around. It was hard, not being able to do the things I wanted to do, but—"

"What did you want to do?"

Grinning, he said, "I wanted to touch you, hold you, kiss you, anything and everything." He paused. "When Joce moved into the estate, I spent my days finding excuses to see you. At night when hunting Malums, I thought about you constantly. It was torture, knowing it would be hours before I had the chance to see you again. So…" His words trailed off. Looking away from her, he reconsidered his confession.

"So…" she prodded.

His gaze shot to hers, thinking what the hell, he said, "After my shifts, I'd materialize at the estate in your room and watch you sleep for hours. Just being around you calmed me, I knew…or I felt you needed time. It gave us both what we needed."

Her eyes widened then her face broke out in a huge grin. "You little voyeur," she teased then burst in a fit of giggles. "No wonder I dreamed about you nearly every night. Your stench wafted into my senses."

He sat up quickly, his hand gripping her hip. "You dreamt about me?"

Flushing that beautiful rosy shade, she nodded. "Well, it was your fault."

"Wait, did you say my stench, darling?"

He didn't wait for her to respond. At immortal speed, he lifted her in one swift movement and headed for the water.

"Cain, no! I'm almost dry," she said between giggles.

"You should've thought of that before you insulted your male," he teased then unapologetically dropped her in the water.

Still laughing, he picked her up again, and headed toward the house.

Her head against his chest angled to his, she asked, "Do you think I'm a doll you can throttle as you please?"

"You are my very precious doll that teases me constantly," he retorted.

"Only when it's well deserved."

He halted just so he could enjoy gazing at her. "God, I've missed you."

She quit laughing abruptly, her expression saddening. He felt it—that same sadness he'd felt in her before.

"What's wrong?"

"You mean the days we were apart?"

"Yeah, and over the last couple of weeks, I knew something was wrong. You weren't acting like yourself. I should've known—"

"Several weeks ago, I decided to leave," she

admitted softly.

He released her, allowing her feet to touch the sand then he kneeled before her and clasped her hands in his. "Mate me. Marry me." He hadn't meant to sound like he was begging, but it did and he didn't care. "I promise I'll do everything in my power to make you happy. I promise I'll spend the rest of my life making up for being a coward."

Her eyes widened even as tears welled. "We haven't even…"

He cut her off because he didn't want excuses, because he wasn't going to take no for an answer. "I'll be everything you need, whatever you want…"

Tears rimmed her eyes and fell.

At the sight, his chest tightened painfully, hating her tears, hating he'd caused them. Cursing himself, he reached out and read her. He realized then she wasn't sad, no, those tears weren't sad ones. She was happy and a bit overwhelmed.

Releasing a breath, his clenched muscles relaxed. "*Meus sodalis*, do you accept?"

She nodded and mumbled, "Yes."

He pressed a firm kiss on her stomach then stood and carried her toward her home.

She shrieked. "You know I can walk."

"I prefer to carry you," he said then firmly placed his lips over hers.

She parted hers, then hesitantly darted her tongue into his mouth. The action so slow and cautious, he knew she was unsure of herself, worried about her inexperience. Endearing him to her, a beautiful reminder he was the first and would be the only. Losing all thought, all sense, breathing her in, he delved into

124

her mouth assuring her. So enthralled in assuring her, enjoying her, he didn't realize they were falling until he lost his footing. Suddenly, panicked he pulled away just as the pool water splashed around them.

Olivia broke away from their kiss, giggling loudly. The sound of it resonated inside him, feeling like a bolt of energy rushing into him. It happened every time she smiled, every time she giggled, every time she laughed, and still he hadn't gotten used to the sensation. He hadn't gotten used to her ability to cause it, so he couldn't help but stare as she threw her head back and laughed that beautiful laugh.

Wriggling from his grasp, she swam to the end of the pool. Grinning, he followed, determined to reach her. Once he did, he snaked his arm around her waist and pulled her toward him simultaneously pressing her back against the wall and planting his lips over hers. This time, when he parted his lips, she mimicked him. He dove in, playing with her tongue gently, relishing in his mate's sweet taste.

He'd kissed hundreds of women, made love to hundreds, but none tasted as sweet as her. Her lips were soft, moist and wet from the water, sliding against his. Her temperature spiked, heating his flesh. When she wrapped her arms around him, he ran his hands down her chest, around her hips and pressed her pelvis toward his, an instinct he could no more control than his love for her. The simple action made her moan sweetly into his mouth. He couldn't help but smile against her lips. Still, he kept his slow, gentle pace as he trailed his mouth across her cheek, toward her neck. In that sensitive spot where her neck met her shoulder, he kissed and licked her, her pulse quickening against his tongue.

"Touch me," she whispered in his ear.

Fuck. He wanted to touch her. He just wasn't sure it was a good idea, and a part of him was scared even a touch would make him lose control. He wouldn't lose control, never with her.

Still, he couldn't help the groan that escaped his lips when he heard her whisper. His shaft pulsed, throbbing against her core. He couldn't deny her and wouldn't deny her, but where should he touch her? Where did she crave his touch? Dragging his hands over her hips, he slid them to her butt and lifted her. Immediately, almost like an instinct, she wrapped her strong, lean legs around his waist. The simple action made the tethered hold on his control slip.

Tracing his tongue along her chest, he untied the string holding her bikini top. It fell away. He pulled away only briefly, to stare at her beautiful breasts, simultaneously running his hands over them. Her nipples tightened with his touch, goose bumps erupting through her flesh. Replacing his hand with his mouth, he fondled them with his tongue. She arched her back, releasing a moan. His fangs lengthened and accidentally nicked her.

A taste of her in his mouth, his muscles shuddered and quaked, reeling from the tiniest taste. Eyes ablaze with desire, craving and yearning, his demon demanded he claim her, drink her.

Battling his demon, every muscle in his body tightened. He groaned deep and guttural, sounding inhuman.

It took every ounce of willpower, but, finally, he summoned the strength, released her and stepped away.

His gaze locked on the nick he'd made, a single drop of blood oozing out, tempting him further.

Her arms went to her chest, attempting to cover herself. Still, he could see that single droplet of blood. Still, it called to him.

"Cain," she said softly.

He drew his gaze to hers. Cheeks flushed, the blue in her eyes spiked with incandescent yellow, like bright threads weaved into the depths. *Beautiful.*

Realization dawned then. He'd nicked her unspoiled, virgin flesh. *Fuck.* Dread crept up and down his spine, fearing she'd cower away for marking her. "I'm sorry. I didn't mean to—"

"W-what? Did I do something wrong? I know I'm not—"

Shit. Why would she think that? "No, Liv," he said gently. "My fault. I…" His eyes went to the nick then met hers. "I didn't mean to, but I nicked you with my fangs…"

His voice fell away when she glanced down and spotted the mark, the blood now trailing down toward her stomach. She shocked him when she closed the distance between them, rubbed the blood off with her finger and hesitantly held it up to his mouth, offering it to him. Her expression unsure, but her eyes now seemed to glow, no blue left.

Assuring her, he sucked the blood off her finger, moaning as he did.

"We can't let it go to waste, can we?" she whispered, then hesitantly pressed her lips over his.

He delved in, not softly, because he couldn't help it. He loved her, loved that she was sweet, loved that she was smart and beautiful and fought like a warrior.

Loved that she hadn't cringed, loved she'd seemed entranced with the nick he'd made, letting him drink what had spilled.

One taste wouldn't tie her to him forever, only a bite would do that, but she tasted like rich wine, taunting him to do just what he longed for, claim her, sealing both their fates forever.

Thinking all of this, he intensified the kiss. Her nails dug into his back. Lifting her off her feet, her legs reclaimed his waist.

"Cain…" she moaned breathlessly.

Everything she did provoked him, but his name on her lips especially made him crave removing her bottom and taking her. He held onto his will with sheer force, but he deepened the kiss, one hand gripping her waist, the other pressing her core against his shaft.

Her hands roamed down his back, one curving toward his front, then she moaned into his mouth and started trembling, not a little tremble but full-blown shakes.

Breaking his lips away from hers, he scanned her heated face. Her cheeks flushed, her eyes avoiding his, she pressed her hands between them and pushed at his chest. Reaching out with his gift, he read her, reading her desire, her need, then her embarrassment. For the latter, he didn't know why.

Her hands at his chest pushed harder, still unwilling to meet his eyes. His arm around her waist, he pulled her closer, silently telling her he wouldn't let her go. She didn't get it or chose to ignore it because the next instant, she pushed harder.

He then lifted her chin with his finger, meeting her eyes and softly whispered, "Quit fighting me. I'm not letting you go, darling."

Her eyes widened and misted.

"Talk to me."

She still shook, so he rubbed his palm up and down her back, encouraging her with actions.

"I-I can't."

"I know your feelings. Just don't know why."

Her cheeks flamed a brighter shade, proving he'd said the wrong thing. Knowing nothing about how to comfort a woman, he was out of his element, and it showed. Still, because she was his, because he wanted to learn, he tried again.

"There's nothing to be embarrassed about."

She nodded. "Yes…there is. I don't know what I'm doing, and…I was…I want you so bad I'm shaking."

Smiling, he said, "I'll teach you. I'll show you. I won't push you. I'll be patient. I promise, and there's nothing wrong with wanting me because I want you too, Liv, just as bad, if not more."

Then he pressed his lips against hers lightly.

That's when the phone rang. With their superior senses, they both heard it from the outside, yet neither of them made a move, neither of them spoke. Her eyes on his, his on hers, they were content to let it ring.

Finally, he spoke. "I don't want to move, but you should get that. It could be Landon."

That jolted her into action. She nodded then pulled away. Reluctantly and with regret, he released her, officially ending the moment.

He materialized at the end of the pool in search of her top. Finding it, he lifted himself out of the pool and strode to her. She'd already gotten out of the pool and was at the other end, her arms wrapped around her chest, covering her breasts. He handed her the bikini top, and watched as she put it on. He reached for her hand then they strode into her home. She picked up the phone just in time.

"Olivia." Cain heard the harshness in Landon's voice. "What is this about you giving Maria the weekend off?"

"I don't need a maid or a sitter, Landon," she said. "I can cook and clean for myself."

"But there were other reasons for—"

"Yeah, I know, so she could watch me and report back to you."

"Can you blame me? I'm worried. You just took off. For what reason?"

"I'm fine. I've never been better, but I don't need Maria here—at all. I promise to check in every two or three days, okay?"

He sighed. "Yeah, okay, I'll let her know."

"Landon, I love you, okay?"

"I love you too, Liv."

Cain watched her hang up, sensing guilt gushing off of her. It was hard to ignore despite his attempts to give her privacy.

He walked toward her and wrapped his arms around her, rubbed her back then feathered a soft kiss on her forehead. "Darling, he's fine. He has Joce."

She nodded.

"I'll make us some lunch," he said then kissed her softly on the lips.

"You're supposed to be on vacation. I'm only allowing you to be my chef once a day," she said, smiling. "We should grab a bite somewhere instead. We have to get the car anyway. We left it in Fira, remember?"

He'd forgotten but nodded in agreement. "I pay," he said then kissed her again.

Chapter 16

Three months ago

As Olivia waltzed out of the elevator leading to the gymnasium at the demon compound, her pine scent hit him like a freight train.

A smile spread across his lips.

Finally, she was there.

He'd been waiting for her since Lucas told him Jocelyn would be visiting her sisters. That had been three hours ago, but Jocelyn always took that long to get ready even if it was an unplanned visit with her sisters.

Cain knew Olivia would come because she always came. Whether it was her growing attraction to him or their friendship, he wasn't sure, and he didn't care as long as he got to see her. If she hadn't come, he would have gone to her. He did it every day—twice a day.

Catching sight of her, as usual, his heart beat a little faster. She was stunning in a pair of dark-wash skinny jeans and a white shirt that hung off her shoulder and exposed her bare skin.

"Waiting for me, I see," she teased, smiling.

"Always," he replied, and meant it.

Words were the only way he could slowly reveal how much he cared. With hints of flirting, he'd been able to reveal truths. His first attempts, he'd admit, were unsuccessful. He soon realized it was all about delivery. If he was too serious when he revealed a fact, she'd flush immediately and cower away. Although he loved watching her cheeks turn rosy pink, he didn't enjoy making her feel uncomfortable, so he tamped his attempts down for several weeks after his first couple of tries. It wasn't until he began delivering truths with a smile, as if in jest, that she'd tease him in return, but perhaps it was that they'd become friends since his first failed attempts. She didn't know he meant it, though he joked as he did with everyone else minus the flirting. That thought troubled him and defeated his true purpose. He wanted her to know, but in time. He had time because she needed it.

"What are you up to?" she asked.

"I just told you. I was waiting for you," he replied, his smile widened, another truth.

"Besides that, of course," she said flippantly.

It stung every time he realized she didn't believe him.

He shrugged as if it would make his chest cease aching. "Wanna fight?"

"Hand to hand or with weapons?"

Tough choice, he thought sarcastically. "Lady's choice."

She pursed her lips as if in deep thought then blurted, "Hand to hand. Definitely."

"Oh yeah?" he said, his heart beating a little faster with just the thought of feeling her skin against his.

"Yep, if I win, it will be all the more rewarding."

He chuckled. "May I ask why?"

"I know you. If we use swords, you'll give me the lighter one because I'm a girl and blah, blah, blah, which means it has less power." She shrugged. "Besides, we dueled with swords last week."

"Do you want to change? Jenna and Ash have clothes you can borrow."

She lifted a brow. "Are you implying I can't fight in my current attire?" she asked, a wicked grin on her face.

Chuckling, he shot back, "Itching for a fight today, huh?"

A second later, she stood inches from him. She moved so quickly she'd been a blur. Her eyes locked on his, but her fist was a centimeter from his stomach. He grabbed her wrist before it hit him. She twisted her hand from his grasp, spinning around him then attempted to kick his legs from underneath him. He spun and caught her leg.

"Why are you holding back?" he taunted.

She sighed, blowing the hair from her face and attacked, swinging her fists and legs quickly, almost desperately. He fought defensively, only preventing her hits from striking him.

It was how he battled with her, even if they weren't engaged in a real fight, even if it was just practice to train or to hone skills, he'd never raise a hand against her.

Olivia swung. He caught her hand and refused to release. She smiled, an obvious taunt, before she flipped over. Her legs swung quickly in front of his face, revealing her flat stomach. He hissed, releasing a breath and her hand simultaneously. Distracted by the brief flash of her skin, she kicked his legs from under him. He materialized before he hit the ground appearing inches from her face.

"Still holding back, Liv."

Olivia hesitated only for seconds, holding his stare as intensely as he held hers. Only then he was lost, lost in her eyes, her flushed cheeks, her full lips and the small puffs of air escaping them.

He loved watching her in battle or after the battle, but then again he loved watching her period. She fought like a warrior, skillfully, swiftly and with tremendous agility.

He discovered weeks ago, she was far from the damsel in distress type, far from her princess title, far from needing her brooding brother's protection or his. His mate could kick ass on her own. From her skills, he assumed she'd been training since she was a child. Although Cain could barely stand to be near her brother, Landon deserved a medal for ensuring Olivia learned to fight expertly. She would never need a man's protection. She could defend herself although knowing this did little to diminish his need to protect her.

Lost in her freshly flush face, she kicked his legs from under him again. As he fell backward, he snaked his arm around her waist, pulling her toward the ground along with him. His back took the brunt of the impact, but it was worth it. She landed on top of him, chest to chest. Her small body pressed firmly against his, every curve, every lean muscle. Her eyes held his as her breathing pitched. He felt her heart pounding against him as quickly as his, quicker than it had during their fight.

He had yet to release his hold on her. His arm still firmly wrapped around her small waist. As he'd been moments before, he was again captivated by her face, her hair, her body, her scent, her. He wanted to kiss her and knew she wanted his kiss.

     Don't ruin it, he cautioned. *It's too soon.*

     "I think it's a draw." He broke the silence.

Chapter 17

"I'm ready," she announced as she strolled into the living room wearing a white linen dress that reached mid-thigh and contrasted against her sun-kissed skin and dark hair.

Clearing his throat, he then said, "You look amazing, *deliciae*."

"Not so bad yourself," she replied. Only he could look like a model in a pair of cargo shorts and a t-shirt.

He grinned. That glimmer in his eyes now back, twinkled. When he opened his arms, she ran to him and wrapped her arms around his waist, tucking her body tightly against his. His hands firm on her hips, trailed down to her thighs.

Heart clamoring, her pulse accelerated. He leaned into her, resting his face in the crook of her neck and inhaled. His breath at her neck, goose bumps erupted throughout her flesh.

Her skin felt so hot she thought it would combust any second, enough to indicate her eyes were already sparkling with hues of yellow.

It was useless to deny, food was the farthest thing from her mind. What she desired and needed for sustenance was him, but he held back. She felt it. She just didn't know why and couldn't help feeling it was her fault. She couldn't help but think maybe he feared being disappointed by her inexperience.

A moment later, they stood in Fira. Hand in hand, they strolled through the tiny, cramped streets surrounded by small white buildings, scoping out restaurants for lunch.

She pointed toward a restaurant and said, "There, it's the best Greek cuisine on the island."

He nodded.

Her fingers entwined in his, she pulled his arm and dragged him toward the entrance feeling his presence trailing behind her.

The restaurant was small and quaint with murals of Grecian landscapes and statues painted on the walls. They were seated near the kitchen at a small table for two. Only a glass separated them from the chef. Cain reached for her hand over the table. His fingers clasped hers. They were warm and soothed her need for his touch.

"Do you like it?"

"I love it if you love it," he said.

She covered her cheeks with her hands, attempting to conceal her blush. Amazing how the simplest of words from him could cause that reaction. "The food's great."

"You've come here before?"

She nodded.

They ordered drinks then their meals, pastitsio for her and souvlaki for him. When their meals arrived a short time later, Olivia could barely touch her pastitsio, a baked pasta dish topped with béchamel sauce. She loved it and usually devoured it instantaneously, but what she craved now hadn't been on the menu. He sat across from her, tempting her: looking at her intensely, his gaze trailing to her chest, saying sweet words, interlacing his fingers with hers, caressing the skin on her hands.

She must still be in shock. Who could blame her? The past day and a half had been a whirlwind: his arrival, his behavior, his confession and then his proposal. All she ever wanted, better than she dreamed. Despite the hours they spent basking in the sun, she still couldn't believe it, so she kept pinching her arm to make sure she wasn't dreaming. It'd been like one of her self-created fantasies, where she and Cain were together and nothing else existed or mattered much. Yet, today had been so much better than her illusions because her imaginings had been just that, and this was real.

"Darling, you have to eat." Cain's voice drew her away from her thoughts.

"I'm just not very hungry."

"Please, eat or…I won't take you dancing tonight," he said, his eyes glimmering.

"Are you blackmailing me?" she asked, feigning shock.

He chuckled. "Yep, and if you keep misbehaving I may have to punish you."

"Me?" She drew her hand to her chest. "Misbehaving? No way!"

"Yep, you know all the teasing you've been doing…splashing water at me, telling me I stink, among other things," he said, his gaze shooting down to her chest.

She flushed immediately and stuffed a fork full of pasta in her mouth. Chewing, she considered what type of punishment he planned to administer, then placed her fork beside her plate, baiting him.

"Liv," he said in warning.

She wanted to tease him, so she took a chance and said, "Maybe I need to be punished. Maybe I'll enjoy it." She should've known better. She couldn't pull off something like that. She was too inexperienced, too naïve in all things relating to men, relationships and especially flirting. Still, because a part of her wanted to pull it off, she said it. Only a split second later proving she couldn't pull it off, she flushed.

He didn't seem to mind. His eyes widened, nearly bulging out of their sockets. Witnessing his reaction, she couldn't help the giggle that bubbled up and spilled from her.

Reaching for her glass of wine, she took a sip. The wine she gulped was halfway down her throat when he uttered, "Mrs. Thaler."

She choked, coughing repeatedly, her eyes roaming the patrons in the restaurant staring at her. Embarrassed, her cheeks heated further.

He was at her side a split second later, patting her back. "Are you okay?"

When her coughing subsided, she met his stare. His expression marred with concern, his pulse beating rapidly. "I'm fine," she said in assurance, wondering why he was so alarmed. As an immortal, it'd take more than choking to kill her. "You know I'm fine."

He sat back across from her, but his appearance didn't return to its usual cheerful air.

"What's wrong?"

His eyes went stark, his voice somber when he said, "Tell me the truth. Do you want to complete the mating with me? Do you want to marry a demon?"

His words came out in a rush, unveiling his deep-seated fear once again—that he wasn't like her, a werewolf. It wasn't the first time.

Because I'm not a werewolf! The angry words he'd yelled that morning replayed in her mind, a bitter reminder he too had lived too long without his mate and with fear in his heart. She could still clearly hear the roughness in his voice, laced in anguish.

She felt the warmth of her previous flush dissolve as her chest tightened, but she managed to say, "You are everything I've ever wanted, everything I've thought about. I never cared that you are a demon. I meant what I said when I agreed to mate and marry you, Cain."

She placed her hand over his. Immediately, the tension in him dissolved, his shoulders slumped slightly then he released a breath.

"Eat," he instructed.

To please him, she did.

They finished their meals and wandered through Fira's narrow streets again, hand in hand, entering several shops. She glanced around at the intricate jewelry made from coral, volcano rocks and precious gems from the island and fiddled through the racks of clothes.

His phone rang. Reaching into his pocket, he fished it out. "Hello," he answered without sparing a glance at the caller ID.

"Cain." Olivia heard Jocelyn's familiar voice. "How's everything?"

She turned and met his eyes just as he responded, "Good."

"Did you—"

"Yes," he answered before Jocelyn could finish her

sentence.

"So everything is—"

"Perfect," he responded.

"I'm happy for you both," Jocelyn said. "Give Liv a kiss for me."

"I will."

"Love you both and take care of Liv."

He smirked. "Love you, and you know I always do," he responded. About to hang up, he quickly brought the phone back to his ear. "Joce, I forgot to say…thanks," he finished then hung up and closed the distance between them.

She couldn't help the questions spilling from her lips. "She knew? Did everyone else know, too?"

His hand went to her face, cupping her cheek, he nodded. "I didn't tell them, but they knew."

"For how long?"

"Remember the party Jenna threw for Joce?"

She glanced away from him then nodded. It had been just days after she met Cain for the first time, days after he'd saved her. Landon had still been denying Jocelyn, who'd just come into her powers. It didn't mean he'd been ignoring her though. The minute they got to the impromptu gathering, Landon headed straight for her. Because he'd been so focused on his mate, he'd left Olivia to her own devices. Cain had kept her company. They'd talked for close to an hour. That was the night he promised to teach her about other immortal breeds, which she knew little of. He kept that promise in the weeks and months to come.

"Remember how Jacob and Benjamin made a comment about there being lots of mates?"

"Yeah, and you told me possessiveness streamed

off of demons when they find their mates."

He nodded. "They knew from the moment I found you."

"Then Lucas told Jenna who then told Jocelyn?"

He shook his head. "No darling, they saw me with you and figured it out."

"But..." She didn't know exactly what she wanted to say, but knew exactly how she felt, just as she had earlier, ignorant. It seemed she was the only one who hadn't realized his feelings for her. Her inexperience with men and her naiveté with all things within the immortal world had prevented her from deciphering what he'd clearly expressed with actions.

"I didn't tell anyone. I didn't discuss my decision to wait with anyone either, not Lucas, not Joce, not anyone," he said, continuing to rub his hand on the side of her face.

"But..." Her words fell away again.

"Tell me," he urged.

"I just...I feel like an ignorant—"

Leaning into her, he snaked his arm around her waist and said, "Don't finish that thought. You aren't ignorant."

"Thanks to you, maybe not as much as I used to be," she whispered.

His eyes softened, a tender glint in them shining through. She loved it when he looked at her like that. He'd done it before, many times. She noticed and loved it then, too. She'd just never noticed how with that one look it was clear he cared for her deeply.

"It's always harder to interpret things when they're happening to you. You're too close to the situation and your emotions get in the way."

She shrugged. "I guess, but..." She trailed off when a thought occurred, then she asked, "Did Joce tell you where to find me?"

Hesitating only briefly, he admitted, "Yes," then quickly added, "I hope you don't think she's picking sides or—"

"I wouldn't." How could she when the result was all she'd dreamed of for months? "I owe her...for you."

He kissed her lightly on the lips and smiled. "You're beautiful, you know that?"

Though she didn't believe it for a second, she blushed. "No."

"Yeah, you are," he contradicted.

"I'm average."

Lifting a brow, he shot back immediately, "Nothing about you is *average*."

"I am. Average height, average hair, average—"

Placing his fingers over her mouth, he silenced her. "You're beautiful, Liv. I know so, and everyone thinks so."

Shaking her head, she said, "If I was, don't you think I would've been kissed before now?" Immediately, she regretted her admission. She looked away from him and attempted to turn.

His arm, firmly wrapped around her waist, tightened, not letting her. "None of that." Her gaze went to his, then, as if knowing exactly what she thought, he said, "I *love* that I was your first kiss. I *love* more that I'll be your last."

He said it with such emotion, the air in her lungs escaped her, and she found herself gasping for breath.

"You grew up around your pack, isolated. Your brother's alpha of that pack. No one wants to mess with the alpha, so unless you were someone's fated, no one would've made a move. That's why you've never been kissed. It's not because you're average, and it's not because you aren't beautiful."

She held his eyes, not knowing what to say. After several moments, he spoke again.

"You know I love it when your face flushes. I get a kick out of it every time." He winked.

Because he actually winked at her, because they were now official, she couldn't help but ask what she'd had the urge to hundreds of times before. "Are you...are you flirting with me?"

His hand at her waist drifted up her spine, then under her loose hair he gripped the back of her neck. "Mrs. Thaler, I believe I am."

She was sure she was as red as a tomato, and once again cursed her inexperience with all matters pertaining to men. Jocelyn would never flush repeatedly for a simple compliment.

"Don't act coy. You flirt with me, too."

Her eyes widened. "I don't," she said immediately. She didn't know how to flirt.

"Really? So all that talk in the restaurant about me administering punishment, what was that?" he asked, his eyes glimmering mischievously.

"That's flirting?" she asked, surprised.

"Yes, my sweet. You're rather good at it. It's not the first time you've flirted with me."

"But I...I thought that was just teasing. We joke like that all the time. You joke like that with everyone—"

Shaking his head, he said, "No, Liv, I *don't* joke like that with everyone, only with *you*." Smiling, his eyes darkened.

It was news to her, and it lifted her spirits to think maybe she wasn't as far behind as she thought. Maybe she knew a bit more than she believed.

"We should get going if we want to go dancing tonight. Don't you think?"

She smiled and nodded.

Chapter 18

Cain insisted on taking her dancing. Whether in an effort to postpone the inevitable, making love, or because he'd promised he would take her, Olivia didn't know but felt it was probably a bit of both.

She knew he was an honorable man who never made a promise he couldn't keep, but her instincts told her there was a part of him that was hesitant to take their relationship to the next level. She feared what it meant.

Immortal males couldn't control their need to claim their mates. Cain had. Being a demon, part of the most reviled, volatile and feared immortal breed, it was unheard of, and again, Cain had. Why?

If she was his, and he'd waited months, his needs should rule him by now. Unless…

Stop it, she scolded herself, hating the negative path her thoughts took. She trusted Cain. He wouldn't lie—certainly not about being her male.

Although she loved to dance and hardly went because of her overprotective brother, tonight she wasn't tempted by the prospect of it. Dancing was the farthest thing from her mind. The only temptation was Cain. Having spent decades dreaming about what it would feel like to make love to another and a century waiting for her male, she needed him in the most carnal way.

After perusing her closet, she finally decided on a blue backless, fitted dress. She picked it because the short dress, which left little to the imagination, was blue, his favorite color. It hugged every curve and ended inches too high.

She dressed quickly and applied some make-up then went downstairs toward the living room. His eyes met hers, and they sparked, briefly igniting the fire in them. His jaw went hard, his hands fisted at his sides in a battle with his desires. The air suspended around her too thick to inhale; she held her breath.

"Olivia," he said, his voice hoarse, laced with need. He mumbled in Latin, words she couldn't comprehend.

She took a step toward him.

He held out his hand to stop her, the action surprising her.

"Give me a minute," he rasped as if in pain. Closing his eyes, he breathed deeply.

Slowly, she walked toward him. His eyes snapped open suddenly, his gaze intensified, but she didn't flinch. She continued to tread toward him until they stood mere inches apart, until she could feel his deep, cool breaths on her skin.

"What is it?" she asked.

Cupping her cheek tenderly, he said, "I want you so bad, darling. I've waited a long time for you, and that's made it worse. You're...innocent. I *can't* lose control with you. But because I've waited so long, because I want you so bad, I don't trust myself to be gentle."

He wanted her so bad he feared his desire would overwhelm him and he'd hurt her? Was that it? Was that why he hadn't made a move? Why he hadn't claimed her as destined? She couldn't believe it. She just couldn't come to grips with it because it was nearly impossible for an immortal male to control his need to claim his fated especially for so long, and yet he said it, so she believed him because coming from him it made sense.

He'd always been extremely cautious around her, terrified of hurting her, as protective as a mate. Immortals who found their mates were consumed with the need to protect, guard and defend them. Why hadn't she realized she was his? Hindsight was twenty-twenty after all.

Releasing a breath, she reminded him, "I'm a werewolf." Pausing for only a split second, she said, "You won't hurt me. I know you won't."

"I'd never hurt you deliberately, Liv, but we both know I've hurt you unintentionally."

The somber tone of his voice gouged a hole in her chest because she knew he truly believed it. She shook her head. "That doesn't count, and you've never *physically* hurt me. You shouldn't be afraid to hurt me when we…" Her cheeks flushed, and she silently berated herself. "It's why you're holding back—"

Feathering a light kiss on her forehead, he said, "Darling, it's more than that…even if I could manage to be gentle…" His words trailed off as he ran a hand through his hair.

"Tell me," she urged.

"Remember I told you about a demon's need to—"

"Mark their mates," she finished for him.

"I'm afraid I won't be able to stop myself from marking you."

Her heart dropped to the pit of her stomach. "W-what…Why does it matter?" she stuttered, afraid to hear his answer.

"Every immortal will know you've been claimed. Before it comes to that, there are some things we need to work out."

Her chest constricted. What things could they possibly need to work out? She was his and loved him, and he claimed he loved her. What else was there?

Pulling away from him, she asked, "What things?" Her voice rose, her cheeks heating in anger.

His eyes widened in response. "I'm just thinking of you."

He tried to grab her hand, but she drew away from him. She couldn't think with his hands on her. She could barely think at such close proximity to him, and right then, she needed to think, to understand what he'd said.

"So, we have things to work out and you're doing this for me?"

Eyes on her, scanning her face, confusion muddled his expression, but he didn't say a word.

"I was under the impression I was your mate and you loved me, but you admit you don't want to mark me because we have things to *work out*."

Shaking his head, he said calmly, "It's not like that, Liv."

Her eyes welling with tears, she asked, "What's it like, then?" She couldn't keep the quiver from her voice.

"Your brother, Liv."

She froze, feeling every bit of the idiot she was. He was thinking of her after all, of them, and she assumed the worst. Her eyes dried instantly.

Truth was she hadn't considered how she'd broach the subject with her brother. In fact, she hadn't thought of her brother at all, not even after she'd spoken to Landon that afternoon, but Cain was right. Landon needed time to adjust. Her brother was a domineering, macho and overprotective alpha who often treated her like a child, overlooking the fact she was more than a century old. If Olivia waltzed into her home with her male's mark on her, Landon would…what would he do? Have a stroke? Scream and yell? Try to kill Cain? But did it matter? She feared when confession time came, Landon would lose his temper either way. She loved Cain, and she was *his*. That meant he was *hers*. Why should they have to wait?

It's the least you can do for your brother after everything he's done for you, her conscience sneered.

Guilt seethed into her anew, and she cursed the emotion altogether. Meeting Cain's gaze, she said, "You're right, but—"

He silenced her with a quick kiss then he pulled away and said, "Don't apologize, darling. I didn't explain it well. I don't want you to feel guilty about this either. I've had months to think about it…You haven't."

She nodded, feeling his hands run down her bare back in a soothing and comforting gesture.

As his hands roamed lower, below her mid-back, realizing the dress left her bare, his eyes flared a deep crimson. He hissed. "Liv," he said in a warning tone as his fingers continued to trail down her bare skin.

"Let me worry about my brother," she said.

"No," he retorted, too quickly and too harshly.

"He's my brother," she pointed out. "I'll deal with

him."

"No, when you want to tell him, we'll do it together, Liv," he insisted, his tone sharp.

Releasing a breath in frustration, she pulled away from him and snared him with a lousy glare. "Why?"

"Because I've had to watch him treat you…" He looked away then met her gaze. "…*unfavorably* for months, and I'm not doing it anymore," he barked, his voice steeped in anger. "I've waited for you, Liv. I've waited a *long* fucking time. I've stood by and watched him…" Running his fingers through his hair, he released a breath. "I heard him scream at you during the first Guardian meeting you attended. I've never wanted to kill anyone with that ferocity—not even the men responsible for killing my family and making me an orphan."

His eyes now glowed, his body practically shaking with rage, his demon an inch from the surface of his lovely exterior.

"Every cell in my body told me to avenge you against your own blood, and while every cell in my damn body told me to kill him, I had to sit back and watch—for *you*. I'll rip my own heart out of my damn chest before I sit back and let you face him alone."

She'd intended to defend her brother. The words were about to tumble from her lips, yet all she could think of was the angry Cain that stood before her, and the overwhelming conflicting emotions in his admission: rage, remorse, desire.

"Okay," she said. She closed the distance between them, and softly grazed her fingers down his chest.

Instantly, his eyes lost their animosity and calmed. His muscles relaxing, he laid his hand over hers then lowered his head and shook it before his eyes met hers again. "I'm sorry, darling," he said. He gripped her hand, pulling it to his lips and kissing it. "Sorry for losing it again."

A soft smile tugged at her lips. "I love you," she blurted. She had intended to finally justify her brother's tantrums, but instead she'd been overcome with love. Her male cared little for her brother the alpha or status within the pack, but cared deeply for her.

He kissed her, cupping the back of her head, and pulling her lips toward his. His tongue lapped against hers softly. When he released her, there was a broad charming smile plastered across his face.

"You know, when I lose my temper, sometimes you should try to get upset with me...or at least pretend." He feathered several soft kisses on her cheek, drifting down toward her neck. "When will we ever fight if you're so accepting of my irrational moods?"

She laughed because there was too much truth in his statement. "Yeah, well, I can say the same."

Suddenly, her laugh died, and she turned serious. "Cain, I love my brother. You can't kill him," she said firmly.

Pulling away from her neck, he chuckled dryly. "I would never kill your brother, darling. No matter how much I want to. I know how much he means to you. I'd love to rearrange his attitude."

"He's just temperamental—"

"Yeah, to my *mate*, and that ends now."

"He's a good man, Cain. I wish you could see him the way I do."

Sighing heavily, he said, "I'm grateful to him. I never understood until...you told me everything he's been for you: a father, a mother, a brother. I'm glad you had him, your own brother, to raise you. Hell, of all people I *can* understand that, I would've had no one if Lucas hadn't taken me in, but he tries to control you and mistreats you in the process."

"He's controlling, overbearing and intrusive, but he's never raised a hand to me in anger, ever. I know it's hard to believe but he's loving and caring. Until recently, he never raised his voice at me and that had more to do with his situation," she said, referring to him denying his female, Jocelyn, "…than anything else."

"I know, but it doesn't make it right," he said. "He won't be happy about us, Liv. You know that, right?"

She nodded, then her gaze fell away from his.

He lifted her chin with his index finger, forcing her to focus on him again. "You are mine, Liv. I've waited for *you*, not for his acceptance. I'll fight for you if I have to. I meant everything I said. I want to mark you so bad my soul aches. Nothing would gratify me more than you bearing my brand. I want to marry you in that church you mentioned. I know your brother's approval means a lot to you, so I've held back today because I don't want you strolling back home bearing my mark without talking to him first."

"But you can't wait any longer and neither can I. I trust you—"

"I've waited too long. I might turn when we—"

"So, turn. I couldn't care less," she cut him off. "It doesn't matter to me whether you mark me. I love my brother, but this is you and me. You're my male and as far as I'm concerned I don't have to consult with anyone to bear my male's mark."

"You care and you'll be miserable if you don't

154

discuss this with him—"

"You're right, but there's no more waiting, Cain. If it happens, it happens."

He smiled. "You are a beautiful contradiction, darling, naïve and vivacious, shy yet stubborn, beautiful and strong and I love you for every bit of it."

"Well, well, I don't know whether to be insulted or flattered," she commented, her voice tinged with sarcasm.

"Flattered," he said automatically. "Can't you see beauty in contradiction?"

His lips lingered too close to hers for her to summon the strength to formulate a response. He traced her lips with his tongue then ran his fingers through her hair, wrapping it around his wrist and pulling slightly, tilting her head back. His lips then trailed down her neck as his other hand ran up and down her back, trailing fire and ice with a single touch. Desire melted within her, pooling at her center. He pressed her closer. She felt every muscle and every tendon as she drew her hands down his chest toward his neatly outlined abs.

He pulled her away slowly. "Darling," he urged. "I think I asked you a question."

"You're a tease," she said breathlessly. "So I can't remember the question."

He chuckled; his breath hit her in waves. "Dancing," he said. "I promised you dancing."

A second later, they were in Fira, and she'd never been more disappointed. The cool breeze made her shiver as soon as he pulled away from her. He ran his hands up and down her shoulders briefly then turned her toward the small capital of the island. Draping an arm around her shoulders, he led her forward. The narrow pebbled streets were cramped with tourists: some loud and rambunctious, some couples lost in lust. Both made her wish they'd never left the comfort of her home.

He leaned into her ear and whispered, "Where's the best place to dance?"

He wouldn't let it go. She couldn't be mad because he was honorable, and she wouldn't have it any other way.

Olivia pulled Cain toward the first bar she spotted with blaring music. As they passed over the threshold, a new song started, one of her favorites. She began swaying to the beat, shifting her hips, letting the music guide her. He grabbed her hand, let her tread forward and spun her, then he placed his hands on her hips, pressing her back toward his chest as he swayed with her.

She'd forgotten what a good dancer he was.

He turned her quickly, so she faced him. His hand pressed firmly on the small of her back, crushing her body to his. The suddenness made her breath hitch, but not for long.

A second later, his lips pressed against hers; his tongue spreading her lips apart then invading her mouth, forcefully exploring her. Their kiss was over as quickly as it'd been initiated.

He led her to the bar. "The usual, Mrs. Thaler?" he whispered in her ear.

She nodded, still unable to speak and smiled. There wasn't much about her he didn't know now and vice versa. He knew what she liked and what she didn't. It fascinated her as deeply as it comforted her. Small details like those allowed her to, in reflection, look favorably upon the time they'd spent as friends when they should've been mates.

The bartender placed their drinks on the bar top. Cain handed over his card without a glance at the bartender, then grabbed her drink and handed it to her.

"To my bride," he said, tapping the edge of his drink against hers. "Need to get you a ring."

"I don't need a ring. Everyone will know once I'm marked."

"Not mortals," he pointed out.

Mortals? An immortal mating was much more significant than any mortal marriage. There were no divorces, no annulments, no "we were drunk and in Vegas" or irreconcilable differences. It was truly till death do they part or forever.

Her expression must have given away her thought because the next instant he said, "Humor me. I'm the typical four-hundred-year-old demon, and I don't fancy reading lust streaming off of men—immortal or otherwise."

"No one is interested in me—"

His eyes sparked. "Ah, right, another thing I love about you. You're humble, maybe too humble." He paused; his eyes scanned the room before they met hers again. "I've read lust streaming from every damn man we've passed and it was for you, darling."

"That's not true."

He raised an eyebrow, suspiciously. "Are you saying my abilities as an empath are lacking?"

Smiling, in a teasing tone, she said, "I would never—"

"That's what you're implying."

"I would have noticed if men looked at me," she

insisted.

"You only see what you want to see, but for fun and because we still need to finish our drinks before we head out to the dance floor, how about we test my abilities?"

She took a sip of her martini then asked, "How do you plan to do that?"

Before she finished her sentence, he grabbed her drink, and placed it on the bar top. He tucked her body against his; her hands immediately went to his hips. His heat engulfed her, filling every crevice, spiking her temperature to new heights. As he trailed his hand down her spine, her heart thumped louder and louder until she heard it above the sound of the roaring music. He bent slightly, tucking his head in the crook of her neck, running his tongue along her pulse. She was hot, too hot, and she wanted him, then and there.

"You want me, Liv," he whispered huskily.

Hands fisting the sides of his shirt, she moaned, "Tease." He chuckled against her, then slowly moved away without releasing her to look into her eyes, his expression mischievous and amused. "I'm only trying to demonstrate my mad skills."

"That doesn't prove anything. You've had lots of practice, and I'm your mate. Destiny…" Her words fell away when his expression hardened.

Taking a long swig of his drink, he finished it then placed it on the bar and ordered another.

Noticing the change in his mood, she asked, "What's wrong?"

"I haven't been with anyone since I met you," he said, his expression torn. "But I've felt guilty about…"

He left words unspoken, yet he projected his

feelings. She felt guilt and remorse but still couldn't grasp the reason why. "Why…"

"You've been alive for more than a century, and I never searched. You were in the same state, sometimes in the same city…"

Her heart swelled with the thought: her mate, guilt-ridden for never searching for her…as if it would've made a difference. She ran her hand down his cheek, loving the roughness of the blond stubble against her palm. "Even if you'd searched, you may have never found me. You found me when fate decided it should be. We're together now, and that's all that matters."

She spoke the words from her heart.

Chapter 19

As the night wore on, it had become breezy, drifting warm air through the bar. They each had two drinks as they talked, laughed and danced.

Thus far, it had been the most memorable day in Olivia's life. A day when she realized dreams did in fact come true, a day when the love of her life confessed his love for her, and hopefully soon it would be the day she gave the greatest gift she could give him in return, herself. Whether he knew it or not, he was already in possession of her heart and soul, but her body had never been touched, until today it had never been kissed or caressed.

A slow melodic song sounded through the speakers, Cain pulled her body against his in an inescapable hold, swaying with her to the soft beat of the music. Her hands crossed behind his neck, her fingers in his hair.

The song sounded familiar, too familiar. He ran his hand down her back, his fingers lingering over her skin. She shuddered loving a simple touch.

It happened every time. No matter how insignificant the graze, whether his arms wrapped around her or whether it was a soft caress to her cheek, her body imploded with desire.

He sang the lyrics slowly and wonderfully against her lips. His voice drifting through her, comforting her.

As the song continued to play, in those enduring moments suspended in time, nothing existed but them, and the lyrics he uttered. His eyes never left her, seemingly as captivated by her as she was by him.

Too soon the song ended, replaced by yet another dance mix, but neither moved. They were still hanging in their moment, preferring to remain in each other's arms.

After a long moment, he leaned down, and grazed his lips against hers. The softest, sweetest kiss.

A soft smile spread across his lips, that glimmer in his eyes shining bright. He tightened his arms around her, the arm around her waist and the one around her back, then he buried his face in her neck. Her hands in his hair, she trailed down his back.

"Home," he whispered.

"Home," she agreed, then he led her toward the exit.

Moments later, they materialized in her living room. She pulled her head away from the comfort of his chest to stare into his too blue eyes, but he didn't release her and she didn't release him. Instead, he leaned toward her and pressed his lips against hers, a beautiful kiss. Despite the hunger and fierceness in his eyes, the kiss was soft, sweet and sensual.

His lips then roamed down her cheek and lingered over the throbbing pulse along her neck. There, he whispered, "I crave you."

He'd held back for too long, kept buried his desires as she had. With that simple declaration, she knew he'd given in, made the decision to have her, all of her. Finally. It was about time he gave into what they both longed for.

A chill swept through her just thinking of it. It was all it took to get her heart racing, her temperature spiking, and her hands shaking. There was no use hiding the nerves. She wanted him. She loved him. As much as she'd dreamt of the moment, she was scared, too, because she didn't know if she could please him and wanted to.

Despite her nerves, insecurities and rambling thoughts, she managed to mumble, "Yes."

Pulling away slightly, she slid the strap of her dress off her shoulder. Holding her gaze, he hissed, the sound coming from the back of his throat. She knew his eyes would soon ignite red, ablaze with hunger—for her.

She was glad for the blue nearly-there dress she'd worn. Perhaps it was her lucky charm, one she would treasure forever. More than likely, it had nothing to do with it; they were fated. Yes, she agreed, it was her beautiful destiny to lay in his arms, a cosmic gift she'd never be able to repay.

"Thank you," she whispered.

His hands trailed down her hips toward her back. "For?"

"You," she mumbled.

His eyes sparked moments before he placed his hand on the back of her neck and met her lips again, forcefully spreading her mouth open with his tongue and delving in with reckless abandonment. The kiss was hungry, passionate, so unlike the other. She couldn't decide which she preferred.

She would soon be lost, lost in him, but worries of her inexperience assailed her, and she pulled away.

"What's wrong, darling?" he asked. The fire in his eyes, his desire, ebbed with concern. "We don't have to do—"

"It's not that. I want to...I just...I don't know if I'm good at this...I've never..."

"You are plenty good, darling. You just don't know it."

He kissed her again, a soft, comforting kiss. Running his hands down her back, he cupped the underside of her derrière. Lost in his kiss, she barely recalled when her weight was no longer on her feet. He'd lifted her effortlessly, and she willingly straddled him. Her dress hiked up. The cool air hit her now bare backside briefly before his hands covered her.

Groaning, he tore himself away to say, "Liv, please tell me you weren't out without underwear."

Immediately, she covered his lips with hers, her arms encasing him, holding on for dear life.

Breaking away from the kiss, he muttered, "Liv." An attempt to question her again, or scold her, but lost in the moment, it lacked the strict tone. It came out heated and hungry and only made her need unbearable.

Her heart drummed louder in sync with his when his hand crawled down her breast and clutched her lightly. She moaned, the sound deep, heated, startling her.

"Darling, I need you," he rasped against her ear.

Her back hitting a soft surface, he continued to taunt her with his tongue, running it along her neck toward her chest then suddenly he was gone.

Her eyes snapped open landing on his, swarming in red. *What a sight*, she thought, realizing then he'd materialized them in her room.

She watched him as he slowly rid her of her dress then her thong. The relief she'd worn one was palpable in his crimson eyes. Tossing her clothes aside, he stood tense, muscles bulging, hands in fists at his sides, eyes hungry trailing every inch of her body, taking his fill.

She couldn't help it. Under his intent gaze, her face flushed, wondering if he liked what he saw. Despite the insecure thought, she fought to keep still, to let him see her, all of her for as long as he wanted.

He murmured in Latin allowing her to catch a glimpse of his protruding fangs.

After minutes without a caress, his gaze shot toward hers. "You're the most beautiful woman in the world, Liv," he said. Those red eyes riddled with blatant desire.

She sighed, relieved.

Removing his shirt then jeans, he only left his tented boxers. Her eyes widened. He was big, bigger than she'd thought any man could be. Would he fit her? Would he get any pleasure at all? Panicked, her breaths grew rapid.

As if reading her mind, he assured, "I won't hurt you, darling. I can't."

She nodded, still unable to mask her worry.

He moved, hovering over her body. His hands glided up and down her chest then he pressed his mouth over her nipple, sucking and tugging lightly.

Pleasure searing and daunting overwhelmed her, so she couldn't help but arch her back and moan in desire. Raking her fingers through his short-cropped hair, she held him to her, never wanting him to stop.

He moved to her other breast, paying it as much attention as the first, kissing and caressing softly. Her breaths grew so rapid she was gasping. His hands trailed toward her core. One soft touch and a shot of pleasure rippled through her, making her ache. Her body tensed as a moan slid out of her lips. His tongue wandered lower and lower, licking his way toward her moist center. One flick, then two as his fingers rubbed her.

She wanted to scream, wanted to encourage him, hold him, pleasure him, but she couldn't speak. All she could do was feel the ecstasy he created so magically inside her.

His tongue's strokes continued, driving her toward a steep cliff of pleasure. With each, her moans became louder and louder, drowning out her pounding heart.

Then he slid a finger into her. Her hips bucked, her body trembling uncontrollably. An explosion of passion, wave after wave of pleasure ascended her and wouldn't stop.

She felt the aftershocks long after his arms went around her shoulders, and he silenced her moans with a gut-wrenching, searing kiss.

Still trembling in his arms, aching from her mind-shattering orgasm and desiring more, she rasped, "I…"

"Your eyes are beautifully glowing, darling," he whispered against her lips.

She didn't know how he could tell. Her eyes were at half-mast, and heavy-lidded. "I need you…" she managed finally.

The muscles in his shoulders tensed. "Maybe we should—"

Her arms, wrapped around his neck, clutched him to her. "No, I need you now." She'd waited over a century for him and wouldn't let him get away now.

His eyes darkened, his expression hardening. His shaft throbbed against her stomach, so she knew he wanted her, all of her, but he battled with himself, his desire and honor. Wanting to help him make up his mind, wanting to pleasure him as he pleasured her, she kissed him. When he groaned into her mouth, she knew desire had won.

His jaw clenched, eyes ablaze, he removed his boxers. Hovering over her, he fisted his shaft then positioned himself at her core. He slid into her slowly, stretching her.

She thought it would have been different, painful even, especially the first time, but all she felt was pleasure, overwhelming pleasure, so much so her nails dug into his shoulders, a loud moan escaped her lips. Immediately, he stilled. When he did, her gaze shot to his.

His face was flushed, holding his breath. His eyes lingered over her, deadly and fierce. "Does it hurt?" he croaked.

"No…it feels…you feel…amazing," she whispered, then lifted her hips to meet his, taking more of him inside her.

His eyes widened. He moaned then slid out and back in slowly. Placing his lips against hers, he kissed her as he continued to withdraw and thrust into her again. The muscles in his shoulders tightened and flexed with every thrust. As he'd done before, he increased his pace, the intensity of his kiss heightening, matching his deep thrusts. Several more and she was where she'd been before, near the edge.

Suddenly, it overwhelmed her, another beautiful mind-blowing orgasm. When she thought it couldn't get more intense, that same intense pleasure radiated into her, leaving her breathless as wave after wave rippled through her. Her arms tightening around him, it was all she could do—make sure he didn't let her go.

Chapter 20

Two weeks ago

Twilight was beautiful in Northern New York. As the sun receded, the sky became a rainbow of colors above the plethora of trees and land. The temperature had dropped slightly. Olivia loved it, all of it. The reason, around this time every day, she went for a stroll in her garden. Her mind as of late filled with thoughts of Cain. She knew why and tried her hardest to fight it. It had her contemplating another run.

But she couldn't. Since Jocelyn had been attacked at the estate, Landon refused to allow her to run unaccompanied at night. It seemed like it had been ages since then. She didn't care much for company on her runs. It was her time to enjoy, and being accompanied would ruin the feeling of utter freedom.

"Liv," his voice resounded behind her.

She hesitated, attempting to control the thundering of her heart before she confronted him. Finally, she turned to face him. Her heart clenched in her chest, struck once again by his handsome features. Every day she fell in love with him a little more.

"Are you okay?" he asked.

Of course, he sensed her disillusion. He was an empath. It was useless even to try to hide anything from him, or any demon for that matter.

He had to know she was in love with him. The thought distressed her more. Did he pity her foolish feelings for a man she could never have? Was that the reason he came to see her every day?

Drawing a step closer, he said, "Liv?"

She lifted her chin, a poor attempt to act confident, then lied, "I'm fine."

Avoiding his stare, she strode toward him and took a seat on the bench surrounded by calla lilies.

"Mind if I join you?"

A dry, humorless laugh bubbled from her. "Of course, Cain. Why would you need to ask?"

After a moment, he sat beside her, not too close, and released a breath, then he said, "You don't seem to want company."

His somber voice made her head snap to face him. It wasn't like him.

"Don't tell me my awful mood has rubbed off on you," she said with a smile, her best attempt to jest and lighten his mood. "I'll have to kick you out."

He laughed, but like hers moments before it held no humor.

She lifted her head and admired the stars. From the corner of her eye, she realized he'd done the same.

"What do you want most in the world?" he asked, surprising her.

Shifting her attention to him, her eyes sought his. Just in time, he turned looking her way, waiting for her response. With that one somber look, she realized the glimmer always present had dimmed.

You, she thought in response to his question, but left the word unsaid, wondering exactly what to say.

Looking away from him, she whispered, "To be

loved, truly loved by a man." Before he could comment on it, she turned the tables on him. "What do you want most in the world?"

****

"What do you want most in the world?"

You, he thought but left the truth unsaid.

What could he say? He wanted to seek shelter in her arms and comfort in her touch. He wanted to come home to her face, her smile—her. He wanted her barefoot and pregnant with life they created growing inside her. He wanted her to love him so much she couldn't fathom living and breathing without him. He was already there.

"I want a lot of things, too many," he finally said.

A cop-out, so the moment he'd spoken the words, he regretted them. He needed her to trust him, but his situation made it difficult. He couldn't tell her the truth, only a version of it without revealing too many details.

"I want my fated to love me," he said it so simply.

He hoped she would respond. More than anything he wanted her to ask him if he'd found his. Because he knew if she did, he'd never be able to lie and, finally, she'd know. He waited for her to say something, but she never did, so he found himself gazing at the stars praying he could magically cure her sadness.

He didn't get his wish, but he did sit with her for hours. He didn't speak, only listened to the sounds of their breaths, wishing for more.

It was inevitable to want more, more of her, all of her, but for now, sitting in the dark, gazing at the stars was enough.

Chapter 21

His Olivia was heaven, a well of desire and unforgettable ecstasy: her taste so sweet, her skin so soft, her warmth so gratifying. Every moan she uttered was sweet surrender, surrender to him.

The moments of passion with Olivia were gone, but his mind refused to give them up. Relishing her lush body beneath his, her breaths at his neck, he couldn't force himself to move, couldn't force himself to stop reliving the moment. Catching his breath, he recalled their first time as a true defining moment in his life, a glimpse of what their lives would entail together. Bliss, true unhindered bliss, bliss beyond anything he'd ever experienced.

His mate clutched him still, her arms around him, her nails digging into his back as if she feared he'd disappear. After having waited so long, it was excruciatingly gratifying.

He couldn't blame her. He was doing the same, one arm around her waist the other around her neck, holding onto her, vowing he'd never leave her.

It had been well worth the wait, the torment and the pain, the anguish of watching her live without him because now she was his to guard, protect and love endlessly.

He placed his lips over her neck, the spot he'd imagined marking. His gums still ached, throbbing with the unbearable desire to claim her. Perhaps, lingering over the spot he wanted to mark wasn't a smart thing to do. It would only succeed in reminding him what he so desperately craved. Except he wouldn't because he understood how much her brother meant to her, because he knew she wanted his blessing.

His eyes fluttered closed. He buried his face in her neck and inhaled her scent, remembering the sweet sound of her moans with every touch, with every flick of his tongue and with every thrust allowing him to sink deeper and deeper into her.

A nasty thought then reared its head. He'd been out of his mind with desire, with need. He'd tried to be gentle, as gentle as he'd promised, but had he? Were her nails digging into him in pain instead of passion?

He pulled away from her quickly to stare into her sea-blue eyes. She looked like an angel with her swollen kissed lips. Her dark brown hair fanned around her like a halo, except for the *tears* spilling from her eyes.

His worst fear confirmed. He'd hurt her. He'd been too rough, too demanding of her virgin body. It should have been perfect for both of them, not just him. He'd never forgive himself.

Swallowing the bile rising in the back of his throat, he managed, "Darling, I'm so sorry…I—"

Despite the tears, she smiled. Her hands cupped his face, then she lifted herself slightly to press her lips against his.

He couldn't pull away, not even to finish the apology she so deserved.

When she did, she whispered, "That was…incredible."

Incredible? But he'd hurt her! "But I hurt—"

"No," she said, adamantly. "You didn't."

He hadn't hurt her? Then why was she in tears? "Why are you crying?"

She swallowed, her fingers softly grazing his cheek. "I've never been so happy in my life."

A warmth filling his chest, he reached out with his senses, felt what she did. He then cupped her face, his fingers grazing her skin. "Me neither, darling."

Her gaze drew away from his then she said on a whisper, "I think…I think I felt your release."

He nodded. "I tried to hold it back, but couldn't…" He'd lost hold of his emotions and involuntarily projected them. He'd been holding back too much: his strength, the need to claim her, and his emotions. Something had to give. The least damaging to her was how he felt. He'd planned to show her in time, but her first time he hadn't wanted to overwhelm her.

"I'm sorry—"

"Don't be," she smiled. "It was wonderful."

He held her for several more moments, unwilling to let their moment end, then shifted his weight and nestled her on his chest.

After a long moment, as he laced his fingers through her hair, he said, "Darling, I'm running you a bath and then you have to eat."

Snuggling closer, she whispered against his chest, "No, a little while longer."

He smirked then materialized them in her en suite bathroom, appearing with her body pressed against his, his arm around her waist, holding her up. Her hands clutched him, nails digging into his skin, she gasped, startled, then laughed.

"Mrs. Thaler, you will do as I say." Shifting away from her, he turned on the faucet in the bath and tested its heat.

"I'd rather lie in bed with you and maybe…"

He knew where her thoughts were headed. His had been headed in the same direction moments after their release. No one could blame him. She was his mate, the one he'd waited for, for centuries, the one he'd watched over for months, and she'd been lying naked beside him. He'd had her. Not all of her, he hadn't claimed her, but he had taken pleasure, given her pleasure and that meant he now knew what he'd been missing. His mind would never roam far from taking pleasure in her again.

"There's nothing I would love more, but we should wait until tomorrow, you may be sore…that's why you should bathe. The warm water will help."

"I guess…" she mumbled. "Are you joining me?"

He kissed her forehead then said, "Anything for my mate." As she climbed into the tub, he said, "I'll be right back, love."

He didn't waste time. Materializing in the kitchen, he rummaged through the cabinets to find a tray, wine glasses and a plate. He then opened the fridge to grab several cheeses, some deli meats, grapes, and white wine. After arranging the meats and cheeses on a plate along with the wine, he materialized in the bathroom again.

"Room service," he said.

Smiling, she said, "I'm not really hungry, for *food*." She blushed.

Come to think of it, neither was he. "Humor me. You haven't eaten since this afternoon."

He placed the tray on the side of the tub then turned off the faucet and settled in behind her, straddling her. When she laid her back against his chest, he handed her a glass of wine.

"I didn't know you drank wine."

"Not usually, but there comes a time when—"

Angling her head to meet his eyes, she teased, "Like when you're forcing your mate to bathe and eat?"

Running his hand down the side of her arm, he smiled. "Exactly."

They sipped their wine for several minutes before he reached for the assorted deli meats and a slice of cheese and fed her.

"Thank you. You know I was just teasing you before."

"I know, darling," he said, lightly kissed her temple before he reached for a slice a cheese for himself.

"How long do you think this will last?"

Not liking the sound of the question, he tensed, forced himself to swallow then asked, "What?"

"You know when couples first start dating they can't keep their hands off each other. It's a phase—"

Fuck. Why on earth she'd think *this* was temporary? They were immortals, destined for one another. It was much more than what mortals experienced. They were *fated* mates and what they felt would *never* fade.

"Where would you get the idea this is just a phase?" With every word, he fought to keep his tone level.

She shrugged. "I've read about it in magazines and—"

He gripped her chin, turned her face to the side to

meet his then said, "Liv, this *isn't* a phase. Whatever's mentioned in magazines doesn't pertain to us. We are mates, fated. This is how it will always be with us."

"But after a hundred years, you won't be as attracted to me—"

She wasn't getting it, so he said it more firmly. "You're *my mate*, Olivia. You are the *only one* for me. I will always be insanely attracted to you. I will always want you. I will always love you a hundred years from now, or a thousand, or however long I live."

Her face softened then her gaze fell away from his when she said, "But I'm not experienced in—"

"You're the best I've ever had," he said without thought. He meant it. She was the best of everything. Everything with her was like the first time, and he loved he was her first and loved more he would be her last.

The tension in her shoulders dissolved, slumping slightly. He released her face, allowing her to turn it away from him.

Inwardly, he cursed, hating her insecurities. It seemed every compliment he'd ever given her hadn't sunk in. His Olivia was a beautiful, naturally quick-witted woman, but had no self-esteem to show for it because she'd been too sheltered. He blamed her brother; it was Landon's fault for keeping her secluded at the estate and away from men who weren't terrified of him. It should be a crime no man had ever told her just how beautiful she was.

Now, it was Cain's job to make her realize she was beautiful, special, beyond anything and anyone, and especially, to make her understand she was all there was for *him*.

Then an ugly thought reared its head: his own insecurity and deep-seated fear. Would her insecurities cause her to leave him again? There was no question Landon wouldn't be thrilled she was his mate. That meant he'd do whatever it took to keep them apart. What he feared was Landon playing on her insecurities, making her run from him, again. Was it a matter of when instead of if?

After feeding her several more slices of meat and cheese, he grabbed the soap and lathered her back then chest, arms, legs, exploring every bit of her body. As he did, he told her why he found each bit of her beautiful. It was all he could do to assure her, so he knew he would do it again, over and over until she believed.

After their bath, he dried her and tucked her into bed then nestled himself next to her with her head on his shoulder and his arms tight around her. He pressed a kiss to her forehead, shutting his eyes tightly.

Tonight, he wouldn't think about her leaving. Tonight, he would enjoy her in his arms.

Tomorrow, he'd wake with her beside him and continue to tell her she was beautiful, and every day after that, too. Eventually, she'd believe him.

****

Cain dreamt and dreamt, the sweet dreams he dreamt replaced with a new dream. He was alone, cold and empty, subconsciously, realizing the warmth that soothed him throughout the night was gone.

He reached for her, but his arm landed on the cold, empty mattress. Immediately, his eyes snapped open, scanning his surroundings.

He was alone.

Olivia was gone.

The dream became reality.

He couldn't prevent the panic, fear or dread that enveloped him immediately. He wanted to believe the day they'd spent together meant as much to her as it meant to him—everything. He wanted to believe she hadn't left him, possibly she'd just needed to use the restroom, but before he even searched the bathroom, he knew he wouldn't find her there. The sheets next to him were cold, too cold, as if she left some time ago not just minutes. Either way, he searched the bathroom and closet, and just as he'd expected, she wasn't there.

With trembling hands, he searched the second story of the home, just as he'd done the day before, room by room. In a flash, he materialized on the stairs. There, his gaze landed on her, feet from him, climbing quickly, holding a tray of food and coffee.

Relief swarmed him. Struggling to tamp down the panic that clawed him, he didn't act fast enough. Olivia collided with him. The tray of breakfast hit his chest before tipping toward her, spilling coffee, food, utensils, plates and cups. She gasped and stumbled. He snaked his arm around her waist, steadying her. The crashing sound of their breakfast, broken plates and cups, smashing into the floor came a second later.

Her eyes burning him with awareness, she said, "I'm sorry I didn't see you."

He took in her appearance. Her hair hadn't been brushed, her face was cosmetic free, and she smelled of him. *Stunning*, he thought, especially wearing his shirt that showed off her long lean legs. Now, it was drenched in coffee and so was she.

His mate had been making him breakfast, and he thought she'd left him. Who was the insecure one? His panic had ebbed, but the dread and fear were harder to tame.

"Cain?" she asked. "Are you okay?"

He nodded. "I'm sorry," he said. "You should go change. I'll clean this up."

"I can help—"

"No," he said, firmly, avoiding her gaze.

As if picking up his bleak thoughts, she asked, "What's wrong?"

He didn't trust himself to answer, so he said nothing. Instead, he kneeled and began to pick up the pieces of broken glass.

"You're not going to tell me?" she asked, so softly, so solemn he barely heard.

When he didn't respond, she turned and headed upstairs. A moment later, he heard the shower running.

Idiot, he scolded. Why hadn't he just told her? His pride? Did he have any left when it came to her?

He finished picking up the pieces of glass and began picking up the food. Sighing heavily, he continued to berate himself. He moved into the kitchen in search of a mop when he heard the shower turn off. Finding the mop in a closet off the side of the kitchen, he took it, headed back toward the stairs and began mopping.

When he finished, he looked up and found her at the top of the staircase, looking down at him, wearing a pink knitted dress that, in his opinion, revealed too much cleavage. She'd showered and washed her hair, which now hung dripping wet around her.

Sighing heavily, she said, "Sometimes I feel like I don't know you anymore. You've changed so much...I don't understand. I know I hurt you by leaving, but it hurt me, too. I know it's my fault, and I *am* sorry. I want to make things right, but I can't if you won't tell me what's wrong. I want to help…please."

Her blue eyes beseeched, pulling and tugging at him. Unable to bear the sadness in her voice, or the pleading in her eyes, he caved. "This morning when I woke up, you weren't where I left you."

Looking confused, her brows drew together. "I went to make breakfast. I thought I'd surprise you," she explained.

He figured as much, but it hadn't soothed his fear, his dread that she would leave again. "I thought you left," he admitted.

She met him mid-staircase, then she wrapped her arms around his waist, resting her cheek against his chest and said, "I'll never do that again, Cain. I didn't know I was yours. If I had, I would have never left. I would've waited. I would've—"

Because he couldn't help it, he said, "But you have doubts."

She pulled away from him slightly, and tilted her head back to meet his gaze.

"You have doubts. If you didn't, you wouldn't wonder when this *phase* will fade. It won't." Harshness seeped into his voice. "It *isn't* a phase. This *is* real, lasting, consuming, can't-live-without-each-other love. We are mates. We will always feel this way."

Her arms fell away from his waist. When they did, her eyes rounded. "I'm sorry I just find it hard to believe you are attracted to me," she said, her cheeks growing flushed. Attempting to conceal the blush he loved so much, she drew her hands to cover her face.

It pissed him off in a way it shouldn't, but because

he was still angry from what she'd said last night his temper spiked. "Because you don't know how beautiful you are. Does it even matter how many times I tell you? You'll never believe it, will you? Do you own a mirror?"

Her eyes narrowed and flared, interweaving the blue with sparks of gold. "Don't patronize me," she fired back, her voice rising. "I haven't slept with hundreds of men who flattered me constantly."

She said she didn't care, said she didn't blame him for not looking for her, but she did. It hurt him because she lied, especially because she blamed him and had every right to. His chest tightening, eyes ablaze, he shot back, "And you hold that against *me*."

"Don't put words in my mouth, Thaler."

Did she just call him by his last name? After all the time they'd known each other? After yesterday? After last night? She was driving a wedge between them, distancing herself from him as she'd done the weeks before she left. A pure and profound frustration seeped into him.

No, she wouldn't; he wouldn't let her.

Wrapping his arms around her roughly, he crushed her body against his then planted his lips on hers. She fought briefly, pressing her palms on his chest attempting to push him away, but when his tongue parted her lips and he delved in, she quit fighting and gave in to him. Her tongue stroking his eagerly, she wrapped her arms around his neck deepening the kiss.

Images of her body naked and pliant, her face flushed with pleasure assailed him, and he could barely control his desire to make love to her right then and there.

He released her and pulled away, adjusting the bulge in his shorts. She stood dazed, her eyes heavy-lidded then her thoughts focused, she scowled.

"Why'd you do that?" she demanded.

"Because I can, and I will," he countered, hoping his soft tone would soothe her temper.

"Arrogance? Really? See what I mean? I don't even know you. I thought I did, but apparently, all those months you were pretending to be someone you aren't," she accused.

It stung. He couldn't help but cringe. For the first time, he realized he didn't know his mate as well as he thought. She wasn't one to fire painful retorts—not even toward her brother, who often deserved them. Love complicated everything, didn't it?

He couldn't blame her though. He had changed, too. Never quick to lose his temper, yet it seemed that was all he'd done over the past several days. He'd never been one to pick fights either, but then again, he'd caused this one.

"Apparently, I don't know you either," he said dryly. The moment he said it, he wanted to take it back, knowing in the pit of his stomach he'd only made matters worse. Because he couldn't take it back, he bit his tongue hard, causing it to bleed.

He steeled himself to hear another scathing remark, but instead, she retreated. "Well, I guess that settles that," she said, sadly then turned and walked away.

He watched her walk up the stairs. With each step she took, a piece of his heart shredded, and yet he stood there immobile, hating what he'd said, how he'd behaved and having no clue how to fix it.

In some respects, he was as inexperienced as she

was. Having no family, his life had always revolved around his duty, and truth be told, he didn't know much about women. He took pleasure in them repeatedly over the course of his existence, but sex had just been sex, no strings attached. There was no point in strings when you were bound to find your mate at any point in time. He and Jocelyn were friends, but that didn't mean he knew what made her tick, and they'd never fought. Up until now, Olivia had never been angry with him. He'd never hurt her like this either, so he had no idea how to handle the situation—the situation, he reminded himself, he created. Though, honestly, even if he'd been experienced in relationships, it wouldn't have mattered. This wasn't just any relationship with any woman; this was the *only* relationship that would ever matter with the *one and only* woman for him.

It was a stupid fight, and he was a stupid man. Hadn't Olivia once asked him how often Jenna and Lucas fought? She hated how often Landon and Jocelyn argued, their tempers often besting them. Olivia and Cain had never fought before. Why now? Because he was insecure, afraid out of his mind she would leave again? That wasn't fair to her.

Running his hands through his hair in frustration, he released a heavy breath and followed her. He found the door to her room closed and knocked.

"Please…leave me alone." Her voice hitched.

Fuck. She was crying. He'd made her *cry*. Nothing could have stopped him from reaching her then. Heart squeezing, guilt swarming him, he materialized inside the room, and found her in tears, sitting near the window. Pain ripped through his chest, so similar to the pain he felt drifting from her in waves. Each tear sliding down her gorgeous face a dreadful reminder he was a coward and a fool.

She didn't turn to address him, "I need some time...alone. Please."

Materializing behind her, he effortlessly lifted her in his arms. She didn't fight him. Maybe because she knew it'd do no good. He then sat where she'd been and settled her on his thighs. Cupping the back of her head, he cradled her against his chest and rubbed her back tenderly.

"I'm sorry, *meae deliciae, meus sodalis*. Terribly sorry." His thumb wiped her tears away. "I'm terrified of losing you, but it's no excuse for hurting you."

She didn't utter a sound.

Tightening his arms around her, he said, "I was terrified again this morning when you were gone. I was upset about what you said last night about our happiness being a phase. It isn't a phase, Liv. I've lived four hundred years. I've never loved any woman, ever, until you. I'll always love you. You are strong and stunning and you give me reason to live, but you don't know it and when I tell you, you don't believe me, and that hurts."

She shivered. When she did, his arms instinctively clutched her tighter.

"I didn't mean to patronize you. I just...I've told you every chance I got before and now I tell you all the time. I'll always tell you. One day, you'll believe me. Even after, I'll continue to tell you just how beautiful you are."

Sighing heavily, he bared his thoughts, his feelings and his heart. "When you called me by my last name, I thought you were trying to distance yourself from me.

After all the months I've waited, after yesterday and last night, I was angry, so I kissed you thinking you wouldn't be able to distance yourself after. When you asked me why I'd kissed you, I didn't mean to sound arrogant. I was trying to..." He shrugged. "I don't know."

She angled her face to his.

Meeting her gaze, he said, "Darling, I have changed, and so have you. Love changes us. I've never been so hot-tempered in my life. We know each other as friends, not as mates and lovers. We'll learn new things about each other now, and in the process we may fight a little. It doesn't mean I love you any less or that we aren't meant for one another. I picked a fight because of my own insecurities, and I *am* sorry."

Finally done, he exhaled. He'd said everything he needed to say, everything she needed to know and could only hope he hadn't said something else to hurt her. He wasn't expecting her to forgive him immediately, but he would hold her until he no longer sensed her sadness because he couldn't stay away knowing he caused the tears she shed. He'd sit with her draped across his chest forever if he had to.

She lifted her head, drawing her lips toward his and kissed him lightly. "I'm sorry, too, Cain," she said, taking him by surprise.

"But...you didn't do anything wrong," he pointed out. "I picked the fight."

"Maybe you were fishing for a fight, but I wasn't any help. I said some mean things too, and I'm not like that."

He smiled. "You're amazing, you know that?"

Olivia chuckled, then she kissed him again.

Chapter 22

Lost in thought, Olivia watched the flames dance in the fireplace, highlighting the dim living room with light. Only moments before, Cain, wearing a collared long-sleeved white shirt and jeans, had stood before it throwing logs then poking and prodding until the fire raged to his liking.

"I have to make sure my mate's warm," he said.

She watched him then, maneuvering ever so effortlessly. Watching him without fear of being caught was a newfound freedom that had quickly turned into a habit. She watched him so intently she often felt like a voyeur—a poor one at that. Many times, he'd turn and smile her way as if her gaze seared him with awareness. Now as she sat on the area rug in front of the fire, she tried her hardest to fight the need to turn and watch him again, watch him prepare their dinner. If he hadn't been humming, she would've failed.

Suddenly, he squatted in front of her, pressing his lips to hers. She smiled into his lips and wrapped her arms around his neck to deepen the kiss.

"Liv," he warned, pulling away. "We'll never eat if we get started."

"So?" she pouted, flushing.

He handed her a glass of white wine.

She took a sip, immediately determining it as Chardonnay. "Sometimes you make me feel like a…a sex fiend."

Much to her disappointment, they spent the day in Oia, the northern part of the island. Her male insisted, and she caved. Instead of spending a lazy day indoors exploring each other's bodies, they shopped and had lunch. He also insisted they visit the church she mentioned days before where she admitted she dreamt of being married.

Eyes softening in the way she loved, he cupped her cheek. "That's ridiculous, darling."

"It's true. You never—"

Cain placed his lips over hers silencing her, simultaneously grabbing her wine and placing it on the floor. Leaning into her, he deepened the kiss, probing her mouth with expertise until her back lay flat on the thick carpet, and he hovering her, his body dwarfing hers yet melding perfectly.

The kiss burning her with awareness, with him, she tugged on his shirt attempting to bring him closer as if their bodies weren't already merged. He ran his hands through her hair then down her body. His kisses lingered long after his mouth trailed fire down her neck.

Resting his weight on his elbows, he broke away breathing heavy, and shook his head as if to dispel their moment from his mind. When she parted her lids, his beautiful red glowing eyes were the first thing she saw.

"Dinner," he barked. His brows drawn, a bewildered expression on his face as if trying to determine what the word he said meant. "Dinner," he repeated.

Lips still tingling, she repeated, "Dinner."

"I want you as bad if not worse, darling," he said then straightened and stood.

Unconsciously, her gaze floated down his body, stopping when they reached his tented jeans. A deep flush coloring her cheeks, she smiled.

When her eyes met his again, he returned the smile. "My darling, Olivia, I wonder if you'll flush like that after the first century."

She shrugged. "Probably," she said, then remembered he said he liked it, and hoped she would.

He turned and walked toward the kitchen, her gaze following him. Reaching the stove, he stood immobile for several minutes, so she prodded, "Cain?"

"Huh," he said, turning.

"Should I set the table?"

"Yeah, yeah," he said quickly.

She walked toward him then asked, "What's the matter?"

He shook his head then poured the thick tomato sauce in the pasta and stirred. "I…" His attention on his task, he ran his hand through his short blond hair then with a smile he admitted, "I forgot what I was doing for a while. I just kept picturing you lying on the carpet flushed and…" His head snapped up even as he trailed off, so she caught sight of his still deep red stare.

She couldn't help but smile, flattered with the thought she could unnerve him.

She then set the large dining room table for two: Cain at the head of the table and her next to him, then returned to the living room to grab her glass of wine and set it on the table as well. From behind her, one arm went around her waist, clutched her to him as he pressed a kiss to her neck. His other arm went around her as he set the garlic bread on the table. Pulling away too quickly, he headed back to the kitchen and served their meals. Finally, he sat beside her.

"Liv," he said, pulling out a box from his jeans. "I got you something." He opened the small box to reveal a beautifully intricate coral necklace. "I wanted you to have something to remind you of our first time here."

Her eyes widened, admiring it. Smiling, she said, "It's gorgeous."

He removed the necklace from the box and stood behind her, fastened it around her neck then took his seat again.

"I love it, Cain. Thank you."

"You look beautiful tonight, Liv."

Still uneasy with compliments, she glanced down at herself wishing she wore something fancier instead of the simple green dress and flats.

"Thanks," she whispered.

He placed his hand over hers firmly. "I love that dress on you...Actually, I love everything on you, but I like you naked the best."

Trying her best to hide her surprise, she replied, "I like you best naked, too." She would have pulled it off if she hadn't flushed.

Shaking his head, he laughed then took a sip of his untouched glass of wine. "We should eat while it's still hot, love," he said then immediately dug in.

They ate in silence, stealing glances in each other's direction. After dinner, Cain insisted on watching a movie. Despite her best attempts to stay awake, before she knew it, her eyes became too heavy and she drifted to sleep.

****

An hour into the movie, Cain was still awake. Olivia's head rested on his thigh; her eyes closed in slumber, her breaths even. She'd fallen asleep shortly after they'd started the movie.

His plan had worked. He'd tired her out so completely, dragging her from store to store throughout the day she'd been too exhausted and unable to stay awake past midnight. He'd planned it that way. Though he wanted nothing more than to enjoy her body as he'd done the night before, he wasn't a fool to think he'd be able to contain his demon a second time. Because he'd held back for so long, his need to mark and claim her, he didn't think he'd be able too much longer.

She made it hard enough for him, teasing and taunting him with barely-there dresses, seductive glances. Then again, it wasn't her fault. She had no idea how easily she provoked him: every time her face flushed, every time she touched him even in the simplest of ways, every time he caught her staring at him, her eyes sparked in that incandescent color. Constantly, he was tempted and fighting his baser instincts.

His duty to protect her was his top priority. He couldn't allow her to confront her brother bearing his mark when they returned to New York because although she said she didn't care, he knew better. Besides, for him, it was enough to hold her as she slept, lie with her, dine with her, kiss her and hold her—for now. He dreamt of just this more often than he dreamt of her naked flesh under his. This was peace; his peace was her.

With those thoughts roaming his mind, he, too, fell into a deep sleep.

****

Olivia's heated skin raked against his. She sat

straddling him. Her long lean legs nestled against his thighs, tormenting him with kisses along his mouth and neck, her moist lips and sweet tongue causing havoc inside him.

Just what he wanted.

Just what he needed.

And it felt amazing, like he'd died and gone to heaven.

He was dreaming and knew it, and because it was a dream he could give into her, give into what he wanted.

Allowing his hands to wander, roaming up and down the sides of her sleek body, his mouth crushed hers with blunt force. His tongue explored her mouth and flicked her tongue with power and speed.

He'd never kissed her like that before; he'd been too afraid to scare her, but there was no fear now. He couldn't hurt her in a dream. In a dream, he could give into his craving, show her just how desperately he wanted her.

She moaned, the sound resonating in his soul, then her fingers were unbuttoning his shirt, her nails biting into his pecs. Her mouth left his.

Missing her tongue, he growled until the warmth of her mouth caressed his chest. His hands went to her back. Gripping the top of her dress, he ripped it, ran his hands down her braless back, then cupped her rear and pressed her against the length of his arousal. He removed her torn dress then tugged her body against his. Her nipples hardened and puckered against his chest.

Feels too good to be just a dream. Just as the thought occurred, his fangs sprang to life, snapping his eyes open.

Fuck. It wasn't a dream. Olivia straddled him, her lips on his chest, her tongue tasting and teasing him. And he'd been rough, the force of his kiss and the tearing of her dress.

Stiffening, he fought his desire, shame running through him.

As if sensing his retreat, her glowing golden gaze found his. "I need you," she said, then as forcefully as he'd kissed her, she kissed him, nicking her tongue against his fangs in the process.

Tasting her blood before he smelled it, he growled. Every muscle in his body clenched, his demon begging to be unleashed. He fought him, fought every fiber in his body, fighting his instincts demanding he claim what destiny granted him. Weakly, he managed to rasp, "Trying to kill me, darling?"

"Just trying to love you, Cain," she countered, her voice so soft, so sweet.

He didn't know what it was: the desire he fought for too long, the feel of her naked flesh against his or the sweet way she'd said his name, probably all of it made his control snap, shredding his composure, destroying his will. By the time he realized what happened, it was too late. He couldn't stop if he tried.

No one could blame him. Aside from her thong and that coral necklace he'd bought her, she sat naked on his lap, offering herself to him. No man could resist, and he wasn't just a man; he was an immortal, but she wasn't just any woman, she was his fated mate. Resisting as he'd done for as long as he had was difficult enough. He couldn't resist this. The control he prided himself with gone, so he gave in, surrendering—to her.

The only thing he could do was hope she didn't have second thoughts because a bulldozer couldn't pry him away now.

"I'll punish you for this later, Liv," he said huskily.

Materializing them on the large thick area rug in front of the fire, him on top of her, he didn't hesitate, flicking his tongue over the exposed flesh above her breast. He descended until he met her nipple then grazed it, caressing her other breast with his hand.

She inhaled sharply and arched, his sharp fang cutting her. Savoring her blood once again, her nails dug into his back, egging him on.

Ripping the rest of his shirt, she moaned, "Yes…"

His tongue trekked lower and lower, kissing her stomach, thighs and everywhere in between. Removing his jeans and boxers, he then roughly placed his mouth over her core. Her taste spread through him. Instantaneously, the impact of what she felt struck him, making his cock jerk.

Died and gone to heaven.

"Ah…" she moaned, wrapping those lean legs around his head.

His hands roamed them, his fingers clutching with little restraint.

Don't turn. Don't turn, he thought. He couldn't ruin this moment with his demon. It was their moment—his and hers, and he didn't want to share with anyone, even if the demon was just an extension of himself, his wicked half.

She unwrapped her legs, then pulled his head away from her core, toward her mouth, and pressed her lips against his. He slid into her simultaneously, then pulled away slightly, hesitating. He hesitated because she was warm and wet and wanting, arching and aching for him, ready to burst. Her face flush; her eyes ablaze in their golden glory, and he wanted to remember all of it. He wanted it seared into his soul.

She pulled away, then met his hips with a force he thought her incapable of. He doubled over her, the pleasure excruciating. Her eyes met his, her nails scored his backside, encouraging him to continue. He obeyed, sliding out then into her again. Gasping for breath, she let out a small startled scream.

Now that he'd started, he couldn't stop. He thrust into her repeatedly, his demon purring and begging to be unleashed.

Mark her! his demon chanted.

He couldn't. He just couldn't, so he dug his fangs into his lower lip hoping the temptation would diminish.

Then it hit him. Overwhelming ecstasy, pleasure beyond imaginable overtook him and her. He felt his release as he felt hers, her body quaking and clenching against him. She cried out his name, and nothing was ever so sweet.

Exhausted and drained from fighting too many desires, he collapsed on top of her.

He couldn't think, could barely catch his breath, but he knew he'd been less than gentle. He knew he'd been rough.

Removing himself from her, he held his weight on his hands, hovering over her and scanned her body, searching for even the smallest of injuries. None that he could see, yet.

"What...are you...doing?" she asked, fighting to catch her breath.

Shaking his head, breathing heavily, he said, "We *can't* do this anymore…Promise me…"

"What?" she croaked. Her eyes trailing the blood dripping his bottom lip.

"I wasn't gentle…" He paused, staring into her gorgeous blue eyes, interwoven with hues of gold. "Fuck! What did I do? Promise me…"

"You…" Her breathing hitched. She sat up, pulled herself against him until her body was nestled close, her eyes on his. "I can't and won't promise you that," she said. Her expression softened then she said, "I wish you'd stop acting like I'm going to break. I'm not. I'm strong. I'm a werewolf."

Astonished and relieved, he exhaled. "I didn't hurt you?"

Smiling softly, she assured him. "No, you didn't." She then shocked him when she said, "And we're spending the rest of our vacation making love."

Then she lifted herself until she could reach his mouth and ran her tongue along his bottom lip drinking him in. Her eyes imploded gold and glowed.

His mate drinking him, tasting him: nothing could be more pleasurable. He released a deep moan. His eyes of their own accord went to her neck. His fangs throbbed, wanting so badly to sink into her.

Control. Control, he mentally chanted then gripped her shoulders and pulled her away. "You're trying my control, my darling."

She smiled. "You try mine all the time." Again, she said it softly. He knew if her face hadn't been heated from their moment, she would've flushed. "I wasn't trying to, but I couldn't help myself, and you'll heal faster, too."

No, his Olivia wouldn't tempt him to do something rash. Her saliva, because she was a werewolf, healed. Combined with his superior healing, the marks he'd made in desperation were now gone. The thing was she didn't have to try too hard. Everything she did stirred his desire. It would never end, even after his mark branded her.

He laughed humorlessly, then grabbed a blanket sprawled across the couch, laid down, taking her with him and covered them.

Tugging her body closer, he buried his face in her hair and whispered, "*Meae deliciae, meus sodalis.*"

Chapter 23

Cain and Olivia made love, lots of it, over the next several days. They made love at dawn when their urges woke with them and the sun seemed as if it were merely a mist. They made love in the afternoons when they were tired of pretending it was far from their minds. At twilight when the sun cast an array of colors inside the home they shared, and after dinners that left them both hungry for something more.

They hadn't left the house, savoring their time together. When they weren't making love, they were eating at Cain's insistence. In the mornings, he made breakfast. In the afternoons, she made lunch, and at dinner time, they cooked together or ordered in. It was perfect bliss. Their bliss, but the days were passing, and there were too many unanswered questions in their future that neither one of them could postpone much longer.

Cain had a duty as did she. While he controlled his primal urge to mark her flesh, there would be no denying they tempted fate and desire. She, too, had battled her urge to mark him. During their hours of intimacy, her canines elongated, the predator inside her craving to claim her male as his demon craved to claim his mate.

Tonight after dinner and dessert, they made love and lingered by the fire. She lay in front of him facing the flames. He lay behind her resting his weight on an elbow. His front pressed close to her back, his fingers buried in her hair. She stared at the fire, seemingly lost in thought. Sensing her apprehension, he knew her thoughts were right where his were—in New York.

"Darling." He broke the silence.

She angled herself until her back lay on the floor. Her eyes met his quickly. "Don't say it," she said softly. "I know it's time."

He nodded and impatiently waited for her to continue. They had only briefly spoken about their situation when he insisted he not mark her until she spoke to her brother, but questions plagued him for days. When would they tell her brother? When they returned, how long would it be before he could hold her again and make love to her? He spent night and day with her for days, was he strong enough to give that up now even for a single day? Even the simplest of questions, such as where they'd live, pestered him. He lived in the city, surrounded by skyscrapers and crowds of people with his king and queen where he could hunt for Malums. She lived in the northern part of the state, surrounded by nature and animals with her brother where she could turn and run and explore. Could he tear her away from the only home she'd ever known, away from her kind? Could she stand to live in the city surrounded by so much? Would she be happy?

She was a loved and respected princess, part of the council of her breed. He was an orphan, second in command to his king, a warrior. When they returned to their lives, would she discover he wasn't good enough for her, that she deserved a king or a prince? Would she care then he wasn't of her breed? Would she discover they were polar opposites with lives running in different directions? Would she leave him, again?

She said she loved him, and claimed his breed didn't matter, but his fear was innate, a threat that could rid him of his greatest gift—her.

He didn't have the answers and couldn't answer any of his lingering questions, only she could, when the time came.

One thing he was sure of, if she asked for more time, he wouldn't deny her. The only thing he could deny her was not seeing and being with her every day because he needed her; he belonged with her. Nothing would ever keep him away.

"I think…you should let me tell him, alone," she said, breaking into his thoughts.

Tensing, he shifted until his body hovered over hers. His anger spiked. His voice gruff when he said, "No, Liv. We agreed to tell him together. Tell me when, and I'll be there. We *have* to do this together."

Eyes saddening, she whispered, "He's not going to take this well—"

"That's why *I* need to be there. I'm not afraid of your brother," he reminded her, firmly.

"I know. But what if—"

Cupping her face, he said, "We'll deal with anything as it happens. The only thing you need to decide is when."

She paused. It seemed for endless moments, then she said, "I think we should give him a couple of days before we tell him."

Hopes falling, he nodded. He had no will to hide the disappointment in his expression. So, he lay down beside her, his body facing hers.

Not a second later, she propped herself on her elbow, facing him. Instinctually, his hand went to her hip. Her eyes pleaded when she said, "Talk to me. I know something's upsetting you. Tell me."

His gaze darting to her, he was honest. "I'm going to miss you a hell of a lot."

"Miss me?" she repeated. "Why? Where will you be?" Panic seeped into her voice.

He loved it for what it meant. That she, too, didn't want to be without him. "I'll be with you every second I can, Liv, but until we tell your brother, we'll be hiding."

She placed her hand over his heart. "We don't have to hide. Everyone knows, right?"

He nodded.

"We just have to keep it from my brother for a couple of days. We'll still be together every chance we get."

Lifting his brows, he asked, "Yeah? Will we get to share meals, make love? Will I get to sleep with your body pressed against mine?" He tried his hardest to keep his voice calm but didn't accomplish it. Fear seeped through and with it came anger.

"Yes, yes and yes," she said, smiling then she pressed her lips against his for a light kiss that ended to soon.

He wanted to believe her, wanted to believe going back wouldn't be the nightmare he envisioned, but he wasn't so sure.

****

Olivia awoke the next morning as she had for days, draped across Cain's chest, one leg over his. Her body pressed close, his scent surrounding her, his hand leisurely caressing her back.

That morning, she didn't want to wake. She wanted to lay with him in bed. She couldn't. He couldn't either. It was time to return to their lives—their separate lives: Olivia, the werewolf princess, sister of the beloved alpha; and Cain, second in command to the demon king.

But not for long, she vowed. As soon as she arrived and after Cain left, she'd tell her brother. Just thinking of her deceit, guilt rushed through her. Although she and Cain agreed they'd tell Landon together, she couldn't. Telling her brother was something she needed to do, alone. After all, Landon was overbearing and overprotective because of her. Because she'd needed him so long ago after their parents' deaths, because she feared she'd lose him too, she'd changed him. In her heart, she knew it was her fault, and she knew her brother better than anyone. She and she alone would be the one to tell him she'd found her male, a man who would love and protect her forever.

"Darling, are you…"

She turned her head to look him in the eyes, smiled then placed a light kiss on his lips, instantly overwhelmed with desire for him. Willpower allowed her to pull away.

"Don't worry. Everything will work out," she said, hoping to distract him from his previous question. "You can materialize us at ten tonight, four in the afternoon New York time, then we'll eat, head to bed and *not* sleep."

His eyes sparked red hinting at his thoughts. "What will we do all day then?" he asked, but he left no time for her to respond. The next instant, his full, soft lips were pressed against hers.

****

His soft lips met hers firmly. She parted hers, letting him in. She needed more than just a touch. He delved in quickly then pulled away. *Heaven ended too soon*, she thought just as he pressed her body against his and buried his face in the crook of her neck.

"Close your eyes, darling," Cain whispered in her ear, his cool breath making her shiver.

Wrapping her arms around him, she reluctantly closed her eyes, knowing she was leaving behind precious memories of the time they'd shared.

Everything she hadn't thought possible weeks ago, was. Her dream came true: he was hers and she, his. Nothing would separate them again. She savored their time alone and knew she was at the cusp of her new life with Cain, yet she couldn't help but feel sadness, sad to have to leave the memories behind.

When Cain pulled away from her slightly, she knew she was home. The cool, crisp air in Northern New York and the scent of the trees and nature lingered in the air. Slowly, her eyes drifted open.

"Home," he said, somberly.

The spark of life in his gorgeous blue eyes was gone. It had become too easy to read him by simply searching for that spark. There were worries he kept hidden from her, she knew. She asked last night, and he answered, but not completely. She supposed some things were better left unsaid. What was the use in telling her he was sad to have their time end when she felt the exact same way?

She nodded, unwilling to speak just yet. He placed his hand on the small of her back and together they walked toward the place she called home. Finally, she shifted her attention away from him and toward the large colonial-style mansion with a wraparound porch covered in ivy, equipped with two-story library, game room, several offices, sun room, music room, theater, conference room, wine cellar, and numerous bedrooms. Everything she needed and more. Strange that gazing toward her home inspired no feelings of comfort and security as it once had.

Once she reached the French doors, she hesitated. With her hand just over the handle, she turned to stare into Cain's eyes.

"I love you," she whispered, barely audible so the high tech security system at the estate wouldn't pick up her words.

He smiled then whispered, "And I love you, darling."

The door sprung open before she could open it. Jocelyn's smiling face greeted them. Wearing an empire knee-length dress, she rushed at them wrapping one arm around her and the other around Cain in a group hug, pulling them toward her.

"I'm so happy for you both," she whispered. "I've missed you so much," she said more loudly, then drew away.

Olivia placed her palm on Jocelyn's belly, where her niece and nephew currently resided.

"How are they?" Olivia asked.

"Craving chocolate and steak," Jocelyn replied, cheekily.

"How are you?" Cain asked Jocelyn.

"Oh, it's been so hard eating all the chocolate and steak," Jocelyn replied, sarcastically. "Don't worry," she whispered in a tone Olivia thought she was incapable of. "I'll run interference."

In spite of the dread creeping up her spine, nervous to see her brother again, Olivia smiled then glanced in Cain's direction. Tense and un-Cain like, he was smiling, but again the glimmer wasn't there. Without thought, in an effort to console him, she reached for him, grasping his hand in hers and squeezed. At the moment, she couldn't care less if Landon caught her. Screw her brother, her male needed her.

"Baby! Who's there?" Landon's booming voice resonated from inside.

Reluctantly, Olivia released Cain's hand and exhaled. Moments later, Landon appeared at the top of the staircase. His eyes registering her, his mouth hung open just before a smile tugged at his lips. He launched himself from the second-story and landed perfectly poised at the bottom, then rushed at her, wrapping his arms around her tightly. She reciprocated, wrapping her arms around his waist.

"Liv, God, I've missed you," he said then kissed her forehead before he pulled away, placing his palms on her cheeks to look into her eyes.

"I've missed you, too," she said, smiling. And she had. She hadn't realized it until she saw him—her brother, her protector.

"You look radiant, Liv…Really beautiful," he said.

"It's the tan." She shrugged.

"No, it's…" He paused, his eyes lingering over her lovingly. "Don't know, but something's different."

Landon's gaze was so soft, so comforting yet intense and different, as if seeing her with new eyes, seeing her as an adult for the very first time.

It's because I'm not a virgin, she thought and flushed. "It's just the tan," she repeated.

"No, it's not..." He pulled her toward him again. This time the hug was soft and less forceful. When he pulled away again, he said, "I didn't think it was possible for you to look more like Mom, but you do. And you look...happy."

It startled her when it shouldn't have that her brother recognized she truly was happy for the first time in her life. Not that she was unhappy before, just unfulfilled. Cain had done that for her.

Brows furrowing, he said, "You're happy, right?"

She nodded as tears threatened to spill.

"Gosh, Liv, what's wrong?" he asked then laughed and said, "Don't tell me you missed me that much."

She chuckled. "No, it's just...I don't want you to think...I wasn't happy...I'm just happier—"

"I'm happy if you're happy...I know a lot's been going on lately. You've been working a lot with the council, and it can be overwhelming. I did miss you though. Everyone did."

She nodded, thankful at least Landon wasn't hurt. She couldn't handle her brother believing he had been nothing but great to her when he'd done everything to ensure her happiness, security and comfort.

"I can't believe it. Why didn't you tell me you were coming? Where's your luggage?" he asked, hugging her again.

"Cain brought me and spared me a flight and he'll bring my luggage later."

Landon's gaze snapped to Cain. "Hey," he said in greeting, then shook Cain's hand. "Thanks for bringing her back."

"Not a problem," Cain responded.

"Well, come in," Jocelyn said. "Dinner will be ready soon."

They headed toward the high-vaulted ceiling living area on the first floor and took seats. Olivia and Cain on the love seat several feet apart and Jocelyn and Landon snuggled close opposite them.

"Liv, Cain, would you like something to drink?" Jocelyn asked.

"A glass of Chardonnay for me and Cain will have a whiskey," Olivia said without thought.

She realized her error after she'd spoken; she'd ordered for Cain. Flushing, she turned to glance in Cain's direction, who hid a smile. Luckily, Landon didn't seem to notice, or regard her mistake as anything out of the ordinary.

"Baby, I'll get the drinks," Landon insisted when Jocelyn moved to stand. "Do you want some apple juice, love?"

Jocelyn nodded then repositioned herself. Landon headed toward the small bar at the end of the living area and prepared the drinks.

"So, how did it go? What did you do? Did you rest?" Landon asked.

"It went well. I did the usual. You know shop, eat, sunbathe…" Olivia responded.

Landon handed Jocelyn apple juice first then handed Olivia wine and Cain whiskey. He sat beside Jocelyn again, and placed his hand on her belly.

"Has anything new happened around here?" she asked.

"Yes!" Jocelyn burst. "We received the furniture for the babies' room."

"Yeah," Landon added.

"I'm so sorry you missed that!" Jocelyn said sardonically. Her eyes glimmered with humor. "You should've seen Landon trying to put the cribs together." She giggled.

Olivia laughed, too. She was sorry she missed it. For everything her brother was, he wasn't handy. He'd never built anything in his life.

"I did a good job," he insisted.

Jocelyn rolled her eyes. "Baby, there's no need to lie. Liv knows you better than I do."

"What would possess you to build anything?" Olivia asked her brother.

"He wants to be a part of everything relating to the babies," Jocelyn responded for him. "Which is sweet but..." Her words fell away. "He spent four hours trying to build one crib then, finally, I recruited Ethan to help."

"Is that why he came up?" Landon asked.

"Yes, baby, that's why," Jocelyn admitted, patting his knee.

Landon frowned. "I could've done it."

"Sure," Olivia chided then laughed. She hated to admit she'd missed their loving quarrels.

"Of course, you could've," Jocelyn said. "But you know we want to be sure the babies will be safe while they're sleeping. Two minds are better than one..."

Landon's eyes flashed. "I wouldn't endanger my kids. I would've climbed in the crib myself before I let—"

"I know, baby. I know," Jocelyn said, then grazed her lips against Landon's. Debate seemingly forgotten, he wrapped his arms around her to deepen the kiss, then

Jocelyn tucked her face near his neck.

Olivia's stomach clenched at the sight. It was exactly what she had with Cain an hour ago. Already, she missed him. Cain hadn't spoken a word, maybe, missing her as much as she missed him.

She spared a glance in his direction. Immediately, he turned as well. Their eyes met and held for a moment speaking volumes they couldn't reveal.

"Liv." Landon's voice drew her away. "One of the wolves from our pack and his mate discovered another werewolf pack."

"What?" she asked, although she'd heard every word. Her brain scrambled at the knowledge. Another pack when they believed they were the last of their kind?

"I know. I'm meeting with their alpha soon."

"How many…Do they know of other packs? How could we not know? The last—"

He laughed. "Yeah, I know. It's unbelievable, huh?" He took a sip of his drink. "Their pack is two thirds the size of ours, two hundred, give or take. They've been reclusive for the last three hundred years…They didn't fight in the last vamp-wolf war. I'm not sure why exactly, but maybe their alpha will tell me more when we meet."

"I-I can't believe it."

"I was just as shocked when I got his call. Trust me, but I think this is good news, Liv. The alpha knows of Malums. They've had several murders in the last few months. When he phoned me, he wanted to meet in person to discuss an allegiance. I spoke to him briefly about the Guardians. He thought I was joking when I told him we'd allied with vamps and demons." Landon chuckled. "But I think once he meets the Guardians, he'll come around."

Quirking a brow, she asked, "You think?"

Growing serious, he said, "I *know*. Even centuries ago, werewolf packs were reclusive, stuck to their territory and didn't wander, but we've never been enemies. These are different times. The Texan alpha realizes that, too."

"Texan?"

"Yep, Texan, and he sounds like one too, not that it makes a difference."

"But their home is in Texas, why would an allegiance with a pack that far away help us or them?"

Cain tensed beside her. She glanced in his direction and realized his expression had grown grim.

Landon sighed heavily before he continued in a serious tone. "When the Malums strike, they will strike big—"

"They strike all the time. They're killing every day," she said, cutting him off.

"No, Liv," Cain spoke for the first time.

Her gaze snapped to him.

"When they're ready for the war, when they refuse to wait any longer, they'll attack in big way: bombs, explosives in all the major cities and military camps. They'll simultaneously wipe out millions, before anyone can fight back."

Olivia felt her face grow pale.

Cain's hand grasped hers, his warmth radiated through her as her eyes met his. She read the pain and torment of the truth everyone had held from her, clear in his face. There would be a fight, a big one, good versus evil. The few killings and attacks were the tip of the iceberg. When he squeezed her hand, suddenly the knowledge of the possible future didn't seem so disheartening. She'd fight alongside Cain, for immortals and for mankind.

Moments later, Cain released her hand. She wanted to reach for him again then remembered where she was.

"I want to hunt with the Guardians," she said immediately then braced.

"No!" Cain and Landon bellowed simultaneously.

She knew they'd disagree, knew they weren't going to make this easy on her, but she had to fight for what she thought was right, so she pointed out, "Both of you do, and I'm trained for battle."

The room grew thick with fury and tension. Her male and brother combined were a force to reckon with, but she couldn't let them stop her.

"Hell no!" Cain and Landon snapped as they stood, towering over her.

"Oh boy," Jocelyn muttered under her breath.

She wouldn't cower. She couldn't. It meant too much. It wasn't just about doing what was right for mankind and immortals alike, it was about her, too. She wanted to stand on her own for the first time in her life, to be something more than a sheltered princess.

She shrugged. Cain and Landon eyed each other, then hesitantly took their seats. Jocelyn rubbed her palm over her belly and took a deep breath.

"That's fine." She met each of their gazes then and said, "I'll just go out on my own then."

They spoke again simultaneously.

"You'll go with me," Cain said, resigned.

"You won't," Landon dared then shot a glare at Cain.

Olivia smiled. "Okay, Cain, I'll go with you then."

Jocelyn laughed loudly, muttering, "Well played, Liv."

"Liv," Landon warned.

"Landon," she said, her tone mocking his. "I trust Cain. He wouldn't let anything happen to me. I'm safe with him."

"But—" Landon began to argue.

Standing her ground, she said, "Either I go with Cain or I go alone. What will it be?"

Landon scowled. Nonetheless he relented, but she knew it was temporary.

"Dinner's ready," the maid, Cristal, announced.

"Oh, great," Jocelyn exclaimed. "I'm starved."

Chapter 24

Fearing the red tint in his eyes, Cain angled his face away from Landon, knowing the alpha's gaze was centered on him. He trailed Olivia instead, watched her as she stood, her thick brown hair swaying. Her tantalizing scent drifted toward him. Even as angry as he was with her, desire sparked. He held his breath because if he didn't, he might do something he'd regret like drag her away and lock her in his room at the compound where he knew she would be safe, always.

Aroused and enraged was a bad combo. His mind debated what he should do the second they were alone, delve into her or scream at her. All because he loved her so much, his body ached without her near. Hell, he hurt more every second she was in the same room and not in his arms.

Since the moment he'd materialized them to the estate and he'd pulled away from her, a dull ache claimed him. Then the stunt she pulled insisting she hunt Malums. What the hell was she thinking? He'd never been this livid, ever. Now, he had no choice but to keep his word.

Fuck it, he thought. If there's no Olivia, what was the point of honor? He'd break his word for the first time in his life. It'd sting, but the pain compared to the thought of Olivia in danger was nothing.

He continued to watch her patiently as she and

Jocelyn headed toward the dining room before he veered his attention to Landon, who continued to eye him suspiciously.

"You aren't taking her with you," Landon spoke.

"I'll do everything I can not to," he said, honestly. "If I can't—"

"Why in the hell did you agree?" Landon cut him off.

Not in the mood for the alpha's temperament, his eyes narrowed. It wasn't smart of him, considering the alpha was quick to temper, considering he didn't need to get on the alpha's bad side. At the moment, though, he couldn't help it.

He spent a magnificent week with his mate. Now, he was a foot away from her scent, her skin and her lips, and he couldn't touch her, comfort her, whisper sweet little nothings to her. His fear—that she'd leave him when she realized he wasn't worth her—tormented him more than ever. It hadn't been an hour, but he was sure he was in the seventh circle of hell. The worst kind of torture: the knowledge and beauty of living with something you once had, that you could no longer have. He wanted to scream, rage, and curse.

Gritting his teeth before he answered, hoping no anger resonated, although he was sure his eyes were ablaze, he said, "Did it look like I had another option?" He paused. "I know her. She threatened to go alone. You called her bluff, but she wasn't bluffing. She'll go. She's a fighter who's tired of sitting on the sidelines waiting just because she's a princess. *I* wasn't willing to take the chance. I'll do everything *I* can to convince her not to hunt. I'll even ask Jocelyn to play ill, but I *won't* let her hunt alone. She's better with me. I'm sure we both agree."

Landon remained silent for a while, seemingly absorbing Cain's point of view then lifting his chin, he asked, "What's it to you?"

The sound of his bitter laugh resounded. It was a little late to play catch up. "The same it's been to me, always," he retorted, then stood and strode away because he was tired of explanations, but mostly because being near Olivia, whether or not he felt her skin against his, was better than being without.

****

Although barely dusk, after the steak dinner Cain had barely eaten, he bid farewell. He wasn't in the mood to pretend he wasn't livid just as he hadn't been hours before.

As the dinner dragged on, his appetite diminished. His rage, on the other hand, hadn't. It stewed so by the end, it had been at the cusp, his demon begging for release. He'd barely controlled himself, only done so not for the sake of his honor or breed or his mate's brother, but for the sake of confronting her.

How could she? Why would she? Didn't she realize the danger? Didn't she realize she was no longer just herself—that she was a part of him, too? Didn't she realize if anything happened to her, his life, too, would end?

Rage festering, by the time he bid farewell he had barely spared a glance in Olivia's direction. He'd been too consumed with his anger to notice the somberness in her.

He dematerialized from the dining room only to appear in her room. Enraged, he waited for her to enter. It felt like eons when in fact only minutes passed.

Finally, she entered, somber and distraught. Her gaze scanned the room then landed on him, her face brightening immediately as she ran to him.

He didn't smile, didn't move.

Noticing, she hesitated inches from him. "You're mad?" she whispered, so softly he'd barely heard.

He cursed then, cursed her innocence, her beauty and her. Why didn't she know?

"I don't—"

"You *know*, Olivia," he snapped, letting his anger speak. "You know how much I love you. You know I don't want you in the line of fire. You know I'd strike a fucking copper knife through my heart before I'd let anything happen to you."

His body shook, shuddering uncontrollably. The change…began…The rage, he'd held back for too long. For months, he fought his need for her. He hadn't touched her, kissed her, or loved her. For a week, he hadn't marked her. He ignored his demon, his need to turn. Now it ended…She provoked him unconsciously, yet still there was nothing he could do.

His body morphed, tearing his shirt. His height stretched, towering over her at over seven and a half feet tall. His back broadened. His muscles expanded, his horns elongated, his fangs lengthened. All he could do was take a step away from her.

She didn't flinch or cower. Holding her ground, unafraid of him, or the demon that possessed him, she gazed at him with that innate innocence of hers, yet with a determined glint in her eyes. "You hunt. Why can't I—"

"Olivia," his voice was rough, fighting with himself to control his anger. "Are you trying to *kill* me?"

She shook her head. "You know I would never hurt you."

He growled. "Doesn't look like it!" The words laced in rage. "Do you know how worried I'll be? You'll be a distraction in the field. I won't be able to think of anything but protecting you. After five months of waiting for you, how much more do you want to torture me?" he asked, taking several steps toward her, closing the distance between them.

Her eyes went wide and round. "I…would never want to torture you. I…" She angled herself away from him. When she spoke again, her voice cracked. "You think it's been easy for me all these months? Worrying about you while you're hunting?" Then she faced him again.

That was when he caught sight of the tears streaking her face. His heart clenched; the rage that had conquered him moments before dissipated. His demon left him as quickly as he'd come, leaving guilt in his wake.

"You can leave me if you want, Cain, so you don't have to worry about me," her voice broke. "But I'm hunting."

Leave her? Was she out of her damned mind! Was that what she really wanted? For him to leave, so she'd be free to find a werewolf mate? As quickly as the thought came, his anger flowed once more.

He grabbed her elbow and pulled her toward him, his body shifting again. His demon unleashed. "My darling Olivia, I'll *never* leave you. Even after there is no breath in my body, I'll find a way to come back to you," he said. "Is the thought of me leaving titillating?

Would you prefer to be rid of your *unworthy, orphan, demon* male?"

Her eyes widened, welled with tears that fell, tainting her cheeks anew as deep hurt flashed across her face. That same hurt, the one he'd caused, sliced through him, her pain striking him.

It hurt. It hurt so much, like her heart had broken. He wasn't sure how she withstood it, how she managed to stand there with tears flowing down her too pale face. With a pain that deep, you expected blood.

He'd done it. He'd gone too far. Deep guilt washed over him mixing with the ache of her pain. His demon vanished, then he released her elbow, and drew away, wondering why he continued to hurt her, the precious gift he was fated.

The demon who once had so much control was out of his mind. Unable to control his rage, he turned demon twice in a matter of minutes, near his fated, and in the process put her in danger. He couldn't help it. His need to protect her, to keep her safe, overruled every action, every word, riling his demon.

"That's never mattered to me, and you know it," she said. "I've given you everything I have, my heart, my body and my soul—"

After what she said, nothing could have prevented him from pulling her body against his. Gripping the back of her neck, he crushed his lips against hers. If she'd planned to say anything more, she couldn't now as his tongue delved into her mouth, parting her lips. His anger still lingered, subdued with desire and every ounce of love he felt for her.

He freely explored her with his hands and materialized them in his room at the demon compound.

Without sparing a glance around, he tore her clothes off, needing to feel her skin against his. When she was bare, he pulled away to admire her. Her eyes dazed with passion.

Embracing her once again, his lips slammed hers with the full force of his craving. He guided her toward his bed where they lay and made passionate love.

Hours later, soothed by her flesh, his anger had melted away, and he gained enough composure to speak.

Lying on his side, facing her, he caressed the side of her face. "I'm sorry, darling. I hurt you, again."

"Next time, you should make love to me before you speak," she smirked. "It seems to cool your temper."

She'd forgiven him, that quick, that easy. She hadn't rubbed it in or held a grudge, instead she'd made light of his faults, a stark reminder that he didn't deserve her. And yet, he knew he'd never let her go because regardless she had been given to him and that meant he'd keep her.

****

Cain slept peacefully and soundlessly as he had for the past week. He woke content because Olivia lay in his arms. Her head rested on his shoulder, her arm slung over his stomach, one leg tangled with his. Drawing her closer, he smiled, then buried his face in the crook of her neck and inhaled her exquisite scent.

Then he begrudgingly spared a glance at his alarm clock, and realized it was six a.m. Past time he took her home, before her brother realized she wasn't in her bed.

Groaning inwardly, he kissed her cheek and whispered, "Darling, we have to get you home."

She mumbled incoherently and shifted, tugging him closer.

"Liv, it's morning. We have to get you home," he whispered, kissing her lips this time.

Her eyes snapped open. "What time?"

"Six," he responded.

Shaking her head, she mumbled drowsily, "One more hour."

He couldn't deny her. They would stay in bed, but they wouldn't sleep.

****

"Cain," Lucas called from his office.

Cain walked the short distance, standing in front of his king, surprised to find him alone.

"Congratulations are in order, I presume," Lucas said.

After retrieving their luggage from Santorini, Cain materialized in Olivia's bedroom at the estate, kissed her one last time, then materialized on his king's floor. He'd been gone a while, and needed to check in. He also needed some advice.

"Thanks," he replied. "We're holding off until we talk to her brother," he added, noticing Lucas's gaze lingering on his neck as if searching for Olivia's mark.

"Five months you've waited to tell her. When you finally do, you hold off marking her for more than a week?" His eyes wide then he smiled. "I'm impressed."

Cain knew Lucas enough to accept the praise for what it was. The demon king didn't often compliment, then again, he'd changed since he found his mate, Jenna. He was content, even happy.

Lucas had marked her within a short period. It had been accidental, so to speak, and Lucas had been wracked with guilt over it—not that he'd admitted it, but Cain sensed it. Still, why Lucas would be impressed was still beyond him. Lucas may have marked his mate, Jenna, within a short period of time, but he'd been burdened with dreams of her for centuries before he found her. The dreams had never given him the knowledge of where to find her, so the king lived with glimpses of a woman just out of his reach. Centuries of dreams compared to Cain's five months of waiting were nothing.

"There isn't much to be proud of. I've barely held myself together." Clenching his jaw to battle the anger that surfaced with just the thought, he continued, "I've nicked her several times, and I've lost my temper and lost control more than I'd like to admit. I don't even know how or why she's put up with me."

Quirking a brow, Lucas asked, "Losing control? You hurt her?"

He glared. "I would *never*—"

"You proved my point then."

"There's nothing to prove. I've been...*rough*," he admitted on an exhale.

"You deny your need to mark what fate destined as yours. The reason you lose your temper, and you'll be rough, even after you mark her."

He couldn't believe he heard Lucas correctly. He'd hoped after he marked her he'd have more control. Eyes widening he asked, "What?"

"Desire is an overwhelming emotion, but what we feel isn't just that. It's an instant connection, love, even if we can't understand why until much later. It's maddening, desperate and uncontrollable, and sometimes that leads to being a little rough," Lucas advised. "I *am* proud of you. I've carried guilt long enough because of the past. Finding Jenna has helped me. I think it's time you leave your past in the past."

Cain sensed where this conversation was headed. Right now, he couldn't hide his emotions any more than he could stop himself from loving Olivia, and he knew Lucas read him like a book. Hating the thought of being read so easily, he shoved his hands in his pockets in frustration.

Lucas opened a drawer in his desk and pulled out two velvet jewelry boxes, a small one and a larger one.

"I've always considered you part of my family, but I don't think you've ever truly considered me part of yours. I adopted you, brought you into my home. Had it been out of pity, as you assume, I wouldn't have given you my name." He sighed, then meeting his gaze dead on, he said, "Then again, it's not completely your fault. I haven't been the best at expressing myself. I should have made this clear years ago, I never told you, so in essence it's my fault." He paused then said, "I had you instated as prince."

Cain tensed, disbelief coursing through him. Prince? He was a prince?

"In my defense, I figured you assumed—"

"That I would take over if, God forbid, anything happened to you?" He paused, shoving his hand through his hair. "No, I didn't. I was too busy being thankful I had someone to teach me, someone to look up to."

"I adopted you. You are second in command—"

"Our rules state—"

"As king, I know what they state. In case the king is killed and there is no family left behind, our kind

221

votes for a successor, but I adopted you, and I know you. I raised you, trained you and most importantly, I *trust* you. I know the boy you were, and the man you've become. At twenty, you had more control during your first shift than a demon two centuries old and you have a good heart. I knew then if anything should happen to me, you should reign. On your fiftieth birthday, I went to the council and expressed my will. There was a vote, everyone agreed. You *are* a prince. You were promoted as second in command immediately as well," Lucas said then paused momentarily.

Cain didn't say anything because he didn't know what to say. He was overwhelmed, shocked and touched.

"As is customary, since I married and mated Jenna, if anything should happen to me, she would reign. When Jenna and I have children, our first will be the successor. His or her siblings will be princes and princesses. If Jenna and I should die before we have children, you would become king. The bottom line is you are a prince, not an orphan. With that in mind, I wanted you to have these," Lucas said, pushing the boxes toward him.

He hesitated, still reeling from Lucas's words, then he took the smaller box, and opened it to find a large blue diamond ring. Olivia's face flashed before his eyes, the diamond reminding him of her, the same blue color of her eyes. Imagining the look on her face if he ever gave it to her, his love for her rushed him.

"It was my mother's. My father loved indulging her." Lucas shrugged then chuckled. "What can I say? I'm not much better."

"Jenna should have this," he said, though he still

held the box firmly in his hand. He couldn't force himself to look his king and brother in the eye, in fear Lucas would see how much he would love to give Olivia the ring he whole-heartedly believed didn't belong to him.

"You know Jenna. She considers you a brother as do I. We both insist the family heirlooms should be divided. Jenna's engagement ring belonged to my mother. She loves it along with the black diamond necklace I gave her from my mother's collection. There's plenty more, but I figured there's time to surprise our mates with jewelry in the years to come. Anyway, I thought this was perfect for Olivia. It's a blue diamond, five carats." Lucas hesitated. "There are others if you want to pick a different one, and you can always buy another if you don't like any of them, but I figured becoming princess of demonkind, she deserved a couple of family heirlooms immediately."

He stood still, speechless for several moments then, finally dredged up enough strength to peel his gaze away from the diamond, close the box, place it on the desk, and grab the second. Opening it, he discovered a yellow diamond necklace, the same incandescent color that laced with the blue in Olivia's eyes every time he kissed, touched or caressed her.

"Lucas, I..." He coughed hoping to disguise the emotion welling inside him. "I can't—"

"You can, and you will. They belong to you and Olivia as much as they belong to me and Jenna." Lucas smirked mischievously. "Unless you want your queen to—"

He shook his head, chuckling with just the thought. His queen was stubborn and always got her way. Jenna would nag him relentlessly until he accepted the heirlooms. Besides, she was his queen, he couldn't say no to her. "Thank you, but I still—"

"Cain," Jenna called from behind him. "You're back!" She walked toward him and hugged him tightly then pulled away.

"We are."

Her gaze drifted to the box he still held in his hand. "I see Lucas gave you the jewelry. Do you like them?" she asked with a wide smile.

"Yes, but I still think these should belong to you, Jenna. I have no blood relation—"

"Blood means nothing, Cain. You have been more of a brother to Lucas than his own twin," she said evenly.

Months prior, they'd discovered Lucas's twin brother, David, was responsible for the deaths of their parents and younger sister in Treconomia centuries before, responsible for the rise of the Malums in the mortal plane, and responsible for abducting Jocelyn months before.

"They're beautiful, but—"

Her eyes glimmering roguishly, she said, "Why don't you spare me the trouble of nagging you until you agree, huh?"

He nodded, bowing slightly then said, "Thank you."

She smiled wide then asked, "How was the trip?"

He grinned. "Amazing. Liv is…" His words trailed off because there wasn't just one word to describe her.

"She's wonderful," Jenna finished for him. "She's sweet, kind and beautiful, but she doesn't know it." Pausing, she sighed then said, "She's insecure, too, but

I'm sure you'll help her with that, won't you?"

He chuckled. "Yeah, I've been trying."

"Don't worry about that too much," she said then walked toward Lucas, who immediately snaked an arm around her waist and pulled her toward him until she sat on his lap.

"Something is troubling you, Cain," Lucas stated.

"I needed some advice." He released a breath then continued, "Olivia wants to hunt with the Guardians. She mentioned it yesterday when we arrived at the estate. I don't want her hunting. Landon doesn't either. She gave us an ultimatum: she goes with us or she goes alone." Fisting his palm, fighting anger, he said, "So I caved, but I want her to change her mind. I was hoping you—" He stopped mid-sentence as the sound of Lucas's laughter rang out.

"Ah, well I'm sorry to be the one to tell you. There is no way I know of to change a woman's mind especially a stubborn one," Lucas replied, nodding in Jenna's direction.

Jenna chuckled. "A woman after my own heart."

Fuck. No advice? None at all? So he was supposed to sit back and do nothing while his mate risked her life night after night? Fear rising, he pointed out, "But what if—"

"Olivia is well-trained, better trained than Jenna," Lucas reminded him.

"Yeah, but Jenna can set someone on fire on a whim. Olivia can't," he countered.

"Olivia's a werewolf and has trained for close to a century. She can defend herself. You need to believe in her," Jenna pointed out.

"I do, but I'll be distracted trying to keep her

safe—"

"You'll be distracted either way. If you take her, you'll be worried about her. If you don't, you'll be worried she's out on her own," Lucas said.

Hating the thought, hating he had no choice, he released a breath.

"It never gets easier," Lucas warned. "You'll worry about her constantly just as she'll worry about you. It's a dangerous time. While you were away, the Malums blew up a night club."

Cain's eyes widened. "What?"

"Several vampire Guardians were inside, following a lead. The night before, four women were found in a nearby alley. When Jacob and Benjamin arrived one of the women was still alive but barely. Before she took her last breath, she said two words: the name of the nightclub and 'vampire.'"

"They left her alive?" He asked because it was so unusual, Malums didn't take prisoners. They killed.

"The three others were drained completely. Their limbs removed from their bodies, the usual Malum MO. The last one wasn't, so it's either they were interrupted or she was left alive to tell us about the nightclub, which was bombed the following night. Fifty mortals died."

Fifty mortals dead in one night? Further proof the war between good and evil was escalating. No doubt it would all come to a head soon. Ignoring the guilt that surfaced for being away, for not being able to save those lives, he asked, "Were any Guardians injured? Do we have any leads as to where David is?"

"Injured, yes but not killed. No leads yet. The Guardian leaders agree we need more man power.

Within the next month, the new demon trainees should be ready to hunt. The vampire king has three new recruits. The elf king has two. Landon mentioned the weretigers' leader will join us during the next Guardian meeting," Lucas advised.

"Landon mentioned someone from his pack discovered another pack in Texas. He's meeting with their alpha soon."

Nodding, Lucas said, "Good."

"Don't you think someone should reach out to Julian?" Cain asked, referring to the king of fairies.

Julian and his sister, Aleta, once queen of their kind, had been Guardians until it was discovered Aleta had allied with the Malums. She wanted Lucas for a mate and David had promised him to her. David's intention had been for Aleta to lure Lucas to him to finish the job he'd started centuries before, killing his family, so he could reign. Lucas couldn't be lured; he'd no interest in Aleta and had already found Jenna, his mate. Aleta then attempted to abduct Jocelyn, to use her as bait.

"I've gone back and forth on the issue," Lucas said. "His sister's death rests in our hands. Some people aren't forgiving, whether or not she fought for the wrong side. And, I'm not sure we can trust him. We have no idea if he's involved with the Malums. We trusted Aleta, and she turned out to be a spy. If he holds any ill will toward us because of his sister's death, he could use it against us."

"I thought Kellen reached out to him?" Cain asked.

"He did. Before Aleta's death though, and Julian hadn't been receptive to coming back. He didn't explain why."

"It's a damn shame. We need all the help we can get and their abilities would be useful."

"I agree," Lucas nodded. "You ready to hunt tonight?"

"Always," he said, taking the jewelry. "Thanks, again." He then turned to walk out the door.

"Don't forget to tell Olivia," Lucas warned. "She'll be upset if you don't. Hell hath no fury like a woman scorned and all that…"

She would be upset, and it was the last thing he needed.

Cain turned to face Lucas and Jenna again. "She would, but you'd be surprised. Over the last week, I've given her plenty reasons to throw me out on my ass. She's forgiving."

Smiling, Jenna said, "Because she loves you."

Yes, she did.

He knew it.

He felt it.

He loved it.

Chapter 25

Cain left her room hours before, but Olivia had little energy to do anything but mope.

Her room once had been a retreat with its soft colors and whimsical décor. Now, it did nothing to relax her. It wasn't just her room; it was the estate. It no longer felt like home. It felt like home in Santorini. It felt like home at the demon compound. She knew why.

Home was with Cain.

Wherever he was, she needed to be.

She belonged with him.

Sighing heavily, she strode toward the French doors leading to the balcony. Parting the doors, the scent of the woods enveloped her. The sun hung high in the east, but not even its rays seemed to soothe her.

A knock sounded on her door. She turned and headed toward it, saying, "Come in."

Jocelyn stepped through.

"Morning," Olivia greeted, smiling. "How do you feel?"

"Like a damn cow," Jocelyn muttered. With a heavy sigh, she plopped on the love seat near the walk-in closet.

Olivia sat next to her and placed her hand on Jocelyn's belly, rubbing it softly.

"The real question is how are *you*?" Jocelyn asked pointedly.

Looking away, Olivia whispered, "I miss him." She did, but it was more than that. She was sad, empty, and feeling a little lost. It was so absurd even to her. She'd just seen him. She'd spent a week with him alone. Would it always be like this? Would she feel that sadness every time they parted? Or was it just because they had yet to complete the mating?

"That's normal. Even before your brother and I were on good terms, I'd miss him. The moment he'd leave, I'd get an awful ache in my chest. It was devastating especially at the time. I didn't want to have anything to do with him because he'd waited so long to tell me," Jocelyn admitted.

"I remember. He was just as torn without you, you know."

"Yeah," Jocelyn said smiling wistfully. "When you tell your brother, you won't have to hide anymore."

"I know. I want to tell him, but Cain thinks we should tell him together. Landon isn't going to take it well. There's no telling what he'll do, and Cain hates it when Landon loses his temper. What if they get in a fight and—"

"Don't think about all the things that could go wrong," Jocelyn said. She then shrugged and added, "Besides, if I'm there, I'll just use my power over the wind to pull them apart. Easy-peasy."

She wasn't so sure. "I hope."

"Why don't you go…" Jocelyn's voice dying away as her gaze darted toward the balcony.

Olivia's gaze followed. There Cain stood, as handsome as ever, wearing a collared blue shirt that fit perfectly against the expanse of his chest and a pair of jeans.

Her heart leaping, she rushed toward him and wrapped her arms around him tightly. She felt his deep chuckle as he, too, wrapped his arms around her, bending to place a light kiss on her neck.

There he stayed and whispered, "I missed you too, darling."

"You have no idea," she said, pulling away to meet his eyes.

Cupping the back of her neck, he crushed his mouth against hers, silencing her. The kiss firm but light and short and exactly what she needed.

"I guess I'll leave you two alone." Jocelyn interrupted.

Cain pulled away from her lips. His gaze moved behind her. "Oh, hey, Joce," he said, seemingly noticing her for the first time. "I didn't even see you there."

"Well, of course you didn't. Liv's here. If I hadn't spoken I probably would've caught a great peep show, huh?" Jocelyn smirked.

Olivia flushed bright red. She knew he felt her discomfort because the next moment his arms tightened around her.

"How are you feeling today?" he asked Jocelyn.

"Like a damn whale," Jocelyn shot back, then turned to head out the door. Before she reached it, she turned toward them again. "I almost forgot. Liv, Landon wanted me to remind you. The Texan alpha is going to be here tonight. He wants you to meet him. He should be here around eight."

"Okay, thanks."

"You two have fun," Jocelyn said, then winked.

****

231

With a towel firmly wrapped around her torso, Olivia sat in front of her vanity, and applied her make-up. She spent the day with Cain in bed and regretted having to leave him, but he needed to hunt for Malums, and, although she wanted to be with him, she couldn't. As princess and part of the council, it was her duty to welcome the Texan alpha into their home. If only the alpha had come another day, or she'd told her brother the truth or...

Tomorrow, she pledged. Tomorrow, she'd tell her brother about Cain.

She couldn't stand being away from him, leaving him got harder each time. Lying to her brother and hiding her relationship took its toll on her. Another reason: she'd almost marked Cain again that afternoon.

His skin had been slick with sweat when he'd filled her. She'd been overwhelmed with desire, and her canines elongated. At the moment, she'd wanted nothing more than to rip into his neck with her teeth, marking him as hers. If he hadn't pulled away when he did, she would have.

She couldn't ignore his need to mark her either. His control slipped by the minute. Today, he'd bitten into a pillow instead of her. The look of torment on his face had nearly been her undoing. He'd been so patient with her, waited to tell her she was his when he thought she wasn't ready, and even now he waited. He hadn't once mentioned telling her brother. He was still waiting, and she was making him.

She planned to tell her brother last night after Cain left, but things hadn't gone as planned. After their romantic interlude and watching the anguish in his expression, she intended to come straight home and tell her brother, but then she remembered the alpha's visit.

It would have to wait.

Tomorrow, she promised.

Olivia quickly finished applying her make-up and browsed through her clothes, wondering what she should wear. She wanted to make a good impression on the alpha, but she was more concerned about wearing something Cain would admire when he came to see her later that evening. Finally, she decided on a blue empire-waist dress with fitted top and pleated skirt. She added simple earrings and a couple of bracelets before a knock sounded on her door. She opened it.

"Hey, Liv. You look beautiful," Landon said, reaching to quickly hug her. "When did you get in?"

"A little while ago," she replied.

"How was training today?"

Figuring Jocelyn must have told a white lie, she lied, too. "It went well."

"Drake's here already. Joce is downstairs entertaining him."

"Drake?" she wondered.

"The alpha from Texas."

Oh, right. She'd gone a day calling him the Texan alpha. She never thought to ask his name.

She and Landon took the elevator to the first floor and headed into the large living room. The moment she entered, piercing gray eyes locked on her. The smoky eyes belonged to a tall, broad-shouldered man with disheveled black hair. Drake, although handsome, was the complete opposite of her male, who had blond locks and crystal clear blue eyes.

"Miss Olivia," he said, his voice laced with a Texan drawl. He closed the distance between them and extended his hand.

She clasped his hand and shook.

As his eyes continued to bore into her, he said, "You are as stunning as Landon said you would be."

Shocked at the compliment, she quickly withdrew her hand from his and spared a glance at her brother who beamed with pride. She wasn't sure what shocked her more: the compliment from this man or her brother's reaction. Her gaze met Jocelyn's who appeared as uncomfortable as she felt.

Damn. She'd walked into the lion's den. The meeting was more than met the eye, and much more than what she'd been told. Her overbearing brother was trying to set her up with the Texan alpha. She shouldn't be surprised. It was just like Landon to think he knew what she needed in a male. Worst, she hadn't had a clue. Naïve Olivia played the idiot, again. What else was new?

More distressing than feeling like an idiot and how angry it made her, was the guilt. She knew she shouldn't feel guilty for her brother's doing, and still the emotion overwhelmed her.

Was she expected to sit at a dinner table with this stranger as if they were on a supervised date while her male risked his life fighting Malums? Was she supposed to pretend her heart wasn't taken?

Hell, no. She wouldn't and couldn't. She belonged to Cain and loved him.

Pull it together, she scolded. *You won't be left alone with him. He won't dare make a move in front of my brother and sister-in-law.*

Finally, she turned her attention toward the alpha again.

His smoky intense eyes hadn't left her. "I'm Drake Callaghan," he introduced himself.

Despite her discomposure, her manners kicked in. She plastered on a fake smile, and said, "Nice to meet you."

As if he'd sensed her discomfort, he turned his attention toward Landon. "Landon." He shook his hand firmly. "It's a pleasure to meet all of you. You have a lovely home."

"Thank you. Please, let's have a seat," Landon said, motioning toward the sofas.

Olivia waited until Drake took a seat, then positioned herself as far away from him as possible.

Cristal stepped into the room, and headed toward the small bar. "Mr. Callaghan, would you like a drink?"

"Miss…"

"You may call me Cristal, sir."

"Miss Cristal, I'll have a whiskey neat, please," Drake said, flashing a million-dollar smile.

Her heart clenched in her chest. Whiskey reminded her of Cain, her Cain, her male—the only man she'd ever loved.

Cristal prepared Drake's drink, then proceeded to prepare drinks for each of them. After serving them, she left. Olivia immediately took a big gulp of her apple martini hoping to steady her nerves.

"Did you travel alone?" Jocelyn asked.

"No, I was accompanied by my sister and her male," Drake informed.

"You should've brought them along," Jocelyn said. "They would've been welcome."

But then it would have ruined my brother's plans, Olivia thought with disgust.

"She's my youngest sister and still very young, less than two centuries old. She's never been to New York, and hoped to go to some of the tourists sites."

Olivia bit her tongue to stop the nasty retort that sprang to mind. If he thought two centuries was young what would he think of her age? What would he think of Jocelyn's age, barely twenty-two?

"Or at least that's what she told me. I suspect it has nothing to do with the city itself. She just recently met her male," Drake continued.

"Well, that explains it." Landon chuckled, rubbing Jocelyn's stomach. "Jocelyn and I met less than a year ago."

"And you're expecting. Congratulations." Drake's gaze shifted slightly toward Jocelyn. "Mrs. Waden, you are part of the new breed?"

"Please, call me Jocelyn. I am, so are my sisters."

His brows drew up. "Sisters?"

"Yes, I have four. We were separated after our mother's death. I was just recently reunited with two of them."

"Interesting…and the other two?"

"We're looking for them," Landon replied for her.

"Pardon my questions, but I'm intrigued…" Drake paused. "What abilities do you possess?"

"My sisters and I have the ability to control the four classical elements: earth, fire, water and wind."

"Impressive," Drake said then turned his attention to Landon. "I must admit times have changed since the last vampire-wolf war. I was under the impression my pack was the only one in existence that allowed their wolves to mate outside our breed. It's why I assumed you were joking when you mentioned you'd allied with vampires and demons."

Landon tensed, squaring his shoulders. His eyes sparked, the blue infused in yellow. "We recently changed our laws," he said simply.

Jocelyn placed her hand over his, and his eyes returned to their blue color, calming his temper.

"No offense," Drake said. "As you know, we didn't participate in the last vampire-wolf war. A choice I made and I've never regretted it," Drake paused. "About thirty wolves in our pack found their females or males from other breeds including vampires. The first vampire-wolf war left us nearly extinct. I couldn't, and wouldn't take the chance, causing a rift within my pack. Any fated female or male of any members of my pack, I consider *part* of my pack."

How admirable of you, Olivia thought sarcastically. Just as the thought came, his gaze darted toward her as if he'd heard.

"I can understand," Landon said evenly. "Yearly, several pack members would disappear, it hadn't occurred to me why a wolf would abandon his pack until I found my female. When we told them, some were shocked, even resistant, but it's worked out for the best. Several deserters have rejoined."

"That's good to hear," Drake said, taking another sip of his drink. "I was also surprised to find out there was another pack still in existence. I've bumped into others of our kind, but all of them were loners. None belonged to a pack."

"I was under the same impression," Landon said.

"As you know, my pack has suffered attacks from Malums, not to mention the numerous grisly deaths of mortals in our area. From what you've explained to me, our goals are the same, but I'm still hesitant. I'd like to meet the Guardians first, then I'll decide whether to join the league or not."

"I'll arrange a meeting," Landon said. "How long will you be in town?"

"I leave tomorrow night."

Landon turned his attention toward Olivia. "Liv, who's hunting tonight?"

She tensed at the sound of her name, then cleared her throat. "Benjamin, Lucas, Jenna, two new recruits and Cain," her voice hitched at the mention of her male. "Ashley, Jacob, and Clyde stayed in tonight."

"They'll hunt till dawn. I'll try to set something up for late afternoon or early evening. How does that sound?"

"That's fine. I can always postpone my flight," Drake said.

Cristal entered the living room, and advised dinner was served. Olivia stood, immediately feeling Drake's eyes follow her out the room. Instead of heading into the dining room, she detoured to the bathroom. Inside, she took several deep cleansing breaths. A light knock sounded on the door. It parted slowly, and Jocelyn came through.

"Liv, I'm so sorry. I tried to talk him out of it. I warned him you'd be upset," Jocelyn whispered, placing her hand on her shoulder.

"It's not your fault. I should have told him already. I got myself into this mess."

"It's not a mess. It's beautiful. You found your mate."

Olivia rolled her eyes. She whole-heartedly appreciated her sister-in-law's attempts to comfort her, but finding Cain wasn't the problem, telling her brother was.

"This is bound to get more complicated before it gets better. I had plans to tell him today then I remembered this dinner, so I decided to tell him tomorrow, but now I can't because of the meeting between the alpha and the Guardians."

"You can still tell him tomorrow, the meeting isn't until late afternoon."

"Yeah, right," she said, sarcasm biting her tone. "Landon will flip his lid when he finds out. It could affect our alliance not only with the Texan alpha, but with the Guardians as well." She shook her head in defeat.

"I know it seems like a big deal now, but when it's over, you'll feel a lot better," Jocelyn said. "And don't worry about Drake. He's harmless."

"Harmless? He doesn't look harmless to me. He's tall, dark, and handsome."

Jocelyn cocked an eyebrow.

"Not my type, but he's an alpha like my brother, used to getting his way. Nothing is harmless about either of them," Olivia added.

"Liv, if he tries anything, I'll kick him to the curb myself. I promise."

"I feel…" Her words trailed off refusing to admit her ridiculous emotions.

"Guilty," Jocelyn finished for her. "I was afraid of that, but you shouldn't. This is business not pleasure, regardless of Landon's intentions. Drake may be an alpha. He may be domineering and overbearing like your brother, but I think that's a good thing. I don't see a man like that pushing a woman who doesn't want him. They've got too much pride. Unless, of course, you're his, which you aren't."

Or he'll be more persistent because he's used to getting what he wants, Olivia thought. Instead of saying it aloud, she nodded and together they headed toward the dining room.

The large table was set for four. Landon was already seated at the head of the table. As usual, Jocelyn sat to his right and Olivia sat to his left. Drake sat beside her.

The first course was served. They ate. While the others talked, Olivia remained quiet, unable and unwilling to participate, despite Landon's attempts to involve her in the conversation. She partly listened, her mind wandering to Cain.

"My sister's mate, Lucas, is the leader of the Guardian Demons. He's their king. Actually, he founded the Guardians," Jocelyn said.

"A demon, really?" Drake asked.

"Yes," Olivia said firmly before she realized she'd spoken. All gazes darted to her. "Contrary to popular belief, the demon king is noble, as are his warriors. I train with them regularly."

"I believe you," Drake replied, his gray eyes locked on her, unnerving her. "I doubt Landon would trust many with his sibling."

"He wouldn't," Jocelyn added. "And he doesn't. Lucas and his warriors are the very opposite of their reviled reputations. My sister is stubborn," she chuckled. "Stubborn enough to drive a noble man to violence. He's patient, kind, and loving with her. Every time he turns, he's in control."

"His twin is the leader of the Malums," Landon

advised. "Lucas's father was responsible for teaching their kind to learn to control their demons. His brother wasn't keen on the idea. He wanted demons' natures to remain 'uncontrollable,' and reviled. In an effort to take over, he had their family assassinated in the demonic plane centuries ago. Lucas survived…" He paused. "By accident," Landon added. "He wasn't where he should have been."

"I must admit, I've never dealt with demons before. In the past, they've been as reclusive as weres."

"They prefer to remain in their plane. Excluding Lucas and his men, I've only encountered a couple in five hundred years. My female and her sisters are as thick as thieves, so our destinies are intertwined," Landon said, chuckling.

"I've only encountered a couple of demons myself," Drake agreed.

"Isn't anyone in your pack mated to a demon?" Olivia asked, unwilling to spare a glance in his direction.

Drake shook his head then smirked. "No, but you never know what the future holds. I've always been curious of the breed. The ones I've come across run for the hills the moment they realize I'm immortal."

"I wonder why…" Olivia pondered aloud.

Drake replied, "Perhaps I'll ask the king when we're acquainted."

After dessert, Jocelyn yawned. Landon noticed.

"Pardon me, Drake, I must drag my female to bed—"

"Landon," Jocelyn exclaimed. "I'm not tired."

Landon cupped her cheek. "You need your rest, baby. It's later than you think," he said, then helped her to her feet. "Drake, Olivia can show you around until I return?"

"It's not a problem. I'm tired myself. I should get going—"

"I insist. Olivia would enjoy showing off her garden." Landon's gaze landing on her before he said, "Wouldn't you, Liv? You love showing off your roses."

Great! Alone with the big, bad Texan wolf, she thought. She bit her tongue and swallowed her retort as Landon led Jocelyn out of the room refusing to acknowledge her protests.

The minute they were gone, Olivia felt the heat of Drake's eyes on her. She was on her own, so she took a deep breath and walked past him. He followed as she led him out the room toward the living room and out the French doors leading onto the terrace. The cool air hit her skin but did little to cleanse her bleak thoughts.

Guilt had lodged itself in her heart the moment she'd set eyes on Drake, fully aware of her brother's attempts to find her a male. Here she was entertaining an immortal her brother thought suitable for her while the only male she'd ever needed, the only man she'd ever loved risked his life. Was he hurt? Was he aching for her as she ached for him?

She couldn't blame anyone but herself, in her very own self-created dilemma. Her male had burdened himself, waited for her for months because she needed time, and how had she repaid him? At that very moment, her male risked his life. He could be injured and suffering and she wasn't any wiser, because she hadn't told her brother.

"You're in love, aren't you?" Drake asked.

Immediately, she turned toward him unable to hide

her shock, and wondered how it was possible a man she'd met moments ago could be so attuned to her feelings.

His gaze roamed her face, seemingly searching for an answer then he said, "There's no need to be shy."

"How did you—"

"I have six sisters. In six centuries, I've honed my abilities to guess their feelings…it's quite a gift," he mused.

"Yes, I am," she admitted hesitantly. "He's my male."

"Has he recognized you as his?"

She nodded. "Yes, he has," she added for reinforcement and spared a glance at his gray stare.

"I know it's none of my business, but I'm curious. Why hasn't he marked you?"

Releasing a breath, she admitted, "It's complicated. He's not a werewolf. My brother is not going to take it well, and—"

"It's simple. You're his fated. You love him. If he's told you, I'm assuming he loves you," he countered. "You haven't glanced in my direction more than a couple of times, and you've been deathly pale and nervous since the moment we were introduced, knowing your brother's intentions for us. Just the thought of having another male for dinner stirs you to guilt."

All true. Nothing she could deny.

"How long has he known?" he continued to prod.

"Almost half a year," she admitted without reluctance. Surprisingly, it felt comforting to admit to someone, even if it was the Texan alpha, how she felt.

Drake laughed. Seemingly he thought she'd joked.

When garnering no such response from her, he stilled, then his eyes widened.

"You're serious?"

She nodded.

"What is he a saint? I've never heard of an immortal resisting their fated for so long. The ones I have had the pleasure of meeting marked their females within the week. How has he resisted?"

She smiled, gazing at the stars, soothed by the thought they were the same stars her male could admire as well. "He loves me more than you can imagine, of that I'm sure," she whispered. "He's..." She drew her hand toward her chest as image of Cain appeared in her mind. "He's everything...everything a man should be."

"I suggest you let him mark you and soon."

"He knew I was his five months ago. As my brother mentioned before, our pack is reclusive and has been until recently. My brother is extremely over-protective. I'd never met an immortal from another breed until five months ago. My male thought I needed time to adjust, so he waited to tell me."

"And he waited five months...waiting for the right time?"

"Yes..." She laughed despite herself. "But during that time, we became friends. I fell for him, then ran away. He came after me then finally told me I was his." Tears rimmed her eyes, threatening to fall.

"Because I have sisters doesn't make it any easier to see a woman cry. Believe it or not, it distresses me," he said, then pulled a handkerchief from his pocket, and handed it to her.

She laughed, her tears spilled over then she quickly wiped them away with his handkerchief.

He smiled. "Tell your brother. Soon."

"I arrived yesterday. Today—"

"I see. My arrival ruined your plans. I'll fix this for you."

Her gaze shot to his, jaw dropping. "No, I can't—"

"I've been an alpha for centuries, Olivia," he said simply. "It won't make much of a difference if I meet the Guardians tomorrow or next week."

"Why?" She wanted to know why a man she barely knew would take interest in her personal life.

"You're a beautiful woman, Olivia. Unfortunately, you're not mine, but you belong to someone. I know the burden of living centuries without a fated. Let's not make the poor bastard suffer anymore, huh?"

She barely restrained from launching herself and hugging him. Smiling softly, she said, "Thank you, Drake."

Chapter 26

As soon as Cain materialized in Olivia's room, her lingering scent engulfed him, soothing his state of mind. It had only been a few hours since he'd last seen her, and yet it seemed like days.

Honestly, at times, he felt like he was losing his mind. How was his desire for her growing more and more pressing every passing day? The moment he met her, he thought no one could desire another more than he desired her. Every day he was proven wrong because every day what he felt grew.

Sighing heavily, he ran his fingers through his hair, pushing the thoughts aside.

It was early still, half past one a.m. He had hunted for close to five hours. Although he'd been out for a little over a week, it hadn't showed. He captured two Malums stalking a mortal woman. Along with the two new recruits, Nathan and Hades, Cain questioned the Malums to no avail. He then ended them.

At that point, Lucas insisted he leave early. He wasn't sure if he really wasn't needed as much since they had new recruits, or if Lucas sensed he missed his mate. The thought should have angered him. He was a warrior, second in command to the king of the most reviled immortal breed, and prideful. He wasn't fond of being looked after at his age, or having a weakness. His pride be damned, but he had no qualms of admitting

Olivia was his. In the end, he was glad Lucas dismissed him because his mind had been unraveling with thoughts of her.

Glancing around Olivia's room, he realized it was bare. Disappointed, he expected her to be waiting for him. That disappointment faded fast when worry took over. If she wasn't in her room, where would she be at that time a night?

Striding toward the French doors leading to her balcony, he peeked through the shades. Outside in the terrace, he spotted her. His stomach clenched at the sight of her flawless appearance, wearing a royal blue dress, her hair loose around her bare shoulders in waves, as the full moon illuminated her skin. She smiled at...

He spotted the man, a stranger, whose features were the complete opposite of his own. Where he was fair, this man was dark, and the differences didn't end there. The male was a werewolf.

His heart tightened painfully before it dropped to the pit of his stomach. Dread spiking, a deep ache clutched him, burning the center of his chest then radiated until all he felt was pain.

He couldn't help but think the worst; his worst fear was becoming reality. Fisting his palms, rage coursing through him, he decided he wouldn't let it happen. He wouldn't let her go because he *couldn't* lose her, couldn't live without her. He'd force her if he had to, but he would drag her away with him, take her to demon plane where she'd be his eternally.

Determined and prepared to do what he had to even against her will, he materialized outside, feet from them, growling.

Olivia's gaze caught his. She smiled, and took several steps toward him.

The werewolf tensed, grasped her shoulder and held her back. "Miss Olivia, don't," the werewolf said firmly, eyes sparking.

Another growl escaped him as anger so powerful, so intense rushed him. It felt like nothing he'd ever experienced. As his mind ran wild with all the ways to torture and kill the werewolf who dared put his hands on his mate assailed him, he vaguely heard the sound of his shirt tearing. His demon taking over.

Olivia pulled away from the werewolf's grasp then said, "Drake, he's my male."

The werewolf's gaze left his, and darted to Olivia. When the stare returned to him, it was no longer incandescent yellow but cloudy gray again.

"He's a demon?" the werewolf asked.

Olivia nodded, then took a step in Cain's direction.

Instantly, the were reacted. Without touching her, he put an arm in front of her and said, "He's in demon form, Miss Olivia."

Olivia's gaze trailed away from Cain's and met the werewolf's then assuredly she said, "He won't hurt me." Not a moment later, she closed the distance between them, and wrapped her arms around his waist.

Then Cain released a deep cleansing breath, the warmth of her body against his, soothing him, so much so the anger that had taken over only moments before vanished. Relief swarmed him with the knowledge he hadn't had to force her. She'd come willingly.

He wrapped his arms around her, crushing her to him, then he buried his face in her neck, and inhaled. As the unique pine scent of her spread through him, a smile spread across his lips.

"Thank God you're safe. I was worried," she said, pulling away slightly to look into his eyes.

Overwhelmed with his emotions, he couldn't speak.

"This is Drake Callaghan," she said. "He's the Texan alpha."

Drake extended his hand. "My apologies," the male drawled. "Miss Olivia said wonderful things about you."

One look at the werewolf, and his temper re-sparked. He shook his hand then barked, "Don't touch her, again. *Ever*."

"Cain!" Olivia admonished, pushing at his chest.

Unwilling to let her go, he tightened his arm around her. He caught sight of her face flushing just as he sensed her embarrassment.

The male wasn't fazed. He chuckled, which only further infuriated Cain. The anger didn't abate until he heard the alpha say, "Again, I apologize. Miss Olivia mentioned she was spoken for, although she left out her male was a demon. I was only doing what any man would do for a woman, if he believed her in danger."

Cain read the sincerity in his comment. It pleased him, so he allowed himself to relax, only slightly. "Yes, of course." Though he didn't want to apologize, he knew he should. The war against the Malums was escalating and the Guardians needed as many on their side as possible. The alpha and his pack would help. "I should apologize as well."

Smirking, the alpha said, "No need. I've met many mated immortals from various breeds. You've acted as expected."

"Cain Thaler, Prince of Demonkind," Cain said confidentially. He felt her gaze on him, then she shifted her weight, nervously.

Drake glanced in Olivia's direction then snapped his gaze to him again. "A prince and a princess...A match made in heaven. You're part of the Guardians. Jocelyn and Olivia spoke very fondly of the king, your brother, I presume."

He nodded.

"Landon said he would arrange a meeting for me to meet the Guardians. He'd wanted to arrange it for tomorrow, but I'll have to reschedule. Perhaps, next week."

"I'll discuss it with Lucas and the others," he assured.

"It's been a pleasure to meet you both. I'll leave you. Landon should join me shortly."

Cain watched Drake walk away from them and inside the home. When his eyes shifted toward his mate, he noticed the tense expression on her face.

His arm resting on her hip wandered up her back until it met her neck and laced with her hair. "Darling?"

She took a step back, still close enough he didn't have to release her, then her gaze fell away from his. When they met again, she said, "You thought I was interested in him? Is that why you were so—"

"Yes," he admitted. "It's almost two. I materialized in your room, but you weren't there. I found you with him. I thought—"

"You knew we were meeting with the alpha today."

The way she said it, like he had no reason to be upset, riled him. In so little control of his moods, it was enough to make him snap. "I knew Landon, Jocelyn and you were having dinner with him at eight. I didn't realize you'd be wandering around in the dark at two in the morning with a male."

His temper rose with each word, the sadness streaming from her made him instantly regret what he'd said and the way he said it.

"You don't trust me?"

Releasing her hair, he gripped her arms and brought her closer, close enough her body pressed against his then he said, "Olivia, I don't think *you* understand. I love you so much it hurts. I've never been afraid of anything in my life—not even death, but I'm terrified of losing you."

"I feel the same way, Cain. This is just part of my job."

"Meeting with alphas in the middle of the night?" he retorted, harshly, the jealousy churning through him leaving him with little control.

She took a deep breath. "Let's not fight about something that may change either way," she said, turning away from him.

He grabbed her elbow and spun her around. An inch from her face, he demanded, "Olivia Waden, what the fuck is that supposed to mean?"

Her sorrow-filled eyes searched his. "It means once I...we, tell my brother, he may not want me around anyway."

Shit. That was what she meant? When she'd mentioned things would change, he'd assumed she meant between him and her. Disgusted with himself, he pulled away from her then released a breath. His control slipped daily, and his precious mate had once again suffered for it. He snapped. He yelled. He cursed *at her*. He manhandled her. He knew this, had known it for a while and there was nothing he could do. The guilt of it was eating him alive. How much more would she take before she realized he didn't deserve her?

Voice bleak, he said, "It's horrible falling for a bastard like me, isn't it? I guess it's worse knowing he's your male."

Her eyes widened then she said, "You aren't a bastard, but apparently, you *are* a prince."

The simple comment sparked more guilt. He'd never thought to tell her. He didn't think it mattered because he was still the same man he'd always been. More importantly, he didn't want it to matter to her.

"Lucas told me today. He said he assumed I knew. He had me instated as prince more than three hundred and fifty years ago. I had no idea."

Meeting his eyes, she smiled softly. "I'm proud of you, Cain."

Proud of him? And he kept hurting her. She was killing him. "I'm sorry to keep hurting you, darling." His voice filled with remorse. "I'm sorry for being so jealous…I just—"

She closed the distance between them and wrapped her arms around his waist. "Don't apologize to me for caring, ever."

He couldn't believe it. Even after what he did, she wasn't mad. She should be. She should throw him out on his ass like he deserved. How much more would she take though? How many more chances would he get?

"I admire you. You fight for what you want. I should be the one apologizing. I've been a coward," she admitted.

He had no idea what she referred to, so he was about to ask. He never got the chance because the next moment she pulled him toward her and crushed her mouth against his.

The kiss, sensual, overpowering, and demanding, making him realize he'd missed her much more than he thought.

And the explanation he wanted to ask for died on his lips, forgotten.

****

Cain's scent lingered. She only needed to close her eyes and picture his face and it felt as if he was still there. He wasn't. If he were, his body could have been pressed against hers.

Dreams were dangerous, she knew from experience. She spent months dreaming of him, imagining he was hers and it had gotten her nowhere. Dreaming he was with her would only make her postpone the inevitable—telling her brother.

Today was the day. Her chance to fight for Cain like he fought for her.

Drake was headed to Texas. With no lingering meeting, it was the perfect time to tell her brother. All she needed to do was stop being a coward and confront Landon, admitting once and for all Cain was hers.

Olivia took a hot shower and dressed, then headed down the hall to her brother's office. She knocked.

"Come in," Landon said.

She opened the door, and found him seated at his desk. The moment he spotted her, he smiled widely.

"Liv, come in," he said when she hesitated. "What did you think of Drake?"

"The more on our side the better," she said, taking

a seat.

"I meant what did you think of him as…a man."

Her cheeks flushed. Instead of answering, she said, "That's what I wanted to talk to you about."

"I don't need details, Liv," he warned. "I prefer not to talk to you about this stuff in general, but—"

"I'm not Drake's female, Landon," she interrupted.

"Oh." He sounded disappointed. "Well, maybe someone from his pack—"

"I found my male," she blurted.

He straightened. His eyes narrowed as the muscles in his jaw clenched. "What? I thought you said Drake wasn't—"

"It's not Drake." She paused, squared her shoulders and admitted, "It's Cain."

"What?" He bellowed so loud she thought he'd shattered her ear drums.

Jocelyn raced into the office. Olivia felt the heat of her eyes on her, but didn't bother to turn her way. She was too busy watching Landon as he stood, and walked around the desk. Eyes glowing with anger, he stopped inches from her, towering over her.

She stood to face him, and repeated, "Cain is my male. I love him and he loves me and we're mating and getting married."

"Over my dead body!" he roared. "You're a princess! The sister of an alpha! He's a demon and a warrior! You need a man who will take care of you, not leave you every night to fight Malums!"

"He's a prince, brother of the king," she pointed out.

His face fully flushed with anger, he corrected, "Adopted brother. And he's not a werewolf, Olivia."

"So the new rules apply to everyone but me?" Her voice rose with each word despite her attempts to shield her fury.

"That's different!"

"Landon, calm down," Jocelyn cut in. "You're not resolving anything by screaming."

"Please explain how it's different. I'm all ears," Olivia asked.

"You *are* the princess of this pack. You *cannot* leave your home. This is your home, and *he* is no longer welcome here."

What? That didn't make any sense. What if Drake had been her male? Did that mean he, as alpha of his pack in Texas, was expected to drop it all to move in with her? "If Joce didn't live here, would this be your home?"

"What are you insinuating?" he demanded.

"My home is with him," she replied, evenly.

He shot back, "You won't survive a day living in the city. You wouldn't survive a day living on another plane! Where will you shift and run? You plan to shift in front of all those demons? So they can all stare at you?"

"Cain would never allow anyone to stare at me just as you'd never allow anyone to stare at Jocelyn, and we haven't decided where we'll live yet."

"You didn't think it was important to discuss it?" Landon screamed again.

He had a point, a good point. She and Cain hadn't thought to discuss those matters, because they'd been focusing on telling her brother first. "My biggest concern was you and with reason," she snapped, losing her cool.

Fisting his palms, he turned from her, saying, "Cain? Cain! I can't believe this shit! Right under my damned nose!" He took several steps, running his hands through his hair in frustration.

"Nothing happened right under your nose. Cain only recently told me I was his."

The next moment, he stood an inch from her, facing her. "When?"

"After I left, he went after me."

His eyes widened, almost to the point she thought they'd pop out of their sockets. "But you've known him for months!"

"Five months. We were just friends until I took the trip," she informed.

"He's *lying*! You aren't his. No immortal could wait five months."

No, Cain wouldn't lie. Cain loved her. She knew it, and still, a part of her, that insecure part of her felt her brother had made a valid point because Cain also said she was beautiful, and she knew she wasn't. Even so, she said, "You waited three."

Eyes fully engulfed in yellow, he reminded her. "And it nearly killed me."

That was true, too. She couldn't help but wonder what if Landon was right. What if Cain *wasn't* hers? Shaking her head, she pushed the thought away. *He's mine. I'm his,* she chanted. Still, her voice shook when she said, "Because you denied her. Cain never denied me. He waited for me to—"

He slammed his fists against the desktop. The sound of the wood cracking resounded around the room. "Is that what he said? It's a cute story, but I don't believe it. He's saying you're his to get you in bed!"

On cue, her face flamed, a blush so deep she felt it as it trailed down her neck and chest.

He didn't miss a beat. His glowing eyes widened, his pulse spiking with his anger.

"You had sex!" he accused.

She jumped, startled. Embarrassed, shocked and angry, she couldn't prevent tears from welling in her eyes. She hated to show weakness, especially now, especially in front of Landon who was always so strong. No wonder he treated her like a child. She couldn't even hold back a couple of petty tears.

"You're lucky he didn't mark you!"

Toughen up, she thought then took a deep breath. "He didn't mark me because he didn't want you to find out that way, but I guess I should've let him because there's no way you'd ever take this well."

As if he hadn't heard a word she'd said, he yelled, "He's a fucking coward for sending you to tell me!"

"He didn't *send* me. He doesn't pretend to *own* me. I told him I'd wait for him," she said. "I broke my word because I didn't want you to—"

"Kill him?" he finished for her.

"I didn't want the two of you to fight, and I didn't want to affect our alliance with the demons, not to mention the Guardians."

"You're *not* his!" Landon screamed.

"That's enough, Landon," Jocelyn interrupted. Both of them turned to look at her. "Everyone knows Olivia is Cain's mate."

Relief swelled inside her, that doubt gone because Jocelyn knew, because everyone knew. Cain was *hers*.

Taking a step toward his female, Landon asked, "What do you mean *everyone*?"

"I mean everyone…but you," Jocelyn said.

"So he's been going around talking about *my* sister? I bet he's told all his friends how—"

"No, Landon. He didn't tell anyone, not even me, but demons are empaths. As for the rest of us, it was pretty obvious." Jocelyn sighed. "I mean, it doesn't take a genius to figure it out. He came here every day with some lame excuse."

Eyes blazing, Landon said through gritted teeth, "I thought he was here to see *you*!" He had a point there, too. Jocelyn and Cain were friends, and Landon, all alpha male possessive, had made it clear he didn't like it.

"Yeah, he came to see me, but spent all his time with Liv," Jocelyn shot back, sardonically.

"Damn bastard! Wait till I get my hands on him!" Landon rushed out of the room.

Olivia couldn't do anything, but race after him.

Chapter 27

Cain's fist connected with the dummy, blood pouring from his blistered fists, staining it red. He didn't feel it. All he felt was rage. As long as he'd been at it, hours, that rage hadn't ebbed.

No wonder. He was disappointed in himself and that, he realized, turned to anger quickly.

She said she wasn't upset, but she deserved better than he'd been to her. She deserved much more than a demon mate who took out his frustration on her just because he'd lost all semblance of control.

Because he was so angry, he'd done the only thing that had come to mind, train. It often appeased him. Today, though, it wasn't working.

He heard the elevator doors part, and cursed. He wanted to be alone, so he could stew in his foul mood. That's where his mind was when he sensed it. The rage surrounding him doubled.

Turning, he spotted Landon barging through. Olivia trailed behind him, panic and fear streaming from her. Before he could stop himself, he took several steps toward her with one thought on his mind—soothing her. He cringed, and halted mid-stride when he remembered he couldn't. Then he noticed Jocelyn merely steps behind Olivia; she, too, was worried.

"You!" Landon bellowed, taking menacing steps in his direction.

Cain crossed his arms over his chest, nonchalantly trying his hardest to hide the anger simmering inside. "How may I be of service?" His voice dripped with sarcasm.

"You are *not* fated for my sister!"

Eyes widening, he glanced in Olivia's direction, her eyes pleading. For what? He didn't know. He couldn't read her mind not until he claimed her. What did she want? Not to fight her brother? Not to be angry with her?

"We aren't mated yet, but she is my fated," he replied.

"Hell! Fuck! No!" Landon roared.

Moments later, Lucas holding Jenna materialized near him followed by Benjamin and Jacob.

Noticing, Cain kept his gaze on Landon. "You learned the hard way. Who we are destined for is out of our control." He spared another glance at Olivia, realizing then her eyes were red rimmed. She'd been crying. His chest ached then, hating he hadn't been there to comfort her. Gaze snapping back to Landon, he said, "If I got to choose, I'd still choose her."

"This stops here! Whatever is going on between the two of you, stops now! She is *my* sister. I choose for her, and you aren't it!" Landon screamed, his eyes burning golden with anger.

"At least attempt to control your temper around my mate and your pregnant female," he shot back. He knew it would infuriate Landon more, but he didn't have it in him to care.

"She is not your mate! She's my sister!"

"She *is* my mate and your sister," Cain fired.

Landon's hands began to shake, quivering from his

anger and need to shift. "You aren't even man enough to tell me yourself. You send her. You aren't worthy of her."

Landon was right about one thing: he wasn't worthy of all Olivia's innocence and beauty. That wasn't his fault. The fates had fucked up. Because they did, it meant she was *his*, and because she was his, he'd never let her go.

"Landon, I explained this to you," Olivia interrupted.

Landon turned to face her. "That's enough, Liv. This is between the demon and me."

Cain clenched his jaw as anger coiled around him. Nothing triggered his demon more than his mate being mistreated or threatened. He wanted to kill whoever caused her any pain. But it was her brother. Cursing, at that moment he wished Landon wasn't related to her, wished Landon wasn't married to his friend.

"We decided when the time came we would tell you together," he said through clenched teeth.

"Yeah, I guess you both worked out your story," Landon retorted.

"It's not a story," Olivia interrupted. "I thought it would be best if I—"

"Liv," Landon warned, his tone filled with fury.

Rage, anger, wrath burned deeper. *Control*, he chanted, materializing an inch from Landon's face. "Don't fucking talk to my mate that way!" he yelled for the first time.

"I'm her brother, and her alpha! I'll talk to her however I fucking want!"

Conceited, arrogant bastard. Through gritted teeth, he said, "You'll treat her with respect."

"Landon, that's enough," Jocelyn said.

Landon's eyes on him, he roared, "No!"

"I'm moving out," Olivia said firmly, drawing everyone's gaze to her. Her features seemed set in stone, grim determination in her eyes.

Shit. What would Landon do now? Fear making him act, he didn't think. He moved, materializing in front of Olivia, blocking Landon from reaching her.

"Get away from her! You think I'd hurt my own blood?"

No, he doubted Landon would. Despite his temper, Landon was a good man. It didn't change the fact Landon lost his temper a lot and when he did, he screamed. Cain had stood by and watched it before, his demon begging to avenge his mate, but that was over. He wasn't going to let it happen again, ever. "From the way you treat her, I can't say for sure."

Olivia's slim hand grasped his shoulder attempting to pull him away. Reluctantly, he moved, but his arm went around her waist, clutching her to him so her side was plastered against his.

"If you make me choose, I choose Cain," she said, her voice steady and firm.

His chest puffed with pride, a small smile tugged at his lips.

Shaking his head in denial, Landon's face paled, jaw dropped. "You can't—"

"Yes, I can, and I did," Olivia cut him off.

"But where will you—"

"With Cain."

"But you can't—"

"I tried explaining things to you earlier. What did you think? That you would come here and fight Cain and I'd forget him? That you would huff and puff and things would go your way?" She shook her head. "Not this time. Not about this."

She paused, and that wall she'd built around her emotions crumbled, her expression saddening.

Cain felt every ounce of it, making his chest clench. Instinctively, his arm tightened around her waist.

"You have Joce. Other werewolves are now mated to immortals from other breeds. Cain is my mate—"

"You don't know that for sure. There could be another, a werewolf—"

"I don't want another. I want him." A tear slid down her cheek. Her voice cracked when she said, "How c-can you not understand when you went through this yourself with Joce months ago?"

Cain couldn't stop himself. He cupped her head with the other hand, and pulled her to him until her cheek pressed against his chest. She leaned against him as if for support, and he feathered a kiss on her temple.

Landon growled, his eyes leaving his sister briefly to glare at him.

"I'm sorry, but if you can't accept this then we can't..." Her words fell away. "You have to accept this…Cain and me, or—"

Eyes wide, looking and sounding shocked Landon asked, "You're giving me an ultimatum?"

"Yes…you accept us together, or you don't accept me." Several more tears slid down her cheeks before she pulled away from him and walked away.

He stared after her, fighting the urge to chase her then he faced Landon. "For what it's worth, I don't want you out of her life. Needless to say, she doesn't either. I want you to accept us. I don't want Liv to suffer, like she'll continue to do. But she's *mine*, I *love* her, and I'll *never* let her go."

With those last words, he materialized in front of Liv. "Darling."

Her gaze lifted to his. Then she wrapped her arms around him, burying her face in his chest. He laced his fingers through her hair, gripping the back of her neck as his other arm went around her waist, and materialized them to his room. Lowering his head until his lips were just above her ear, he said, "You shouldn't have done that, Liv."

Pulling away, she angled her face to his. Her puffy, swollen eyes met his. His heart clenched just as she croaked, "What?"

"You should've waited for me."

She had agreed to wait, but for some reason changed her mind. He wondered why, then put the thought aside, and focused on wiping away the tears streaking her face.

"You think it would've changed anything? If anything the drive here calmed him somewhat...Actually, that's not true. It seems the only thing that calmed him was me moving out."

He shook his head then released a breath. "You shouldn't have given him an ultimatum."

"Like he would have understood any other way?" she asked rhetorically, her expression torn.

Running his palm down the side of her face, he pointed out, "This hurts you."

"Being away from one another hurt both of us," she countered. "Besides, what were we going to do? Did you really want to continue to sneak around until he came around? We would have been sneaking around for centuries. I mean he'll never—"

He drew a strand of hair away from her face. "It's fine, sweetheart."

She looked away from him, and her brows drew together. "Do you think I've ruined the alliance between the pack and the—"

"No, darling. You can't ruin anything."

"You aren't mad that...I kind of just moved here...You didn't ask me per se—"

He smiled. "I asked you to mate me and marry me. Did you think I meant to claim you, and live away from you?"

"No, but we hadn't discussed when we would tell Landon, or where we would live and...now I feel like I—"

"Don't even finish that sentence," he said then kissed her lips softly. "I couldn't be more thrilled, darling."

****

A bit unsettled still, Olivia headed into the kitchen at the demon compound. She preferred to be alone after the confrontation with her brother, but her stomach continued to growl, and she couldn't ignore it.

Although Cain had a kitchen on his floor, the pantry wasn't stocked. Neither was his fridge. She figured he hadn't been shopping since before he'd gone to Santorini.

Cain left the compound a little over an hour ago, telling her he had errands to run. He'd attempted to get her to spend some time with Jenna and Ashley, Jocelyn's two sisters, but she wasn't in the mood for company. She knew he worried about leaving her alone, but she assured him she just needed some time alone, which she did. She'd left out the guilt tearing her apart. Then again, she didn't have to say it. He knew what her brother meant to her. He knew she was hurt and probably read it in her emotions, too.

Landon was the only family she had left, but he'd given her an ultimatum before she'd given him one. He wanted her to end her relationship with Cain—the man destined for her. She couldn't live without Cain just as her mother couldn't without her father. She hoped Landon would come to terms with her decision. However much hope she had, she felt it useless. Her brother was as stubborn as they came, and she feared losing him because of it.

As she walked into the dining room leading to the kitchen, she spotted Jenna and Ashley.

"Hi," Jenna greeted her brightly. "Are you hungry? I made some sandwiches."

"Yeah," she admitted then took a seat. "I'm sorry to barge into your lives—"

"Liv, you haven't barged in anywhere. You're as welcome here as you've always been. This is your home now."

"Thanks, I'm sorry you had to witness that—"

"No apologies," Jenna insisted. "We're all aware how stubborn and hot-tempered Landon can be. Don't worry too much. He'll cool off and come around."

"He'll come around," Ashley repeated. "Jocelyn will nudge and nudge until she gets him to admit he overreacted."

Jenna plated a sandwich for Olivia and handed it to her. "I wonder if a brother of mine would have reacted like that," Jenna wondered aloud.

"From what I've heard, you had plenty to deal with, with Clyde," Ashley said. Clyde, Ashley's soulmate, was an angel and had been guardian to Jenna around the time Jenna met Lucas. He'd disapproved of their relationship from the get-go and gave both of them a hard time.

Jenna chuckled. "That I did."

"Five sisters? A brother of yours would've had his hands full," Olivia said.

Ashley laughed. "True. I guess we'll never know."

Taking a bite of her sandwich, she said, "You know who mentioned sisters? Drake. I wonder if he's as overbearing as my brother."

"Drake?" Ashley asked.

"He's an alpha from Texas. Landon, Joce and I met him last night to discuss an alliance. Landon plans to arrange a meeting between him and the Guardians."

"I think Cain mentioned something about the alpha. Oh! Maybe we can invite all the Guardians and Drake over for dinner," Jenna said.

Ashley rolled her eyes and mumbled, "Here we go."

Olivia laughed. It wasn't a secret Jenna loved to play hostess.

"My heart, what're you planning now?" Lucas's voice boomed from behind Olivia.

She turned to glance in his direction, and noticed him accompanied by two demons she hadn't met, which she assumed were the new recruits. Both demons had dark hair and dark eyes, but that's where the similarities ended. While one was model-esque capable of posing for GQ; the other was rugged with a full beard.

"It's not a party. It's a dinner and strictly business. Olivia says Drake, the Texan alpha, wanted to meet the Guardians and since there's no meeting until later this week…" Jenna explained.

Hiding a smile, Lucas said, "That's a good idea, love."

"Olivia, have you met Hades and Nathan?" Ashley asked.

She shook her head.

The model-looking demon, extended his hand to her and said, "I'm Nathan."

She shook his hand.

"Hades," the bearded demon said.

"Nice to meet you both," she replied.

"Are you boys hungry?" Jenna asked.

They spoke simultaneously.

"Starved," Lucas muttered.

"Yeah," Hades and Nathan said.

"Have a seat," she said, plating sandwiches for each of them, then took her seat beside Lucas. Her gaze went to Olivia's and she said, "So about this dinner, how do I get in contact with Drake?"

"I'm sure Landon has his number," Olivia said. "Drake mentioned he may be leaving today. He was here with his sister and her male."

"I see. I should get on that right after lunch then," Jenna said, more to herself.

"Liv, Jenna and I were going to tan by the pool. Do you want to join us?" Ashley asked.

"I don't have a bathing suit," she said, remembering not only didn't she have a bathing suit she didn't have any clothes at all.

"Don't worry about that. I have plenty. As a matter

of fact, I have a couple of brand new ones I haven't had the chance to wear," Ashley said.

"Oh, I don't want to—" she began.

"It's fine. I don't mind, really. Clyde keeps buying me bathing suits," Ashley shrugged. Her expression became somber for a moment.

Jenna placed her hand over Ashley's. "Don't think about that," Jenna whispered to her sister.

Bewildered, Olivia said, "Only if you're sure, I don't want to intrude—"

"The more the merrier," Jenna said. "I've been dying to hear about your vacation."

****

Cain was on cloud nine. His mate was with him in his home, not that it mattered where they were. His home was wherever Olivia was, but they no longer had to hide. It thrilled him.

He left hours ago telling her he had errands to run, which he did, but the errands were for her. He stopped by several stores, spent close to a fortune buying her clothes, shoes and under garments. No cost was too much for her. She deserved the best of everything and had nothing to her name in his home—their home. He supposed he should invest in redecorating too, letting her pick out what she liked, so she'd feel more at home. He'd never spent money and had a small fortune saved; he'd enjoy blowing it all on her.

Tonight would be special. He had plans to make her a romantic dinner. Then finally he'd give her the engagement ring and necklace Lucas gave him, and he couldn't wait to see the look on her face when he did. He'd spent the day imagining her reaction.

Materializing in his closet, he dropped off his

purchases on the floor then stepped into the room. Scanning it, he realized Olivia wasn't there. He checked the rest of his floor, but it too was empty.

He couldn't help it then. Dread began prickling up and down his back, his thoughts wandering toward the worse possible scenario—that she regretted the decision she made hours before, that she left. He shook his head trying to rid himself of his fear then materialized in the security office fully equipped with a state of the art surveillance system. He searched the camera screens until he spotted her on the top floor, sunbathing with Jenna and Ashley. Releasing a breath, he materialized on the rooftop. Instantly soothed with the sound of her giggling, he strode toward her.

Before he reached her, she turned to face him, smiling then she stood and sprinted toward him. He lifted her off the floor, wrapping his arms around her, picking up her scent mingled with sun tanning lotion.

"Darling," Cain said then crushed his mouth to hers.

"Hi," she said after pulling away.

"You look delicious in that bathing suit and taste even better," he whispered. "Speaking of…Have you eaten?"

She nodded. "I went to grab a bite in the kitchen then Ashley mentioned she and Jenna were planning to tan, so she gave me this bathing suit…"

He turned his attention to Ashley and Jenna.

"Hello, brother," Jenna greeted with a wide grin.

"Hello, sisters," he replied. "Ash, I'll get you a new bathing suit to replace this one."

"Don't worry about it. I have tons, and Clyde continues to buy them for me."

"That I do," Clyde said, appearing beside Ashley. Turning his attention toward her, he squatted beside her, kissed her softly on the lips and said, "Angel, I've missed you."

"Not as much as I've missed you," Ashley replied. "Any news from above?"

Clyde shook his head. "Sorry, love." He sat beside Ashley and pulled her onto his lap.

His gaze then went to them. "Congrats," Clyde said. "Ash mentioned the good news."

"Thanks," Cain replied for them both.

Lucas appeared next to Jenna moments later and sat beside her. "My heart," he whispered, then kissed her before he turned his attention to Cain and Olivia. "I'm glad you're both here. I wanted to talk to you about where you plan to marry."

Olivia tensed. The emotions streaming off her were unsettling: sorrow and worry. Silently cursing his insecurities, he wondered again if she had second thoughts about them, about moving away from her home. Because his need to protect and care for her overrode his insecurities and fear, he tightened his arm around her and rubbed her arm in an effort to console her. "Olivia has always wanted to be married in Santorini," he said.

"Well then perhaps we can have a small reception in Treconomia. Our people would like to meet their new princess," Lucas said.

"If it's not too much trouble," Olivia said just as Cain responded. "We'll discuss it."

"I can assure you it's no trouble, Olivia," Lucas said. "It's not every day, the prince finds his mate. The council has already alerted our kind. Needless to say, they are over the moon about it." Lucas paused, smiling. "Welcome to the family."

"Thanks," Olivia replied. "Thank you for opening your home to me."

"This is Cain's home as much as it's mine and Jenna's, and it's your home now, too," Lucas countered then spared a glanced at Olivia's left hand.

She nodded.

"I'm making us dinner tonight," Cain whispered for only Olivia's ears. "Want me to come get you when it's almost ready?"

"No, I'll go with you now. I want to shower and freshen up. Maybe you'll let me help with dinner."

"Not a chance." He kissed her forehead then they bid their farewells.

Chapter 28

Cain materialized them in his room. Not a moment later, he pulled her slightly away from him. His eyes, bleak and somber, bore into hers.

"You regret it, don't you?"

Her heart squeezed in her chest, and she felt the color drain from her face. "W-what?"

"Do you regret leaving the estate, Olivia?" The somberness in his eyes seeped into his voice.

"Why would you think that?"

"I know you're sad and worried and feel guilty. All those feelings doubled when Lucas mentioned the wedding." He turned away from her and ran his hands through his hair taking several deep breaths.

"I—"

"Don't." He faced her again. "If you want to leave, you can leave, but I'll follow you," he warned, his eyes darkening.

"I don't want to be anywhere but here, Cain," she said, her voice loud and firm. "I'm sad my brother doesn't understand. I'm worried he'll never understand. I'm worried he'll refuse to walk me down the aisle when we marry, and never meet our kids. I shouldn't feel guilty, but I do because, although I know I'm right, he's hurting, too. None of this has anything to do with you."

Eyes flaring, he shot back, "Of course, it does. I'm

the reason for all of it."

"No, Cain Thaler, you are my gift, my fate," she replied, her hands gripping his sides. Her voice steady yet filled with so much emotion. "*Mine*. I can't turn my back on you even if it means losing my brother. I don't want to live without him in my life, but I will because I know I won't survive without you."

He disappeared, and reappeared moments later, an inch from her face, holding up a black velvet jewelry box, and handing it to her. "I was going to wait until later, but I think you should have it now."

She opened the box slowly. Inside lay a necklace, a yellow diamond set in the middle surrounded by smaller white diamonds.

Her jaw dropped. She'd never owned such an elaborate necklace. Very few werewolves hardly, if ever, wore jewelry because they shifted and couldn't wear jewelry when they did.

"It's a family heirloom. It belonged to Lucas's mother. I hope you—"

Finally, she tore her gaze away from the necklace, and said, "It's beautiful. It's so…Thank you, Cain. I've never had anything this—"

He crushed his mouth to hers. Against her lips, he said, "Only the best for *meae deliciae, meus sodalis*."

****

Cain had plotted and planned, of that she was sure. While she spent the morning in despair over her argument with her brother, he had spent his time running errands and planning the perfect dinner for her.

After she showered, she wandered into his closet wondering what she could borrow of his, since she didn't have any of her clothes, to look semi-presentable for the special dinner Cain insisted he cook, alone. She'd been shocked to find not only a yellow knee-length dress hanging in the middle of his walk-in closet and matching shoes, but at least twenty other shopping bags littering the floor.

"Cain!" she yelled.

Instantly, he materialized beside her, worry marring his handsome face. "What's wrong, darling?"

"What's all this?" she asked, amused.

"I forgot to hang them…"

"Is that what you were doing this morning? Shopping? I assumed you had some Guardian business—"

"It's more important than that. You needed clothes." At her bewildered expression, he added, "It's for you. Can't have you wandering around naked, so I bought you some stuff."

She glanced around the closet once more. "You think you got enough?" she teased.

"Not nearly enough, but…" His words trailed off.

"I don't need all this stuff, Cain, and I have a hefty trust fund."

He shrugged. "Maybe, maybe not, but I wanted to buy it for you." He pressed his lips to hers for a quick kiss then said, "I'd love to stay here, but it's dangerous considering you aren't dressed." He winked. "And dinner will burn."

He left as quickly as he came.

She towel-dried, then donned Cain's blue robe as she emptied the bags of clothes he'd purchased for her and organized them. Half an hour later, she fixed her hair, applied her make-up, and dressed. She heard the shower running and assumed dinner was almost ready so she headed toward the kitchen, prepared two glasses of wine, and strode to the patio for some fresh air.

As if he hadn't surprised her enough for one day, outside she found a small table set for two with a bushel of red roses in the middle and a candle.

"You ruined the surprise."

She heard his voice say from behind her. Turning, she spotted him wearing a black fitted long-sleeved shirt that outlined his broad chest perfectly and black pants hugging his muscled thighs.

She neared and handed him a glass of wine. "If you didn't want the surprise spoiled, you should've told me I wasn't allowed out here," she pointed out.

"This is your home, remember? I can't ban you from entering any room."

Her heart clenched in her chest. Her home with him. It sounded right. Perfect.

"Thank you, Cain…for the clothes and the necklace…" Her fingers grazed the diamond on her neck. "And dinner and for…loving me."

He closed the distance between them and kissed her roughly. His tongue delved into her mouth, soothing her as his arms pressed her body toward his. His warm body roared hers to life. All her worries were forgotten.

"You don't need to thank me for anything, especially for loving you. I can't help it," he whispered against her lips. "Dinner's ready. Let's eat."

They ate salads, steaks, and chocolate cake for dessert. Olivia was still enjoying hers when Cain's brows drew together and he nervously began rubbing his hands together.

"Do I make you happy, Olivia?"

The question caught her off guard, but she replied

immediately. "Yes, you make me very happy."

He looked away from her and sighed. Her stomach knotted and a lump formed in her throat. Unable to eat another bite, she put down her fork.

"I don't know why this is so hard," he said, gazing at her again. "Come here." Then he stood, opening his arms.

She stood hesitantly and closed the distance between them, pressing her body against the comfort of his.

"Close your eyes, *meae deliciae*," he whispered.

She did. Moments later, she opened her eyes and realized they were no longer in New York. The smell of the ocean tinged the air and she felt sand beneath her heels. She glanced around and realized he'd taken her to the private beach outside her home in Santorini.

"What are we—"

Reaching for her hand, he kneeled. "Olivia Clare Waden, I've asked you before. I thought it would be easier this time, but I was wrong. The first time I asked you we were right here."

He reached into his pocket and pulled out a black velvet box then he opened it. Inside laid a large blue diamond ring.

She gasped as tears welled in her eyes.

"Olivia, I dream about you every night. When I'm not dreaming, I'm thinking about you whether you're beside me or not. You've not only captured my heart, but my soul. I love you more than I could ever express. Will you mate and marry me?"

Unable to speak, she nodded through the tears of joy streaming down her face.

He smiled then removed the ring from the box and

placed it on her finger. The next moment, her body was pressed against his in an embrace.

"I love you, *meae deliciae*," he whispered, pressing his mouth against hers as his fingers softly wiped her tears.

His declaration, his second proposal, the way he so effortlessly loved her…all of it made her chest clench, the strength of her love for him spilled from her and radiated around her.

She didn't know how it was possible to love someone so much you ached, but she knew she did. Every time he told her how much he loved her, every time he showed her through his thoughtful actions, even the simple action of wiping her tears, her heart ached. It burned with love for the man she was made for.

"I love you so much," she managed to mumble.

She kissed him passionately for everything he was, and for everything he would be. She kissed him for being hers, for needing her, and for loving her. As she explored his mouth with her tongue, the aching turned to desire that exuded from her until she couldn't think of anything but him. His tongue, his touch, the feel of his body against hers seared into her. She couldn't imagine a week, a day, or a second without him. Her desire for him running deep inside her burned away their surroundings and her logic. It didn't matter where they were. In her mind, it was only the two of them.

She craved him.

She wanted him.

She needed him.

"I need you, now," she said between gasps. She ripped his buttoned shirt down the middle and ran her hands over his skin exploring his chiseled chest.

He placed his hands under her butt and lifted her effortlessly, rubbing his sex against hers. The sensations rippling through her exquisite, she couldn't help but throw her head back as liquid pooled between her legs. She ground her pelvis against his.

His mouth continued to taunt her, devouring her. He groaned deeply. "I need you to tell me. I need to hear it," he said, his voice rough with need.

But in a cloud of haze and pleasure, she barely heard his words. His hands roamed and taunted her and she couldn't think of anything but the inconceivable need coursing through her body.

Running his hands down her thighs, he lifted her dress baring her rear. The cool air on her bare skin did nothing to dissuade her. Nothing could distract her from her need for him and the pleasure.

His hands roamed her bottom, then he lowered the top of her dress exposing her breasts. He kissed down her neck until his mouth was firmly on her breast, eagerly sucking and licking and teasing her.

"Tell me!" he groaned, his tongue circling her nipple. "Tell me you want to marry me…" he rasped.

Marry me was all she'd heard before his hands traveled her body hungrily until they reached her sex, then he rubbed his fingers over her clit sending spasms of pleasure through her. She screamed so loud her ears rang.

Another desire began to burn in her—the need to make him as frenzied as she was. She licked her way down his chest, her nails trailing behind scoring his skin until she reached his pants, fumbling until she unbuckled them. They slid off of him, the flesh of his throbbing shaft pressed against her, teasing her.

He placed one hand on the back of her neck forcing her to gaze into his eyes. "Olivia! Tell me!" he demanded then ripped her thong off her and entered her flesh in one swift movement.

She moaned loudly arching her back. Her canines lengthened, throbbing painfully. "Oh! What? I can't...concentrate...you're making..."

Cain pulled her face toward his again then clenched his jaw. His gorgeous eyes glowed in the dark. She knew he battled his demon.

"Olivia, tell me you want to marry me," he said through gritted teeth, then with each hand at her waist he pulled out of her and delved into her core again.

"I...want to...marry you..." she cried. "I...need your mark...on me," she moaned.

He groaned loudly then slammed his lips against hers. "I can't stop..." His body shuddered. "Losing...control."

Body shifting against hers, it enlarged and grew, ripping what was left of his shirt. She peeled her lips away from his and gazed into her demon's eyes, burning a fiery molten red. His horns stuck out from his head, his fangs peeking from his mouth.

He ran his fingers through her hair then pushed her lips toward his again, stumbling moments before her back hit a soft surface—their bed.

He didn't waste time. Thrusting into her roughly, repeatedly, she lost all reason as flashes of pleasure ran through her, heating her body, her blood, her soul. Just when it began to fade, another flash of pleasure overwhelmed her. She'd thought she'd die of it.

Then his fangs bit into her neck, and the pleasure intensified, overwhelming her. She screamed and moaned, the sound coming from deep inside her.

Growling, he drew away from her neck.

She clutched the back of his neck and dragged his head toward her again, whispering, "Drink...Don't stop...Feels too...good."

He sank his fangs into her again sending more flashes of pleasure through her. She couldn't help it then. Nails clutching him, her canines lengthened, she sank them into him. His tangy sweet blood hit her tongue. The pungent taste sent her reeling, trembling uncontrollably, her undoing.

His body tensed above hers before he groaned, his chest vibrating from the strength of it, then he collapsed on top of her. His demon leaving him a moment later.

The only sound left was their ragged breaths. Neither spoke. Only Cain moved, running his hand through her hair softly.

"Darling?" he asked, lifting his head. "Did I hurt—"

Smiling contentedly, she whispered, "No."

"Let me see..." He turned her head to look at his mark on her. "Holy shit!" he yelled then launched himself from the bed. "Damn it! I..."

She sat up in bed, her hand gazing over his mark on her neck. The skin was soft and smooth, having already healed. "Cain?"

He stopped his pacing and stared at her wide-eyed.

"Nothing is wrong. I'm fine," she assured.

"Fine, huh?" He closed the distance, lifted her off the bed and carried her into the bathroom then plopped her on her feet, facing the vanity.

She gazed at his mark in mirror. It was large, one of the largest she'd ever seen, with four puncture wounds instead of two. He'd bitten her twice in a matter of moments, claiming her. Those four wounds, visible only to the immortal eye, would remain on her neck, branding her as his forever.

She smiled.

"What? Why are you smiling?"

It's perfect, she thought, and he heard.

"Perfect? You can tell how out of my mind I was!" he said, sounding every bit as exasperated as he looked.

I know, she thought, enjoying every second of their silent conversation.

She tilted her head to spare a glance at the mark she'd made on him. It, too, was rather large, considering it was made by her.

"You think that's a good thing? Your…"

His words trailed off, but she knew what he meant to say, that her brother would be furious.

"Some females I know would kill for a mark like mine. It shows how much you desire me."

His expression softened, the tension in his shoulders dissolving. For the first time, he turned to look at himself in the mirror. His eyes examining her brand on him, he ran his fingers over it then he snaked his arm around her waist, pulled her toward him until her front pressed against his and thought: *Every immortal male would kill for a mark like mine.*

She heard.

They had accepted their fates and entwined their destinies forever when they claimed each other by marking and drinking each other's blood.

Their mating was complete.

Chapter 29

Enough was enough.

And Cain had had enough.

Never had he allowed himself to imagine a better life outside of his duty to his king, to his kind. Never had he allowed himself to hope. Never had he thought an orphan like himself would be rewarded with a fated as precious as his Olivia.

And yet, he had.

Still, in the pit of his stomach, he felt he didn't deserve her. That meant he'd do whatever he could to make himself a better man for *her*. It meant he'd go to the deepest bowels of hell just to make her happy.

Since he claimed her, he'd done everything in his power to ensure her happiness. He pampered her, making her breakfast in bed, ran her baths every night, and took her shopping. He spent every spare minute telling her how much he loved her, holding her, simply loving her. Though he hated the thought of her anywhere near the brewing war, he even let her hunt with the Guardians, with him. It went against every protective instinct, but he did it to make her happy.

And she was. He sensed it. God only knew why he made her happy. Sometimes, though, that happiness was shadowed with a deep sadness. He knew why. It didn't take a genius to figure it out. He'd done nothing but wait because he knew Landon well enough to know no one would change the alpha's stubborn mind. He waited days. Now, he was done waiting. He had to do something even though it was a long shot.

Taking a deep breath, he materialized outside the alpha's office door at the estate, and knocked. Silence, then he heard a thud and a series of quick steps drawing closer to the door. The door parted, and Landon came to view, eyes wide, surprised to see him.

"Come in. Have a seat," Landon said, motioning toward the seat in front of his desk.

"She doesn't know I'm here," he said in way of greeting, then he walked past him, and sat.

Landon returned to his desk, and took a seat. He opened his mouth to speak, but Cain beat him to the punch.

"I've come to beg you," he said stoically.

Landon's eyes widened.

Cain felt every ounce of shock streaming him, and he knew why.

He was a warrior, with a warrior's pride, and yet he willingly sacrificed his pride for Olivia.

It infuriated him, though, because Landon shouldn't be so shocked. Having a fated, Landon should know pride meant nothing compared to one's mate.

Clenching his jaw to hide the anger, he said, "You can't imagine her suffering. I can't stand to see her hurt."

It was his turn to be surprised, then, at what he felt streaming from the stubborn alpha—guilt, loads of it, rushing from him. Still, he went on.

"She hasn't said it, but she doesn't need to. I know. She thinks she's weak and that's why you sheltered her so much because she wasn't strong enough," he said in a clipped tone.

Finally, the alpha spoke, "What?"

"She wants to be strong, but I know she's hurting. I've caught a couple of stray thoughts here and there." Although they could now communicate telepathically as mates, there were still ways to keep certain thoughts to themselves. Olivia had tried her hardest to and often succeeded, but sometimes when he'd caught her by surprise he heard several thoughts. As an empath, he knew exactly how she felt. "You raised her yourself. How can you…" His eyes briefly sparked crimson, and he sighed in frustration, saying finally what he came to say. "I want you to accept me, so you can be a part of her life. I'll do whatever you want. *Except* stay away from her or do anything that would hurt her in any way."

Landon closed his eyes briefly, and shook his head, a look of defeat washing over him. Releasing a breath, Landon admitted, "I didn't want her to be fated to a demon."

At his words, Cain's eyes flashed, seeing red. Rage gushing out of every pore in his body, his demon battled him for release.

"Because," Landon added, "I was afraid you'd take her to your plane, and I'd never hear from her, or see her again." He paused. "It has nothing to do with you, Cain. Despite my poor way of showing it, I think you are a good man, and a great warrior."

Fucking ridiculous assumption, he thought. He believed him though because he heard the sincerity in his tone, and read it in his emotions.

The anger coiled inside him dissipated, tension dissolving. "You don't know me well enough then. I

285

would never keep her away from her only living relative."

"I've sheltered her because..." Landon ran his hands through his hair. "She may be my sister, but I've felt more like her father. We lost both our parents. Olivia and I are the last of our line..." Landon's eyes fell away from his then after a moment's pause met his again. "If anything ever happened to her, I don't know how I would cope...It's never had anything to do with her not being strong enough."

Damn. So much love...It wasn't just what the alpha said, the love spilling from him told the tale. Landon was impossible: stubborn, domineering and worse had hurt *his* Olivia, but Cain realized he couldn't hate him, not even a little because he could never hate anyone who loved Olivia as much as Landon did.

Only then did Cain allow himself to relax, releasing a deep breath.

"You've seen her fight. She's skilled and fierce," Landon continued. "I had plans to go see her, but I've been working on something, and I wanted it to be ready before."

He arched his eyebrows. "I don't think she—"

"Come," Landon said, taking a stand. "It's for you, too."

Hesitantly, he stood and followed Landon out. As he did, he muttered, "You realize it won't matter what you've got up your sleeve. She'd forgive you without an apology."

****

It was late, past one, and Olivia was exhausted. She and Cain had spent the last five hours hunting Malums, along with Ashley and Clyde. Since the Guardians had upped their numbers, the shifts of hunting for Malums had been divided in two. She and Cain had taken the first shift tonight.

It wasn't the first time Cain had taken her along. She'd been out with him three times so far. He'd been nerved-wracked the first night, and she hated to admit so had she, but with her keen nose, she'd been able to lead them to Malums easily, finding two hiding out that night. Cain had been proud of her and spent the next day bragging about how his mate was a natural.

Cain, she missed him even now and she knew he was in the same building just fetching them some food. It had been a week since she'd told her brother Cain was her male, one of the best weeks of her life. He filled her with such happiness, but she had lost her brother in the process.

She sighed sadly, as tears threatened to spill, then blinked rapidly hoping the urge would ebb before Cain returned. He sensed her sadness, she knew, and it hurt him, so she hid it as best as she could. Her brother's disapproval wasn't Cain's fault, despite the fact Cain blamed himself. She loved him too much to allow him to think it, or allow him to suffer, with her.

The elevator's doors opened, and she quickly managed to wipe away a maverick tear, then stood.

"What did you bring us..." Her voice died when she realized it wasn't her male who'd come through the elevators but her brother.

Shocked, she froze, studying his gloomy expression, not believing her eyes.

"Hi, Liv," Landon said.

"H-Hi," she stuttered, taking a step away.

"May I come in?" he asked.

Folding her hands into each her, she hesitated. "I…Cain's coming back soon…I—"

The next instant, he closed the distance between them and embraced her. Reluctantly, she wrapped her arms around him. The woodsy scent, that had comforted her whole life, engulfed her.

"I'm sorry, Liv," he muttered. He pulled away from her slightly, meeting her gaze. "I'm a jerk, and I'm sorry. I want you to come home."

Home? She couldn't. Home was with her male. She shook her head. "I…I can't—"

"Listen, I raised you myself, and I was afraid of losing you. I overreacted, and I'm sorry. I know Cain is a good man and he'll take care of you. I'm sorry for…everything…"

His words trailed off, but she still reeled from his admission. Her brother feared losing her? She couldn't believe he was there, and apologizing? She'd been sure he'd never forgive her and positive she'd never see him again.

"I didn't shelter you because you weren't strong. You *are* strong, Liv. I sheltered you because I couldn't stand the thought of losing you like I lost Dad and Mom and our aunts and uncles…I didn't want you to be with a demon because I thought you'd leave this plane, and I'd never see you again."

She felt tears well and drop silently.

His expression softened, looking sad then he said, "Liv, please…don't cry." He pulled his shirt up to her face and wiped the tears away.

Impulsively, she wrapped her arms around his neck and squeezed.

Landon chuckled. "I've missed you, too. So I'm

guessing you've forgiven me?"

Pulling away, she looked into his eyes, the same color as hers. "Maybe," she said with a smile.

"Maybe?" his brows drew together.

"You have to promise to walk me down the aisle."

He hugged her again then whispered in her ear, "I wouldn't miss it for the world."

Chapter 30

Olivia awoke to the smell of strawberry pancakes, her favorite. Reaching across the bed instinctively, she searched for her male. As her fingers felt the cool empty bed, her eyes snapped open. She sat up just as Cain entered with breakfast.

Smiling wide, he said, "Morning, darling."

"Morning," she said.

"Breakfast is ready. We have to eat quickly, got somewhere to be." He cuddled next to her in bed, and placed the tray in front of them, then dug in immediately.

"Where?"

"My lips are sealed," he said with a mouth full of pancakes.

"Another surprise, Mr. Thaler?"

"I can't say a word."

She couldn't take her gaze off him. He was so strikingly handsome, even as he shoved too much food in his mouth.

"What?"

"You have awful table manners," she teased.

He chuckled. "What do you expect? I'm starved for food and…" His eyes trailed down her body.

Still unused to his compliments, she blushed. When she did, his eyes softened. He did that more and more often now, especially when they made love. Because she wanted him to look at her that way longer, she ran her fingers down his chest then pressed her lips against the crook of his neck.

He hissed. "No, don't. We'll be late," he said with little force.

She knew she'd get her way. He wouldn't deny her, and she did.

****

After close to two hours in bed, not sleeping or eating, Cain and Olivia quickly dressed. Wondering what surprise he had in store for her, she wrapped her arms around him, and closed her eyes. When she opened them, she realized she was at the estate. Her attention shifted to Cain, who smiled from ear to ear.

"What—"

He kissed her. "Shh...I can't say," he said mischievously, that glimmer in his eyes twinkling.

Together, they walked toward the front doors. Before they reached them, Jocelyn parted the massive French doors. A big smile plastered on her face.

"I'm so glad you're here!" Jocelyn said enthusiastically, rushing toward Olivia and embracing her. "I've missed you both so much," she said, then she hugged Cain.

"I've missed you, too," she said. "And Landon."

"Baby!" Landon bellowed from inside.

"Oh, come in, hurry," Jocelyn said.

"Baby! Where could they..." Landon's words trailed off when he entered the foyer, and spotted them. "There you are," he said, smiling. He closed the distance between them, and hugged Olivia, then shook Cain's hand.

"Sorry we're late," Cain said.

"It was my fault," Olivia admitted, then immediately flushed.

"I don't need to know, and I don't want to know," Landon said quickly. His gaze darted away from them as he held up his hand.

Jocelyn erupted in laughter.

"Anyway," Landon said. "Come, it's this way."

Olivia, along with Jocelyn and Cain, followed her brother up to the second floor, and down the hall to the far end. Where there had been two doors that led into guest bedrooms, there was only one. Her brother had apparently done some remodeling after she'd moved out.

Landon turned to face her and smiled before he opened the door. Inside was a sprawling bedroom suite. A large canopy bed sat in the middle. The pale blue and green comforter complemented the earth tone accents. The walls were a lovely shade of beige. A nightstand stood at each side of the bed. To the right of the large suite was the bathroom with hot tub and shower. Beside the bathroom was a large walk-in closet with a vanity. All of her clothes and belongings had been moved.

To the left of the bedroom, a doorway led into a living room with a couch and television. That room then led into another, an office lined with bookshelves, and equipped with a desk, and a loft chair for reading.

She turned to face her brother, who continued to grin. "What is this?"

"It's a mating slash wedding present," he replied.

"You did this all in a week?"

He nodded. "Actually, five days."

"Why?"

Worry lines creased his brow. "You don't like it?

It's only temporary. I'm building you a house on the estate grounds…"

"What? A house!" She spared a glance at Cain who continued to smile from ear to ear. "You don't look surprised," she told Cain. "Were you plotting this with my brother?"

"If you don't like it—" Landon started.

"We don't need a house, Landon." She smiled, touched by the thought her brother had gone to so much trouble because he wanted her and Cain to live at the estate with him and his mate and soon their children.

The truth was it wasn't just about her anymore. She and Cain hadn't discussed where they'd live, and Cain had responsibilities with his brother and king.

Cain took her hand in his. "Darling, don't—"

We haven't discussed this, she thought knowing he could hear her.

You love it. I know you miss it here, he thought.

As Landon shifted his weight impatiently, Cain closed the distance between them, and wrapped his long arms around her, pressing the length of her body against his.

We can split our time, he thought.

But you have duties with Lucas, she replied.

And you have duties with Landon and your pack, Cain countered. *Besides, Joce and Landon are going to need all the help they can get from us when the babies come.*

Are you sure? she asked. She missed the estate. She missed her brother and Jocelyn and her garden and library, but she had given them up for Cain. She wanted what was best for both of them not just her.

He nodded and kissed her firmly on the lips as he

thought, *I'm positive, darling.*

She smiled. *You're the best,* she thought, then pulled away from Cain, and embraced her brother, lightly kissing him on the cheek. "Thank you, Landon, but we don't need the house."

His expression fell and he shoved his fists in his pockets. "But—"

"We don't need the house because this is perfect. We'll split our time between here and the demon compound."

"Yay!" Jocelyn exclaimed in excitement, then turned her attention toward Landon. "See, baby, I told you she wouldn't want the house. You owe me two new pairs of shoes!"

Landon kissed his female on the lips. "Yes, you told me, my love. I'll get you three new pairs."

Epilogue

Olivia and Cain married the following week in Santorini, atop the cliff where she'd dreamed of marrying since she was a child. She wore a silk fitted gown and a veil. Cain wore a tux. His best man was his brother, Lucas. Landon walked her down the aisle, giving her away, and Jocelyn stood as her maid of honor. It was a small wedding, only their closest family and friends present.

The reception was much larger. It was held in the demon plane, Treconomia, where Olivia was introduced as princess of demonkind and princess of the Waden Pack. Demonkind, cheering for her profusely, welcomed her, Landon, and a few other weres from their pack with open arms.

As they stepped out to the dance floor for their first dance, Cain pulled her toward him, and pressed her body tightly against his, his eyes soft, looking at her the way she loved. Immediately, she flushed, desire for her male coursing through her.

He lightly kissed the spot where he'd marked her then whispered in her ear, "*Meae deliciae, meus sodalis.* My darling, my mate, you've made my life complete."

She gazed at him lost in his eyes, in his touch, in the feel of him underneath her fingertips. "As you've made mine."

He smiled, then kissed her passionately.
Demonkind erupted in cheers.
It was the perfect day.

A word about the author...

J. L. Sheppard was born and raised in Miami, Florida, where she still lives with her husband and son.

As a child, her greatest aspiration was to become a writer. She read often, kept a journal, and wrote countless poems. She attended Florida International University and graduated in 2008 with a Bachelors in Communications. During her senior year, she interned at NBC Miami, WTVJ. Following the internship, she was hired and worked in the News Department for three years.

It wasn't until 2011 that she set her heart and mind into writing her first completed novel, *Demon King's Desire*, which was published in January of 2013.

Besides reading and writing, she enjoys traveling and spending quality time with family and friends.

~*~

If you've enjoyed *Awaiting Fate* and would like to read more about the characters, don't miss the Elemental Sisters Series:

Demon King's Desire, Elemental Sisters I
Burdened by Desire, Elemental Sisters II
Heavenly Desire, Elemental Sisters III

~*~

Find out more about the author at:
http://www.jlsheppard.com